Political Intervention

Peter Compton

To John,
A fellow Jumper

Alex Hunt
aka *[signature]*

Political Intervention

Peter Compton

Alex Hunt

Heather Publishing   UPS Box 481
Marana, Arizona 85658

This edition was prepared for publication by
Ghost River Images
5350 East Fourth Street
Tucson, Arizona 85711
www.ghostriverimages.com

ISBN 978-1-7333149-5-4

Library of Congress Control Number: 2020911473

Printed in the United States of America
July, 2020

Contents

Other Books by Alex Hunt

This book is dedicated to

Cpt. Larry Thorne
5th U.S. Special Forces
(Disappeared in the Tri-border area, spring 1965, where
South Vietnam, Laos and Cambodia meet.)

Acknowledgments

You write a few books which get published and you think "am I great or what?" Then reality sets in and you realize that you provided the story but it took other people to bring the final product to print. I ask the indulgence of the following for not recognizing you before:

Cindy Cozzi – for the hours you spent correcting my spelling and atrocious grammar and then typing the manuscript and designing the book covers.

Michael White – for organizing and making sure the books were structurally correct and presentable (making me look good).

Ruthie – my best friend, loving wife, and fellow author - for encouraging me to keep writing my stories.

Thank you all, for as you well know, I need all the help I can get.

Chapter 1

The cold December drizzle had shrouded the Capitol dome in a blanket of grey. Washington seemed to be in hibernation at seven in the morning. The only sound, except for some light traffic, was his leather heeled shoes hitting the wet pavement as he approached the granite steps of the Capitol building. Ascending the stairs, he pulled his green army overcoat a little closer around his neck at the same time tightening the grip on his small briefcase clutched under his left arm. His mind kept going over the events which had taken place the past three and a half months. Finally someone was going to listen to him. He had given up hope when Senator Clifton had answered his letter, inviting him to meet him and a few of his colleagues on the Senate Foreign relation committee. He remembered Senator Clifton when the senator along with the Secretary of the Army and the NATO Commander, had visited his unit in Italy. The tall lanky senator had shown a great interest in the units' readiness posture and the soldiers' morale. His knowledge of each piece of equipment shown him had surprised many of the high ranking officers, especially when he mentioned certain limitations of a new piece of equipment recently acquired by the unit.

As he approached the huge doors at the top of the steps, a man whom he had not noticed stepped from the shadows and opened the door for him.

"Major Compton, please follow me" he said in a soft southern voice. He was in his later fifties or early sixties, and preceded Major Compton down the hallway past heavy oak doors with inscribed brass plates mounted to the left of the doors; probably the names of the various senators who occupied the offices. After a few minutes they arrived at a door which was slightly ajar. Again the man indicated for him to enter. The room appeared to be an outer office. It was relatively small with heavy furniture taking up most of the space. A door opened at the far end of the room and Senator Clifton extended his right hand greeting him.

"Good morning, Major Compton, nice to see you again. This is quite a change from the balmy breezes of the Mediterranean. Hope you don't catch a cold."

He returned the greeting. The Senator must have detected his nervousness for he put his arm around his shoulder.

"You know Major Compton; say it's Pete, isn't it? Well anyway, Pete, get your coat off and if you need to use the restroom it's through the doorway over there behind the desk." The Senator kept talking as Pete removed his coat and hung it on a coat rack and straightened his tie.

"I have five of my committee members in the next room. They know basically your story having read your report but I want to go through your story from the time the unit was formed at Fort Bragg, N.C.; leave nothing out and, of course, the alert status in Italy and especially the direct MSG's from the Secretary of State. Leave nothing out and if we have to continue tomorrow, so be it. This is serious enough to warrant the time. The boys in the next room cannot be shocked in any way. They are here because they want to see justice done and are sincerely interested in your story. Let's go in and meet them and get started." Senator Clifton escorted him into the conference room. It was smaller than he had expected. The Senator's colleagues were seated around an oval table with two empty chairs at the far end.

"Gentlemen, this is Major Compton or Pete as I have come to call him. This is Senator Burgess, Clampton, Stewart, McLean, and Rose". Each in turn shook his hand and welcomed him to the Nation's Capitol.

"Let's take our seats, Pete you sit next to me up here." Senator Clifton indicated the chair on his right at the head of the table.

"I have told Pete that we would like to hear his story leaving nothing out. If any of you have any questions, I prefer that we hold them until Pete here has finished. If any of you have anything you'd like to ask him before he starts fire away."

He told them he would be happy to answer any questions they had.

"For the sake of expediency though let's keep it to a minimum, that way we can get on with it and perhaps finish this today. Since most of our colleagues have left the Capitol for the Holidays, we should not be interrupted by outside calls. Alright then, if you have any questions before Pete starts?"

The other Senators around the table were refilling their coffee cups and getting their notepads out. Senator Burgess seated on Pete's right brought coffee to Pete and Senator Clifton.

"If you want anything in it, help yourself, Pete," Senator Burgess said with a polite smile.

"Pete" Senator Rose at the far end of the oval table was the first one to speak up.

"I have observed you since you arrived here a few minutes ago. You appear to be well decorated, Viet Nam I take". He didn't wait for Pete to reply. "I also happen to know and will pass it on for the benefit of my colleagues, that your military record can only be described as outstanding. You appear to have a bright future in the Army, providing you continue your good work."Pete nodded his thanks and smiled towards Senator Rose.

"But how in the hell can you come up with a fantastic story like the one you wrote Senator Clifton? Are you prepared to call some of the highest ranking officers in the Army and God knows the State Department a bunch of liars, not to mention the President of the United States. I suggest that you forget about all this horseshit and go back to being a good soldier."

Senator Rose's voice had risen as had the color of his face. His outburst had taken Pete by surprise and he was working hard to regain his composure.

"If I might interrupt," It was Senator Stewart. "You know gentlemen, sometimes it's hard to adjust from a war time situation, like Viet Nam with its combat and excitement to a peace time situation, which many professional soldiers find a drag. They don't hand out many medals in peace time, do they, Pete?"

Pete looked around the table, all eyes were on him. His palms were sweating. He looked down at his hands and rubbed them together, slowly extending his fingers trying to collect his thoughts.

"I have come here today hoping to start a process which will eventually right a wrong." Thoughts were racing in his mind. He knew he would be alright, the nervousness had left him.

"The easiest road I could have taken was the one most of my fellow officers and some, not all, of my superiors took, namely go along with the official version of the events which occurred. I am not after another medal, being an officer in a strike unit has more than enough excitement for anyone even in so called peace time."

"Gentlemen," Senator Clifton spoke up, "Pete is not on trial here, this is not a witch-hunt, we are here to listen to Pete and question him. We here are aware of the ramification this could have if it were released to the press in the wrong manner. Heads would roll. Pete has come to us; he didn't go to the press, even when he thought the last door had been slammed in his face. He has gone about this in a dedicated and mature manner. A lesser person, one selling sensationalism, would have gone to the press long ago. After listening to his story, we here have to decide what to do about it and how best to handle it. I suggest Pete that you start off and tell it like it is or was, leave nothing out from the start of forming the unit in to the move to Italy and what transpired."

"Yes Sir, thank you." Pete took a sip of his coffee and fingered the stack of papers in front of him; finally he had gotten his chance. He briefly glanced at the first page, he knew it by heart. Pushing the papers to the side he heard himself start. "The unit was started or formed by Colonel Lawson, the Brigade Commander of the 1st Airborne BDE part of the 82 Airborne Division at Ft. Bragg, N.C. The officers were picked first, then the NCOs and the enlisted men. Total force about eleven hundred officers and men. The competition for slots, especially among the officers, was intense. Boot licking and ass kissing were not uncommon. The unit was formed into an Airborne Combat Team: 3 Rifle Companies, 1 Artillery Unit of 105 millimeter artillery, 1 Engineer Platoon, 1 Expended Medical Platoon with a Doctor and Dentist, 1 Parachute Rigging section, 1 Recon Platoon and a HQ Company. The units NCOs and men's records had to be clean. No courts martial, etc. The Colonel would not tolerate Pot Heads. (In the 1970s it was estimated that 75% of the Army had smoked pot or some form of drugs.) Physical fitness was key; the runs and physical training disqualified many. When the assignment of Italy was made public, Colonel Lawson informed the troops that in Italy the national military police, "Carabiniers" could enter any US post and arrest anyone suspected of smoking or selling pot. As a result, about 60 men left the unit, especially when informed that in Italy you could remain in jail for up to a year or more before your case was heard. In two months the unit was down to its authorized strength. The units' proficiency steadily improved and by movement day it was the finest unit in the entire US Army bar none.

The unit moved in the spring of 1972 to a former US Air Base in southern Italy. The facilities were far superior to anything the unit had been used to. Housing for dependents was plentiful and lavish by Army standards. As a result, the morale was sky high. By July the unit had settled into a regular training cycle and had become part of the US Army Southern European Command (South Com.). The only caveat was that Colonel Lawson was the G-3 in charge of operation. Colonel Lawson was a strict airborne soldier who tolerated no deviation from his orders or plans. There was definite friction between Colonel Lawson and the units' commander LTC Hays and some of his staff. A lot of the men felt Colonel Lawson was basically a bastard and expected too much of them. Everyone had been happy to leave Ft. Bragg and Colonel Lawson behind. Now he was at the base and would probably run the unit.

This was not to say LTC Hays was soft, far from it. The Company Commanders took to heart every order he issued them and carried out his direction faithfully. It was common knowledge among the officers that a strain had developed between the LTC Hays and Colonel Lawson the last few weeks at Ft. Bragg but no one thought too much about it since they would be leaving Colonel Lawson behind. LTC Hays almost didn't get the command had it not been for Colonel Lawson intervention the command would have gone to someone else who was under the impression that he would be the new commander. Colonel Lawson was not particularly fond of this LTC who could, along with his wife, flaunt his influence to the consternation of whichever command he was under. Colonel Lawson called LTC Hays into his office and told him that he would keep his command. Colonel Lawson was not without his own influence. I was at the time Colonel Lawson's adjutant and our wives were on very friendly terms. There were a lot of rumors circulating at Brigade Headquarters and I was under a great deal of pressure to spill the beans, so to say, of what actually was happening. But my loyalty was to Colonel Lawson who had asked me if I wanted the Executive Officer slot of the new battalion. This of course went against the grain of the many West Point Majors within the command and those serving in other commands. I was not a West Point graduate.

Things were moving well in Italy and there was little interference from Colonel Lawson. I was going over a report to LTC Hays one day when LTC Hays asked me to close the door. It was just the two of us in the Lieutenant Colonel's office.

"I know that you and Colonel Lawson are good friends. However, I hope that you are my Executive Officer and not Colonel Lawson's." I was taken aback by his comment. I told him I had been Colonel Lawson's adjutant for about two years and yes we had formed a close relationship. However, I was now LTC Hays's Executive Officer and would serve him to the best of my abilities and no I would not inform Colonel Lawson on activities within the Battalion.

"I will be as loyal to you as I was to Colonel Lawson when I served him. He will not hear anything from me nor does he expect to. Colonel Lawson happens to think a lot of you. I personally have not heard him say anything about your abilities. The only thing I have heard came from the Chief of Staff who mentioned that Colonel Lawson holds you in high esteem. As you well know his wife and mine are good friends and we get together once in a while and the only thing I have heard is positive things about you and the Battalion. And there is no pillow talk in our house about you or the Battalion. There never has been, no matter what unit I have been in. My loyalty is to you and if you find that I don't do my job to your satisfaction or my loyalty is in question, fire me. I know there were a lot of outstanding WPs who wanted this slot and I'm sure you would rather have chosen your own Executive Officer and to be frank with you, had I been in your shoes I would have insisted on it. I threw my hat in the ring at a late date and it was not Colonel Lawson who ultimately chose me; he told me that my chances were slim. It was the Division Commander who called me over to the Division Headquarters and asked me if I wanted the job. His words were that you and I would complement each other. I think you knew the Division General personally having served under him in Vietnam."

LTC Hays stood up and extended his hand and we shook hands.

"I am pleased with you and I know I have your loyalty, I could not have chosen a better Executive Officer. I know it must put you in a difficult situation at times and as you know there are rumors around as to who you work for. I will put those rumors to rest at tomorrow's staff and company commanders meeting. That's it, I'm glad we had this talk; we should have had it months ago. Thanks, Pete."

True to his word, LTC Hays at the end of the staff and commanders meeting the next morning asked me to represent him at the Chief of Staff's meeting. I knew there was no meeting at the headquarters so I excused myself and departed the room. What had transpired at the staff meeting after I left leaked out that afternoon and the next morning, Captain Ryder, the S-2 intelligence officer, came into my office and closed the door.

"So you knew LTC Hays before in Vietnam." Captain Ryder looked at me waiting for an answer. "Yes, I gave him some intel when he was the S-3 in a 1st Air Cavalry. They were the only ones who acted on it and got all kinds of kudos from higher headquarters."

"Well according to the old man after you left this morning if he hears any derogative comments about you, he will personally take care of the individual. He also said that he along with the Division Commander picked you as his Executive Officer even skipping a Medal of Honor recipient. I guess we have to treat you nicer from now on."

"Unless you have solid Intel, Ryder, get the hell out of my office."

"I might in a week or so" said Ryder on his way out.

Saturday night was to be a formal affair at the officer's club. It would be the first one since moving to Italy. Everyone was dressed in their finest, the ladies looked stunning. After cocktails and the meal, just as the music was about to start, an NCO from Headquarters approached LTC Hays and informed him that an alert had been called. LTC Hays sat there stark faced and whispered the message to me."

LTC Hays stood up and called for everyone's attention. He announced the 24 hours alert and for all the officers to go through the alert procedure and get their men into the garrison. Everyone took off leaving some of their wives and girlfriends in a state of shock. The unit had 24 hours to rig and be ready to go. Some officers took off leaving their wives and girl friends behind, some had managed to ride home with their husbands and others were left stranded. People who worked at the officers' club offered to take the stranded ladies home. None were to see their men for the next three days.

Thirty hours after the alert was called, the unit was ready to move. Colonel Lawson directed LTC Hays to pick one company for a mission. The Co-Commander was briefed, loaded his men aboard waiting C-130s and dropped in the rugged plateau area north of the base where an opposing force of Italian Airborne troops acted as the enemy. The chosen company did well and was brought back to base after a day of skirmishes with the Italian unit.

Colonel Lawson was pleased but found many shortcomings. He directed that from now on one company would be on alert status at all times. This task was rotated every two weeks. The unit on alert consisted of about 120 men. A non married soldier had to stay on post. A married man could go home and leave a phone number where he could be reached at all times.

Three alerts were held in August, the last two met Colonel Lawson's 24 hours time limit. The rigging unit was kept busy and opened another drive through building to expand their capabilities.

The Battalion settled in to a new routine, the S-3 section, headed by a Major wrote contingency plans for just about any eventuality. Families made the most of their time off together knowing that is could be days or weeks before they saw each other again.

Each day after the Battalion physical training LTC Hays held his 7 o'clock staff meeting. If he was absent, I conducted the meeting. One of us was always on base and on call.

"Let's get this over with, we have a lot ahead of us today" LTC Hays leaned back in his chair at the same time glancing down at his note pad, which contained unfinished tasks, which he had previously assigned his staff to accomplish.

Each staff officer in turn gave his update on the previous days actions and accomplishments. LTC Hays crossed off an item on his note pad which had been completed.

"We are using up too much ammo that has been allocated to training "The S-4, or logistic officer Captain Baird was saying. "At this rate we will be out of ammo by next month. I have briefed the Company Commanders of the situation but they seem determine to use it up."

"This is what I was talking about last night, Sir. I have discussed this with Captain Baird and the two of us talked with the Task Force G-4, to see if we can pry some additional ammo out of 7th Army. Our chances are kind of slim the way it sounds."

"I don't want to cut back the arms training; qualifications are coming up next month which for us means everything from a 45 Caliber pistol to our artillery. We have a lot of folks high up looking at us and I want this Battalion to come out on top. You dig into this and come up with something. I don't want to get into it until the last resort."

"Yes sir, I'll take care of it".

The motor officer gave his report giving the status of the vehicles and its new sand color repainting.

When each one had finished there was a complete silence in the room. This happened at every staff meeting. Each staff officer knew that the Battalion Commander kept a list of tasks on his pad. Some days he would go over the uncompleted ones asking each officer the status of the tasks. This could get embarrassing for some of the tasks had been on the list for months. It was not that the individual officers were not trying; it was often times the system which they were part of which produced slow results.

"What is the status of the two 81mm mortars S-4; they were damaged a month ago in the mass equipment drop, both Charlie Company and Bravo Company Commanders informed me they are short one 81mm mortar?"

"Sir, they have been turned in for salvage. We should have

the replacement any day" said Captain Baird.

"What is any day Captain Baird, I heard that last week" The Battalion Commander was talking in his low ass chewing voice. "I want you to start calling as soon as this meeting is over and have a definite answer on my desk before I depart tonight."

"Yes, sir" said Captain Baird making notes on his own pad.

"S-1, you promised me a new personnel update three days ago. I also asked you to come up with a new way to manifest our people in the event of a real alert.

"Sir, I have the program. I have been working with the Executive Officer and Task Force and have computerized our personnel system. The reason I'm late is the computer needs maintenance after so many hours of operating and this week has been maintenance week."

"Basically for you sir and the rest of the staff, the S-1 has come up with what I feel is an outstanding manifesting procedure. The S-1 can cross load the Companies in any manner you desire. He has samples available for your perusal and can have them printed out in seconds. It's so simple it's unreal. We ran a test before the computers went down for maintenance, the only thing left to do is update the cards. I talked with the Chief of Staff, Colonel Hassan and he has promised us priority, which should happen tomorrow. The S-1 will have a printout for you tomorrow afternoon."

"Thanks, Pete. It sounds good, when you get a chance I would like to see a run of the manifest, my computer skills are limited to placing a film in the VCR and that is not always a success."

"OK let's break this up. I have a meeting with the General in 15 minutes. You had better come with me Pete; he got a message from his higher last night."

The staff stood as the Battalion Commander left the room and took their seats again.

"I'm going to make this short. Some of you start sweating as soon as the Old Man brings out his pad and starts going through his list. That to me indicates that some of you are not doing your homework. You'd better start going over some of your old projects, refresh your memories a little. When you are called on give an update on every one of your tasks finished or not before he has to ask you about them. Like I told you before it can be a slip of paper, give it to the S-1 or myself and we will put it in his evening update but get it in. If you have a problem, come and see me and I'll help you. I want these meetings to be briefings not excuse periods. If you don't like the SOP around here, remember there are a hundred officers waiting for one of you to trip up so they can get your job and that is always a possibility. Now let's get to work!"

"You're getting a little hard nosed, aren't you Pete?" It was Major Bradly the S-3 operation officer. He had followed me to my office.

"God damn it, Bob, I know most of them are busting their ass but the briefings are starting to sound like excuse sessions and I don't have to tell you that the old man is under a lot of pressure from Task Force. We have to do our jobs so that he will have the answers and not be surprised by those non-airborne "legs" up there."

"OK, OK, no speeches please" Major Bradly held up his hands. "By the way what's up with the General and Colonel Lawson this morning? It sounds important. I thought maybe rumor control had a copy of the message by now."

"Where is the S-2, Captain Ryder?"

"I saw him go into the S-1. I'll get him." Major Bradly left and quickly returned with Captain Ryder.

"What's up?" I said looking up from my desk. Captain Ryder hesitated a few seconds.

"This is really top stuff," said Captain Ryder. "And yet it

may be nothing", he said glancing from Major Bradly to me.

"Cut the crap, just give me the basics so I can brief the old man on the way over to the General" I said curtly.

Captain Ryder closed the door to the office. "I just got this from my contact. It seems the Egyptians are conducting rather larger than normal exercises along the Suez Canal. Some say that all leaves have been cancelled for the past two weeks and an unusual number of Russian supply ships have been in and out of Port Said the past few weeks. There have also been more than the usual meetings between the Aligned Arab countries lately."

"What about Israel?" Major Bradly interrupted.

"I don't know what they are doing. I don't have anything on their reaction to this. I do know they have a big religious holiday coming up and they usually draw down their forces so that as many soldiers as possible can go home to celebrate."

Are you sure this is the message the General got?" I asked.

"Absolutely sir," said Captain Ryder with a smile on his face.

"OK. I've got to go. I'll see you later. I'll brief the old man on the way over.

I briefed LTC Hays on the message as we walked across the parade field which separated the two headquarters.

"Where the hell does Ryder come up with this stuff or shouldn't I ask?"

"He has a lot of friends in the intel community, some that not only owe him their careers but also their lives as well. He was with me in the Special Forces in Viet Nam for over five years. He received a direct commission from Sergeant E-6 to 1st Lieutenant at the personal direction of the Theatre Commander. Two of those five years he was detailed to the Agency on the Phoenix project and project Omega; knows everyone. Probably will never make any more rank than he has but he is happy as long as he stays in the intel game.

"Well keep a tight rein on him. He worked for a friend of mine once in Vietnam. He would disappear for days at the time and come back with enemy information that contradicted everything Saigon was putting out for that particular area, to include weapons which the VC and NVA was not suppose to have. My friend slipped once when asked by the Division Commander how come he was turning in more body counts and weapons than the other battalions in the Division combined. He told the Division Commander he disregarded all the information the Division Intel was putting out and relied entirely on his own intel officer. The division Commander almost fired him then and there."

LTC Hays paused to reflect a moment and said "What I'm saying is, don't throttle him back too much but make sure he stays within bounds."

"Will do, as a matter of fact he is scheduled to go up to Stuttgart next week for a EUCOM Conference. General Peters personally asked for Ryder to be included in the representatives we send. You approved it last week." I glanced at LTC Hayes.

"Yes, I remember; what the hell could I do, the EUCOM Commander asks for him, who am I to say no."

As they approached the Task Force Headquarters building with the massive grill work, two Italian Carabiniers snapped to attention and opened the gate for them.

"I get the feeling I'm being locked up every time I go through these gates" said LTC Hays casting a glance over his shoulders.

They walked up the wide marbled stairs to the second floor where the Task Force Headquarters was located. The building had been built originally as an officers' club for Mussolini's Air Force officers back in the 1930s. The U.S. Air Force had appropriated it along with the airfield at the end of WWII and had only recently vacated it.

They walked into the Chief of Staff's office. LTC Hays threw his hat on an empty chair and addressed Chief of Staff Colonel Hazen who was seated behind his desk enjoying a cup of coffee. "The General asked us to come over. Any idea what's up?"

"Actually the G-3 will be with you in a few minutes. We got a message last night that he wants you to see. I also think he wants to talk to you about that incident at the officers' club last weekend."

"Look, I talked to my officers who were there. They got with the club manager and paid for the damages. They have all been restricted to the base for two weeks. You were there when I briefed the General. He seemed satisfied. Why has this flared again?"

"The G-3's wife, Mrs. Lawson happened to run into the Mrs. Burtrum at the base hospital yesterday. It seems Mrs. Burtrum still has quite a bit of pain where one of your young officers supposedly had bitten her. As a matter of fact the skin was broken and required two stitches. Mrs. Burtrum has not been able to sit or lie on her back since the incident, much to Colonel Burtrum's consternation." Colonel Hazen said with a twinkle in his eyes.

"I thought Lt. Duncan merely slapped her rear" said LTC Hays looking at me. Before anyone could say another word Colonel Lawson emerged from the General's office and gave the sign for us to follow him into his office.

"Sit down" said Colonel Lawson. Before I say anything, I want both of you to read these messages. Here is a copy for you Major Compton. Handing them the messages Colonel Lawson sat back and studied the two officers as they started reading. Puffing slowly on his cigar twirling it ever so slightly, he was satisfied with his choice in the two officers. LTC Hays had turned out a little meeker than he had expected but he was getting the job done and mission accomplishment was after all the most important thing. His officers liked him and morale was high. Yet there was something he couldn't put his finger on that he didn't care for in Hays' makeup. He had only realized it during the last few weeks prior to their move. Looking over at Major Compton his mind quickly changed to the positives. The finest Major he had ever run across. Had all the qualifications an officer should have aside from his top physical condition, he was aggressive, the most loyal officer he had ever met. Compton had been his Adjutant for 2 1/2 years. It had been Compton who had run the staff, made sound decisions but most of all was loyal. He knew Compton was the one who really ran the unit, the one who got down to the nuts and bolts of the entire operation; the one who carried out the unpleasant tasks, the bastard in the unit. LTC Hays played the good guy and Compton the bastard. That was it, he thought. This was the first time he had the chance to observe the two side by side undisturbed. That was it, LTC Hays didn't like to do things that were not popular. He wanted to be friends with everyone. Of course that was it. Compton did all the unpleasant things. He would file that in back of his mind.

The two officers in front of him finished reading the messages about the same time and looked over at him.

"Well, what do you think? Is it worth increasing our readiness posture or should we wait and see?" Having said this Colonel Lawson leaned back in his chair putting his hands behind his head, cigar still in his mouth. I knew him well enough to know he had already made up his mind on what course of action to take. His G-3 staff was probably writing directives at this very moment. He just hoped LTC Hays had read the Colonel correctly and would support the approved course.

"Well sir, the message doesn't say or even imply that we take any action regarding upgrading our readiness. It's strictly information for us not implementation," said LTC Hays.

"I have read the message Hays and understand it" said Colonel Lawson with a slight irritation in his voice.

LTC Hays sensed the irritation and knew what answer the Colonel wanted.

"What I was getting at, Sir, was that short of announcing a step up in our readiness posture, we just start going down our Standard Operating Procedures (SOP) and recheck all of our rigged air drop equipment and set up additional rigging lines in the hangers out by the airfield."

"Good, we are talking off the same sheet of music. Have everything ready in the event we need it. Might be a good idea to rehearse a couple of the contingency plans, war game them. You can use our new War Room, the new topo maps are finally mounted in place. What about you, Major Compton, any ideas on this?"

The Colonel leaned forward and relit his cigar as he spoke.

"The only recommendation I have is that we don't bring any extra aircraft. Keep them up at Aviano or Mindenhall, England. Even extra aircraft at Wiesbaden or Frankfurt will tip our hand especially the C-141s they are real attention getters."

"I see your point but we don't have much choice in that area; I'll talk to EUCOM about it this afternoon; anything else?" LTC Hays cleared his throat and asked about the Israelis. "Have they increased their readiness as a result of this buildup?"

"I just talked to General LeMay last night, he came by the house on his way back to Heidelberg, stayed over last night left early this morning. He informed me that the Israelis are down to 1/3 strength all along their lines. There is a big Jewish holiday coming up this weekend and commanders have been instructed to let as many soldiers go home as possible. They are a bit over confident I'm afraid. I guess after the last shellacking they gave the Arabs they have grown a little complacent. Enough of this work on the SOP. Keep the troops in close next week. Now that God damn incident at the club last weekend keeps haunting me. Aside from the damages which I know have been taken care of. It seems some of your young lieutenants got carried away in another direction. What I'm getting at is someone bit Mrs. Burtram in the ass. Now God Damn it, look into it and handle it. I want to know how this could happen at an officers' club with people all around. Mrs. Burtrum required stitches to close the wound. I want...."

"Sir, if I may speak frankly, Sir?"

"When the hell didn't you speak frankly, embarrassed me more than once, anyway go on."

"I checked into this for Colonel Hays. It was Mrs. Burtrum, whom we all know is quite young and at times take a fancy to the young officers especially after a few martinis."

"I don't want to hear any horseshit Compton, the General is pissed over this incident."

Sir, I have talked to the five couples at the table and they all tell the same story. Mrs. Burtrum was wearing black sheath low cut dress with nothing underneath. She kept pestering Lt. Duncan who at this time was feeling no pain and who was sitting in an overstuffed chair and asked Mrs. Burtrum to get off the arm of his chair and leave him alone. She had started teasing him by leaning over him displaying her charms. He told her once more to leave him alone and get off the arm of his chair, this time in a loud voice. Mrs. Burtrum told him in a huffy manner he could kiss her ass, she intended to sit there after all she was married to a Colonel and he was only a lieu-tenant. Lt. Duncan then leaned over and bit her hard enough on the ass to tear her dress. Mrs. Burtrum screamed and ran from the club with her derriere exposed. End of story sir."

"That dame has been a headache ever since Burtrum brought her over here and married her. You whisper in the lieutenant's ear Hays, if anything like that happens again, he will be up in Germany. Do we all understand?" Colonel Lawson signaled that the meeting was over.

They walked out of the building without saying a word. When they reached the parade field LTC Hays broke the silence.

"He is a strange nut. He wasn't as mad about the club incident as he appeared to be. He was probably echoing the general's words but then you know him better than I do."

"The Colonel married late or should I say when he was a Major. He has been an airborne soldier most of his career. I don't have to tell you that the airborne boys have ruled the senior promotion board these last fifteen years and Colonel Lawson will make General very soon, he is definitely one of the boys. He is at least 3-4 years ahead of his West Point class; has been with the troops just about all his career except for a stint at the Pentagon and the service schools. He understands the soldiers, was a hell raiser as a lieutenant and captain. He knows the troops think he is a bastard and too hard but he doesn't mind for he also knows that the troops know he will back them 100% should the occasion arise, in mass or on an individual basis."

"I agree he has his good points but I wish he was a little further away from our headquarters. It's difficult to command the unit with him peeking over your shoulder constantly. Getting back to the message situation, get the staff together and brief them, include the support company commander and the rigger platoon leader also. I want every effort placed on getting ready should the need arise. I want to be one step ahead of TF on this. I'm going out to observe training and will brief the other company commanders on what is going on. I have a feeling the shit is going to hit the fan this weekend. Oh, and cancel all leaves for the weekend no exceptions."

"Jesus I just remember I promised the family we'd take a trip up in the mountains Saturday and Sunday. Oh well, they are used to broken promises by now."

I briefed the staff on the situation.

"Today is Wednesday. I want a report on my desk by 1200 hours tomorrow giving me the status of the work I have outlined. I want additional rigging lines set up inside the empty hangers. That way we can rig additional equipment for air drop and store it inside. You have lights and power and it's easier than using the gantries. If you need additional help, get a detail from the line companies, per SOP."

"Sir, we are in good shape, bodies wise," said Lieutenant Lise the quartermaster rigger platoon leader. "I'll have everything completed tonight."

"Good, any questions? One more thing, S-1, put out to the entire unit that all leaves and passes are cancelled this weekend. There was silence around the conference table. Each officer weighing the impact the last statement was going to have on his personal life.

"Well shit" said Captain Ryder. "Just when I was getting used to sleeping with my wife again; when I tell her we are postponing our trip to Rome, I'll be back on the old couch again!"

"You're too old to cut it anyway" said Major Bradly, "a little rest may rejuvenate you."

"If there are no further questions let's get to work." Major Bradly stayed after the others had left.

"Aren't we pushing the panic button, Pete" Major Bradly said sitting down at the edge of the table. "After all we are doing nothing but second guessing a situation which may or may not happen. Even the Israelis are going home to celebrate whatever it is they are celebrating. We aren't going to get involved in anything other than maybe go in and rescue some Embassy people who might get caught in the middle. Why screw up everyone's weekend again. The troops have been busting their ass for the past month. The people in my section have been working seven days a week for the last month. They need a break, Pete, they are getting frayed. Do you realize we have a detail plan for thirty-two different contingencies which we could get called out on and that includes viewgraphs and slides for each mission?"

"Bob, I'm not going to argue the point with you, everyone is in the same boat."

There was a knock on the door and Captain Ryder walked in.

"Thought you might be interested in a piece of information I just got from Heidelberg." Captain Ryder didn't wait for a response. "The Secretary of the Army, a Senator and the Army Chief of Staff, the US Ambassador to NATO and the 7th Army commander will arrive here Friday AM. Purpose of the visit is to inspect and be briefed on the unit's readiness, end of info." Captain Ryder looked from one Major to the other.

"Jesus what luck! We'll be ready for Jesus Christ himself by Friday. End of my argument Pete, I got work to do." Major Bradly departed.

"Ryder keep this under your hat until LTC Hays has been briefed and tell Bradly on your way back to your section.

The briefing and equipment demonstration for the Secretary of the Army, the NATO Ambassador and the 7th Army Commander went off without a hitch. The Secretary of the Army was particularly impressed with the caliber of the soldier and their professional knowledge. In his brief address to the unit he stressed professionalism and extolled them to carry out their responsibility as the US representatives to the NATO quick reaction force. He along with the 7th Army Commander officially sanctioned their wearing of the red European Airborne

Beret as a symbol of an elite unit. Morale hit a new high!

As I watched the Secretary of Army and his parties plane depart someone tapped me on the shoulder. I turned around abruptly and looked into the eye of Colonel Lawson.

"I want you and Colonel Hays and your wives at my house tonight for cocktails. That and my treat at that famous restaurant, whatever its name is, downtown."

"I sure will try sir" I said looking at my watch anxiously.

"I'd better tell the Colonel and our wives, babysitters you know."

"I know but arrange it, I'll expect you around 1930 hours" Colonel Lawson said with a grin on his face. That way I'll have a chance to tell Nancy she is having guests for cocktails. The women get their dander up if we don't give them enough lead time."

"Yes sir, I know what you mean".

"Oh by the way that was a good show today. I have never seen a better one. I'm going to send Hays a note. See you this evening."

I saluted and took off for my own jeep, told the driver to head back to the headquarters. God I was glad it was over, everyone had busted their ass to make sure everything went right. Colonel Lawson was a strange guy, I thought as I rode back to headquarters. He knew damn well Colonel Hays would not be able to attend the cocktails and dinner tonight. He had a previous engagement that the General had asked him to attend as his personal representative. He would still have to call him and tell him what Colonel Lawson had said. I knew Colonel Lawson was not overly fond of Hays. It was a hell of a mess and I was caught in the middle.

The phone woke me from a sound sleep. I opened my eyes slowly. The phone kept ringing - why doesn't someone answer it, I thought, Betty or the kids. Then I remembered the wives tennis tournament it started today. There was no one home. The kids were probably in the pool by now. I got up and walked into the kitchen and picked up the phone.

"Major Compton, Sir" He didn't bother answering, he recognized Captain Ryder on the other end.

"Better get over to the TOC (Tactical Operation Center), there is a message Colonel Lawson wants you to read. I strongly recommend you hurry, sir."

I acknowledged and hung up. God I had a headache. Why I drank wine I would never know. It did me in every time, didn't bother me while I was drinking it. It was the next morning, it hit me. How the hell did Betty take it and play tennis but then she didn't drink very much for it to affect her. There was a message there I reluctantly admitted to myself. Captain Ryder met me at the door and buzzed me in.

"I have a cup of coffee for you, sir." Ryder said with a grin on his face.

I accepted the strong cup of caffeine without saying a word.

"The message folder is on the briefing table" said Captain Ryder walking into the crypto section, leaving me to myself.

The red folder looked unusually thick. Opening it I started to read, sipping absently from the cup as I turned to a new page. Well here it was the Egyptians had crossed the Suez Canal and were attacking an unprepared under strength Israeli force. It took me almost a half hour to digest the implications of the message. Captain Ryder had sat down across the table from me.

"Colonel Hays is on his way back with an ETA of about 1400 hrs. Colonel Lawson says not to implement an alert but to continue to get everything ready, he is at the handball court."

"Has Major Bradly read this?" I asked leaning back in my chair.

"Yes, he came by early this morning; you and Colonel Hays are the only ones who have not read it."

"OK, get the staff in at 1500 hours, by that time we should have a follow-up message from Heidelberg and Colonel Hays will be back by then.

"OK Major Compton, when Senator Clifton said to tell everything he didn't mean everything. This is the most boring story I have ever heard. At this rate we could be here a week, not only will I and my fellow senators here be pissed but our wives will probably divorce us. Get to the meat of this pack of shit and let's get it over with or we are walking out of here, do you understand Major Compton?" It was Senator Rose and he was pissed!

"I asked Pete to explain the unit and its inherent problems. What Pete will get into now is information he got from a military attaché at the White House and friends at the Pentagon. It's not hearsay, it's notes and recordings made available to him with the authorization from the Secretary of the Army. Go ahead, Pete, get to the meat of this situation."

"Thank you Senator Rose for getting me off the tangent I was on and back to reality, as you may realize I'm a little nervous to speak to such an august group. I'm a soldier not a politician with an agenda and up for re-election."

"What the hell is that suppose to mean? Are you saying we, my colleagues and I are not serious about this situation?" It was Senator Rose again.

"See, there I go again sticking my foot in my mouth. What I meant was in the service when giving a report you have certain guidelines to go by, in this case I was winging part of it both to show the units readiness and its inherent political problems which believe me are rampant in the military. From now on I will confine my report to actual happenings which I became privy to. I thank you again for your patience."

No alert was called when Colonel Hays had been briefed, we only continued getting ready. Task Force Headquarters alerted our resupply and storage facility in Livorno, Italy approximately an hour flight north of us on the west coast of Italy, they were given a list of supplies needed for an airdrop - top priority. They had also gotten a list from the Pentagon to have everything on pallets for Air Drop. They were not told where it was going.

The Chairman of The Joint Chief of Staff got a call from the White House to report to the Oval Office immediately. He knew what the subject would be having received numerous messages about the situation in the Middle East and had prepared to brief the President on his options. He hated to confront the State Department representative whom he disliked. He knew Sadat was in trouble however even though Sadat had gone with the Russians, he liked Sadat having met him several times, he was not only a good soldier but a great statesman as well. His 3rd Army was surrounded on the Israelis' side of the Suez Canal and was running out of supplies.

His senior aide, Colonel Hammond informed him that a Rep from the State Department, the Middle East desk, and members of the Security Council would also be present. The Admiral merely grunted his acknowledgement as they walked down the extensive corridors and headed out to the waiting car. As they drove into the White House gate and were flagged through, the Admiral tried to put a finger on why he disliked the State Department so much. They were escorted up to the Oval office. Everyone was already there except the Admiral and the President. When the Admiral walked in everyone greeted him. Colonel Hammond stood behind him. The President walked in and everyone stood up. The president took his seat and everyone followed.

"Well as most of you know the Jews have Sadat's forces on the run, after a week or so when the outcome looked dire. The problem is that Sadat's 3rd Army is on the Sinai side of the

Suez Canal and is surrounded. They are running out of food, water and medicine, every time Sadat tries to send in a relief column the Israelis' shoot the shit out of them. The Russians are leaving as we speak either by air or by ship. I got a call from Sadat asking for help. I like Sadat and I told him I would try to help him - that is his 3rd Army with humanitarian help. He told me he would make airfields available to us and any support we need. I informed him I would get back to him later today."

"Excuse me, Mr. President, but surely you are not serious" said the State Department rep.

"Now don't get your head screwed up with logical thinking, if we can do Sadat a favor like this we will have him in our corner and the Russians will be out. Think of the influence we will have in the Middle East if we get Sadat aboard. Who knows, he and the Israelis might be convinced to come to the peace table. That would be a feather in the cap of the State Department."

"I strongly recommend that we not undertake this mission, Mr. President."

The President seemed to have made up his mind and turned his attention to the Admiral.

"Do we have any forces nearby that could be used here?"

"Yes sir, we have forces on standby 24/7 Mr. President. We have a thousand soldiers that could be there in hours."

"Are you saying we have alerted forces already without any coordination" the State Department Rep asked?"

"No, they are part of our rapid deployment contingent part of NATO's quick reaction force which you co-signed a year and a half ago. They are not aware of any contingency. We have not alerted them" the Admiral said in a calm voice.

We have a reaction force that can be there in hours - where is this force located?'

"Mr. President the force is located in Brindisi, Italy. One

company of about 120 men can leave within about 3-4 hours, the rest of the force within 24 hours. It is a paratroop force with HALO (High Altitude Low Opening) capabilities. The main supply area - food, water and medical supplies are located at Livorno, Italy about one hour flight time to Brindisi."

"Admiral, you handle the location of the drop in conjunction with the Egyptian Generals - I'm sure we have some contacts and you with your boss (indicating the State Department rep) get with the Israelis and tell them we are dropping some supplies to the 3rd Army and make sure everyone in the area gets the word; I don't want some trigger happy Jew shooting up our people who are going to secure the drop zone. Which brings up the questions how many troops do we send in?"

"I would recommend less than a company, Mr. President. If we drop too many in the Israelis might get the wrong idea."

"I agree Admiral but you and your staff do the numbers coordinating with the Israelis and the Egyptians. You work with the State Rep and when you are ready I'll call Sadat and give you the final go."

The President got up and indicated the meeting was over. Everyone rose and when the President had left took off for their respective offices leaving the Admiral and Colonel Hammond and the State Rep alone.

"I'll coordinate with the Israelis and the Egyptians to make sure we don't have any screw-up's" said the Secretary. "I'll call you when we are clear."

They departed the oval office and headed for their cars. It was easy to see the Secretary was still mad.

The Admiral and Colonel Hammond returned to the pentagon and called a meeting of the Chiefs of the Army, Air Force, Navy and Marines. He filled them in on the situation and asked if anyone had any recommendations.

The Air Force Chief was the first to speak up.

"If you, Sir" addressing the Joint Chief," will alert Livorno, I can have seven 141s at their airstrip in 3-4 hours. I just happen to have them up at Aviano, Italy about an hour away. In addition, I have 12 F-4-Es at Ramstein in Germany to give close air support should the need arise. I also know the Egyptian Chief of the Air Force. I'll coordinate with him for the use of one of his airfields and send support teams including ammo for the F-4s. I recommend we send the support teams in as soon as I talk to the Egyptian Chief of Staff. We also have transport planes at Aviano we can use for the support teams. As for dropping the airborne troops we have a couple of 141s at Wiesbaden in Germany, they can be at Brindisi in about 4 hours.

"That sounds good - go ahead and notify those crews to be on standby. Have the 141s fly to Livorno ASAP. Colonel Hammond alert Livorno immediately of what is needed and that they are about to get some 141s.

Colonel Hammond and the Air Force aide left the room together.

"What size force do we send in and where do we drop them?" was the Admiral's next question.

The Army Chief of Staff pressed a button and a detail map appeared on the wall of the conference room. He zeroed in on the 3rd Army area and it showed in detail the terrain and the ground. "I would suggest right here" a red arrow appeared on the map. "It's a slight depression but the ground is flat and easily accessible to the 3rd Army. The only thing that bothers me is the ridge to the North. Anyone up there could do serious damage to the men dropping in. Not that I don't trust the Israelis' High Command but there is always that 10% that doesn't get the word or has communication problems."

"What about the size of the force?" asked the Admiral again.

Well, I would suggest an Air Force FAC (Forward Air Controller) would have the radio to both the C-141s and the F-4s should they get into trouble; the main force about 50 troops or less. They can smoke the Drop Zone (DZ). If they get in trouble a fellow on force is not advisable cause then it becomes a turkey shoot."

"I agree with the Army here" said the Marine Chief of Staff. "The smaller the force the better. A large force, which I know they have could spook the Israelis and it could be misconstrued."

"We have a carrier and support ships in the eastern Mediterranean. If we can be of help let me know: said the Naval Chief of Staff. "I'll move them towards the Suez with your permission, Admiral.

"I hate to overdo this, but go ahead and move the Carrier Force and coordinate with the Egyptians for use of their facilities. Move the support troops and all air assets as soon as you have talked to the Egyptians. This meeting is over, go to work and brief me as soon as the assets are in place."

The conference room emptied except for the Army Chiefs of Staff.

"What's bothering you, General" asked the Admiral.

"Well, it's nothing really, but I don't trust the State Department. They have screwed up more situations over the years then I care to remember. The Secretary is a bootlicker, he wants to be something. God knows what it is! He can't become President, he is foreign born, but that's what he wants or maybe a King. I just have this feeling in the pit of my stomach that he is going to screw this up somehow and then step in and save the day. I have nothing to hang my hat on but we have to double check with both the Israelis and the Egyptians. The 3rd Army has been without or low on rations and medical supplies for a week. They must be getting desperate."

"I agree Hal. Between you and me I don't trust the State Department. I'll call on a secure line over to the Agency and talk to my friend and see if he can't use his assets. I know he has a good relationship with both sides even though Sadat has been in the Russian camp for a while. I know the Israelis will listen and get the word out. God knows we gave them enough supplies these last weeks. Get the word to Brendisi as soon as you have determined the places and don't let anyone else pick the drop zone. You send the coordinates to Task force Headquarters over there; I know they have the new maps. Is anything else bothering you?"

"Yes, I would like all Israeli recon forces withdrawn at least 5 miles from the DZ. They are the trigger happy ones. I happen to know from our Special Forces liaison that they just had a meeting at their forward headquarters. One recon force was given 5 additional tanks to go with their half tracks which have quad 50 caliber MG on them. Their order is to put pressure on the 3rd Egyptian Army, in addition the word is they are having trouble with their new radios we sent them."

"Shit, Hal, when did you find this out?"

"Just before I walked into this meeting. I didn't want to say anything in from of the others."

"OK let me get to work. I have to call in some chips."

The admiral was alone in the conference room when Colonel Hammond walked in.

"I just talked to the G-3 at Brendisi, an old friend. He is on the same page as we are. He has 45 troops handpicked and is waiting for the FAC from Aviano - 46 troops in all. He needs one C-141 - maybe another as backup if something happens to one of the planes and would like them one hours prior to boarding. So they can top off their tanks. He has an intel officer in the unit that's going in and this guy is only a captain but with all types of resources, informed him that the Israeli forward forces are to shoot and I quote the shit out of any movement in the 3rd Army area. They have done an extensive map recon and have come up with a DZ that matches ours.

"Is this Colonel Lawson you talked to?"

"Yes sir, he is a soldier's soldier."

"I know him; he will receive his first star in two months. God I know the troops he is sending in are good - because he is a hard man. I think his wife has softened him a little around the edges but he is good. Tell him to stick with the DZ no matter who tells him different - even the President and that I agree with the manpower."

"Yes, Sir, I'll get him on the horn right away."

"The Air Force Chief of Staff walked in and informed the admiral that coordination has been made - an airfield has been designated and the support personnel are getting ready as we speak; should be in place, 4-6 hours. The F 4s are leaving Ramstein, heading for Aviano, Italy. Will be briefed at Aviano and upon the Go word will head to the designated air base in Egypt. They will be armed at Aviano, just in case something goes wrong - a KC 135 will be in the air over the Mediterranean for refueling."

"Have the instructions been given as to what they are to do in case the Israelis fire on our people?"

"Sir, that will be given at Aviano and there can only be one command, destroy the Israeli unit causing problems."

"Good - our careers might be over after this but if the Israelis attack our troops neutralize them with extreme prejudice."

Colonel Lawson, LTC Hays and Major Compton were in the briefing room when Captain Ryder knocked on the door and walked in closing the door behind him.

"Just received this from the State Department."

Colonel Lawson took the message and read it, passed it to LTC Hays who upon reading it gave it to Major Compton.

"What the hell is this crap?" Colonel Lawson said in a loud voice.

"We don't coordinate with the State Department and they don't give us DZ coordinates Ryder place these coordinates on our map."

Captain Ryder took the message and scribbled the coordinates in grease pencil on the plastic covered map. Matching the coordinates with the map, he looked a second time at the location and shook his head.

"Sir, these coordinates have us dropping into a rock quarry, it will be a disaster, sir."

"God damn give me the secure phone Compton. I need to call a friend ASAP, you all stay here."

The call went through.

"Colonel Hammond please, no it's an emergency. Tell him Colonel Lawson is on the secure line. Hammond, Lawson here. I just received a message from the State Department giving me the coordinates for the DZ. No God damn it, I'm not kidding, it's a fucking rock quarry. You're in with the Old man now? Tell him I don't take orders from the State Department and if I show this to my General he'll go through the roof. I have the unit commander and Major Compton who will lead the unit in and smoke the DZ. What the hell is going on?"

"I'll wait your message, give my regards to your better half, she deserves someone better than you. I'll disregard your last statement - out."

Colonel Lawson looked around the room.

"Someone is trying to fuck this operation up and it's not the Pentagon."

Colonel Hammond briefed the Admiral on his phone call from Colonel Lawson. The Admiral rubbed his stubbly grey hair leaning back in his chair.

"Give the Air Force the go ahead to move all assets immediately and give me the word when they are in place."

The Admiral called the Secretary of Defense and asked him if he had five minutes.

"OK, I'll be right over."

The Admiral looked at Hammond and told him to stay in the office in case any more calls came in but to get the Air Force going.

The Admiral walked into the Secretary of Defense's office and took a chair.

"What is the problem today? Are we going to war or is this an internal problem?"

The Admiral explained the situation in detail trying hard to keep his temper down.

"Why in God's name would the State Department get involved in military matters much less contact the unit involved? I am close to Moshe Dayan, the Defense Minister, let me give him a call." The Secretary of Defense pressed two buttons on his phone and waited.

"Sorry for the time difference Minister Dayan but I have a problem on my hands which requires the utmost diplomacy and discretion. I'm sure you have heard that we have received a request from Sadat to help resupply his 3rd Army with food, water and medical supplies. You haven't heard a word? Let me explain the Russians have left or are leaving Egypt. Sadat indicates that he is tired of business as usual and is ready to work with us. I see this as leading to peace between your two countries. Of course, this is between you and me. Our State Department has indicated that they were in touch with your people and that everything is set. What my concern is that your unit located around the 3rd Army does not open fire on our 46 paratroopers dropping in at the following coordinates. They are merely there to secure the drop zone and bring the resupplies in. Sadat has already alerted his troops i.e. 3rd Army or any missile batteries not to fire. In fact he has ordered his troops along the entire front to stand down. After all there is a truce in effect."

"Yes, I believe him. He has given our President his word. I'm also telling you this as a friend, that he has designed an airfield for a squadron of our fighters and support crews in case anything goes wrong on either side - yours or theirs. I'm telling you this to be upfront with you as a friend. Yes, I feel strongly that peace is in the offering, but if we get too many people involved in this humanitarian support, things could get ugly. If you agree to this please inform your Commanders of the situation. If you don't agree please let me know soonest. Thanks, Dayan, I'll await your call." The Secretary of Defense hung up and looked at the Admiral.

"It seems our esteemed State Department has not notified anyone in the Israeli chain of command of the situation and Dayan was less than happy about the situation in its entirety. Thank God we go way back, otherwise it could get sticky."

"The State Department had no intention of notifying the Israelis - at least not the ones who had the clout. We would have had a fiasco and then they would step in and rescue the situation and become the big man on campus. I don't trust them."

"Don't be too hard on them, Admiral, How far are we along on our deployment of men and planes?"

"Planes and support teams are in the air as we speak. When the President says go we are ready. If you would turn your wall map on I'll show you the airfield Sadat has given us and our drop zone." A detailed map appeared on the Secretary's wall and the Admiral pointed out the two sites.

"Any reservations?"

"The only thing that bothers me is the ridge above the drop zone. We know there is a reinforced recon unit in the vicinity with 5 tanks. It could be a turkey shoot if they don't get the word."

"I should be getting a call back from Dayan in a few hours. I'll keep you posted."

As the Admiral walked into his office, Colonel Hammond was pacing back and forth.

"What's the matter?"

"I just had a call from Colonel Lawson, they have received two additional messages from the State Department telling them to hold off any action until they hear from them. They will give the order to go or not to go. I'm getting a little frustrated. I haven't told anyone and Colonel Lawson is talking only to me."

"The Secretary called Dayan, an old friend, and he promised to get back to him in a few hours. I told the Secretary about my apprehension about the ridge and the recon unit in the vicinity. I also reiterated my feelings about our State Department, which I think he feels the same way about. I don't want to go to the President until I absolutely have to. We should be able to handle this amongst the staff. I'll give our Secretary of Defense a call and update."

The Secretary answered his phone.

"What's going on?"

"Two more messages from State to Brendisi telling them to hold off and that they will give the order to go."

"I'll call our Secretary of State and find out what the hell they are doing."

The phone went dead.

"This is the Secretary of Defense give me the Secretary of State - I need two minutes of his time."

"What can I do for you?" came the gravelly voice.

"I was under the impression that the President said for your section to coordinate with the Admiral. Our forces in Italy have received 4 messages from your office telling them not only where to jump but when. The Israelis have not heard anything from you and it's been almost 5 hours now. I'm about to go over and see the President on something else but I'll surely bring him up to date on this most unusual line of communication."

"I have been trying to get Dayan but evidently he is up at the front lines and cannot be reached."

"I just talked to him not 30 minutes ago and he was headed to their Prime Minister and Golda to brief them on the relief situation and its possible long range implications between the two countries."

"Leave the politics to me and go and play with your little tin soldiers."

The line went dead.

The Secretary of Defense was fuming. He called for his military aide and told him they were heading to the White House now. He was escorted in to the Oval office.

"What can I do for you, George, you look flustered." The President sat back in his chair and played with his pen.

The Secretary of Defense briefed the President on what had transpired and the lack of communication between the State Department and the Israelis.

"Are you sure? If that son of a bitch is playing games again with his friends, I'll fire him. We are talking about American lives here. We have lost thousands in that stupid war in Viet Nam and are still losing them. That's all we need to do is lose some more young men in the Middle East and the demonstrators will probably burn down the White House. You handle this; I'll give Golda a call right away and explain to her what we are doing and its long range implications. When Golda was here a few days ago, she seemed receptive to new and future ideas on peace with Egypt, between you and me I think she is physically sick, there is definitely something wrong with her, the old spark is gone. As you well know, Congress is after my ass; the eastern establishment is riding the crest of the wave and is screaming impeachment. Well, we'll see about that, so I have a few things on my plate but I'll call Golda now. You handle the humanitarian relief; don't pay any attention to the Secretary of State.

The President indicated the meeting was over.

The Secretary of Defense returned to the Pentagon and called a meeting of the Secretaries of the various military branches and their Chiefs of Staff.

"I wanted all of you to be here and be brought up to date on our mission to rescue or help the 3rd Egyptian Army. The only progress that's been made as far as coordination with the Israelis and Egyptians is what we have done. The State Department is trying to muddy the waters, they have not contacted anyone regarding the 3rd Army. Where do we stand as far as our air assets?"

"The C-141s are being loaded at Livorno as we speak. The F-4s should be landing in Egypt in about two hours or less. The support troops are in place. The two C-141s at Aviano are fueled and ready for departure to Brendisi when we give them the word," said the Chief of Staff of the Air Force.

"Give them the GO for Brendisi."

The Air Force General's Aide left the room.

"One more thing" the Air Force chief of Staff lifted his hand.

"I have sent a complete crew for each of the F-4s to Egypt along with the support personnel. The French balked at our over flight of their country so the trip got longer. I wanted fresh crews in case we needed them."

"Good planning, if I live to be a hundred I'll never understand the French" said the Secretary of Defense.

"Army?"

"I have talked to the Air Force and we concur. We will fly at normal altitude and then drop to 400 feet for the troops, it will give them less exposure in the air and there will be no need for a reserve parachute and they will use M-C1 stretchable chutes to lessen the footprint on the ground. I talked to the G-3 Colonel Lawson and they are ready to go. A pallet of extra ammo will be dropped also - just in case. They are continuing to receive messages from the State Department and the Ambassador to Italy flew in and gave them hell for not notifying him. According to him he is in charge of all American assets in Italy. Colonel Lawson said he had the distinct impression that the Ambassador was aware of the mission, his departing words were that nothing was to move unless he gave the order."

"I will say this one last time and let there be no misunderstanding among you and pass the word to Lawson. Dayan will contact me, The President is speaking to Golda as we sit here. The President will call me to give the GO word and I'll tell you. Do not be distracted by anyone, I don't care who he is or his title. I have heard enough horseshit today to last me the rest of my life. Am I clear?"

There was a nodding of heads all around the table.

About an hour later Dayan called the Secretary of Defense and informed him that the word had gone out to all the units. There were some problems with some of the new radios but messengers were on the way to notify them and everyone should have the word within the hour.

"You realize of course if there is any shooting at our soldiers or planes they will be dealt with in an extreme manner?"

"I understand, that's why I have ordered commanders to send personnel to these units with radio problems so that we can avoid an unfortunate incident."

"Thanks Dayan. I appreciate your personal cooperation. I think we are on the verge of peace between you and Egypt."

"Shalom, my friend." The line went dead.

The Secretary of Defense sat there even with Dayan's assurance he had a feeling in the pit of his stomach that he had missed something. He pressed the button on his desk and his military aide came in. A One Star General with years of combat experience.

"Mike, brief me on these steerable parachutes the troops are going to use and why so low on altitude?"

"Sir, the chutes have two panels missing in the back, letting air spill out. The soldier has two toggle lines, one for each hand that he pulls on to steer his chute where he wants to land. It's a very effective way to drop in anywhere and the soldiers are well trained in its use. The low altitude is to get the soldiers on the ground faster and not exposing him so long in the air for someone to take a shot at him. The normal altitude is 1200 to 1250 feet that leaves the soldier in the air a lot longer."

"Do all the airborne troops use these chutes?"

"No, only special units; the regular Airborne units have the T-10s which should have been done away with long ago."

"How low below the ridge will they exit the plane?"

"About a hundred feet above the ridge a little lower at the south end."

"All this time the C-141 is vulnerable to ground fire if it's flying parallel to the ridge."

"Yes, sir, that is a concern since the recon unit in the area has quad 50 Caliber Machine guns; they could definitely bring down the C-141."

"Get me the Air Force Secretary and Chief of Staff in here and you join us.:

"Five minutes later they were sitting in the Secretary of Defense's office.

"I don't like the vulnerability of the troops and the C-141 dropping them. We have twelve F-4s ready to assist. Can we send in say 4 F-4s prior to the drop, I mean right prior to the drop and maybe waggle their wings or whatever you call it to show the Israelis that we are friendly and not to fire?"

"There are two things we can do said the Air Force Chief of Staff. One - do a dirty pass right over the recon unit. It's dicey but our pilots are trained to do it. They come in fast on the deck lower their flaps and create a sand storm that will last long enough to get the C-141 out of the area and the troops on the ground. The other 8 F-4s will be stacked over head and if there is any firing after the sand storm clears they take the recon unit out. The second option is fly two F-4s in low do a waggle as you say and do a gentle turn over the troops while 10 F-4s are stacked and ready to attack. We call the first option a dirty pass."

"Do we do things like the dirty pass normally?"

"No, to be honest but the special forces love it and often request it. It gives them time to close with and take out the enemy."

"Do what you think works best; I just don't want any American soldiers hurt."

At the State Department, the Secretary of State for the Middle East desk made a call to an old friend who worked on Dayan's staff and informed him of the U.S. Plan to send in humanitarian help to the 3rd Egyptian Army. He informed the staff officer that he didn't think it was a good idea and wanted to know if the Israelis had units to intercept this aide. He was told that they had a reinforced recon unit that could handle it. The Secretary then briefed the officer on the U.S. plan. The officer was somewhat taken aback when told that a small contingent of U.S. Paratroopers would secure the drop zone. The Secretary gave him the coordinates where the drop zone would be.

"Just pin them down so they can't call in the planes that will drop the supplies" said the Secretary of the Middle East desk.

The Israeli officer was hesitant but told the Secretary of the Middle East desk he would personally send the message to the recon commander who he knew well.

At Brendisi, Major Compton went over the operation with all the men going in including the Air Force FAC who had just joined them. He emphasized that the points on the drop zone each of the five sections were to land. They had good communication in case one section needed help. He also informed them that there was an Israeli recon unit in the vicinity but that they had been told about the operation and would not interfere. The Egyptians were also cooperating and would upon the landing of the supplies send a convoy to pick them up. Upon the termination of the operation CH-53 Air Force Choppers would pick them up and take them to a U.S. occupied Air Base in Egypt.

"As in any operation most of us have participated in, there is always Murphy's Law, What can go wrong will go wrong. I therefore want six extra machine guns, extra ammo will be dropped, and each man carries extra ammo in their rucksack. We should be in there approximately one day perhaps two depending on the Egyptians ability to get the supplies off the drop zone. We have Air Force support in case something goes wrong hence the FAC here. The drop zone is relatively smooth but should anyone sprain an ankle or something we have medics that will place ankle supports on you. The FAC will be in contact with the planes arriving from Livorno and myself and Captain Ryder will smoke the DC in our sector which will signal the designated personnel in the four other sectors to throw their smoke grenades. Are there any questions, we should get the word any time now so grab your chutes. You may have noticed there are no reserve chutes. You will jump at 400 feet so get chuted up and attach your rucksacks on the plane in case you need to relieve yourselves. Again any questions? No one is confused? That's good, saddle up.

Colonel Lawson had been listening to Major Compton's briefing.

"Be sure you stay next to the FAC if there is any shooting. I just had a message from the Pentagon that F-4s will do a fly over and plenty more are on station should some Israelis not get the word. Don't hesitate to shoot back if the shit hits the fan. Brief the troops once in the plane. I did a detailed study of the map, there are some large boulders scattered along the drop zone below the ridge. It could give you cover if you need it. Good luck! Colonel Lawson slapped Major Compton's helmet as he walked to the back ramp of the C-141.

Chapter 2

Captain Hertzog of the 2nd Israeli recon force was halted and sitting atop of his half track eating his breakfast along with the rest of his troops. The tanks were dispersed and all of his vehicles had recently been refueled so he was good to go for the rest of the day. He hated Egyptians. This was the 3rd time he had been called up. Everyone who was able bodied in Israel was in the reserves. He missed his family, not to mention the business he had to run along with his father-in-law. They had just started construction of their 3rd large motel along the ocean not far from Tel Aviv, where he should be instead of sitting out in this God forsaken stretch of desert.

His last briefing had been, if the Egyptians move shoot the shit out of them and keep harassing them. They had destroyed a relief column sent to resupply the 3rd Army. They had used up too much of their ammunition but they had enough, he knew the tanks were low. He had sent a message requesting re-supply but these new radios were not reliable and had not gotten a reply. In the distance he saw a cloud of dust, it was a vehicle heading towards them. When it got closer he looked through his binoculars and saw it was one of theirs. As the vehicle stopped by one of the distant tanks, it quickly picked up speed again and headed for Captain Herzog's halftrack. A sergeant got out of the vehicle lifted his goggles up and handed Captain Hertzog a plastic covered piece of paper. Captain Hertzog took the paper out and read it. What the hell was this, he read it twice. The Americans were coming to resupply the 3rd Army? It must be some mistake. The Americans were their friends and had supported them with planes, tanks and ammunition in each of their battles with the Arabs. This must be a mistake. A small force of American paratroopers were to secure a drop zone not a kilometer away from where he was sitting and transport planes would come in later and drop supplies to the 3rd Army humanitarian supplies it said. What was going on? It was signed by Dayan.

He started to ask the Sergeant some questions but realized this was only a messenger. He handed the paper back to the Sergeant but was told by the Sergeant to sign the message. The Sergeant handed him a pen. Hertzog reluctantly signed the message and handed it back to the Sergeant who got back in his vehicle and departed. They were not to interfere with the air drop. Why were they here? Why had he lost soldiers dead and wounded? He told his radio operator to try headquarters again, static was all they got. He was tempted to drive NE to a place he knew he could reach headquarters but that was a waste of fuel. He'd wait a few hours. His men needed to rest, they had been on the go all night. He had dozed off and was rubbing his eyes, looking at his watch he realized that he had slept almost 3 hours. His troops were still asleep except for the guards. He looked around; everything was quiet except to the NE. There was another cloud of dust. He grabbed his binoculars and looked, it was one of theirs. This time the vehicle did not stop at the tanks but headed for his track. The same Sergeant got out lifted goggles and handed Captain Hertzog a plastic bag with a note in it. Captain Hertzog opened the bag and started reading the message. What the hell was going on? The message said to pin down the paratroopers, prevent casualties and not to fire on the transport that dropped them. It was signed by one of Dayan's staff officers. He looked at the Sergeant and asked for the pen. Captain Hertzog wrote a note on the back of the message, for headquarters to clarify the two messages and handed the paper and pen back to the Sergeant who replaced his goggles and took off. What was going on? How could he pin down the airborne troops without hurting them? These were Americans their best friends. He shot a green flare up, a signal for everyone to gather around his track. The rumble of the tanks could be heard as all units started gathering around him.

When all were assembled Captain Hertzog explained what was about to happen. He didn't mention the first message. His men looked at each other and some raised their hands. Was he telling them to fire on American paratroopers? And when were they arriving? Captain Hertzog explained that they were merely to pin them down and not to fire on the transport plane dropping them. Some of his men wanted to know where the drop zone was and how were they to pin them down with quad 50s? The Americans would fire back, then what? They are dropping a kilometer north of here and we will deploy on the ridge above the drop zone. One of his soldiers pointed out that a kilometer north was a stone quarry. They are not jumping in there. There is a flat area about 2 kilometers back there. You must have gotten the wrong coordinates. Captain Hertzog checked his map, the soldier was right. He told his men they would cover both places. They should be coming in about an hour from now. He divided his forces assigning a small section to the quarry the rest to the flat area. The Tankers wanted to know what their roll would be. Use your machine guns but not the main gun was his answer. They split up and headed north. They were barely in place when 2 U.S. F-4s came in low and waggled their wings and made a lazy turn to the West gaining altitude. A large C-141 dropped down to about 500 feet above the drop zone. They could see the pilots who waved at them.

Inside the C-141s, Major Compton had done his checks and the green light came on. He exited the plane and the rest of the men followed. Major Compton was in the air and looked around. Ryder was a little above him. He slipped the pins for the toggles and grabbed one in each hand. He steered for a rock outcropping below the ridge; he was on the ground. He collapsed his chute, Captain Ryder and the FAC landed fifty feet away from him. He looked around - the troops were on the ground in their respective places, collapsing their chutes and hitting the release mechanism on their chests. All of a sudden there was a roar of two F-4s above the ridge waggling their wings and doing a gentle curve gaining altitude over the drop zone and disappearing north. The pallet with extra ammo sat in the middle of the drop zone. The troops rushed to get the extra ammo and returned to their original positions. All of a sudden Captain Ryder grabbed his arm, blood was pooling in his upper arm. Major Compton grabbed him and yelled at the FAC to get under the rock outcropping. Heavy machine gun rounds were peppering the drop zone. Major Compton cut Captain Ryder's shirt arm open with his knife. The bullet had grazed Ryder's arm. He quickly bandaged the arm and asked Ryder if he was OK. He got the thumbs up sign. Bullets were now peppering the drop zone where the troops had no cover. Three of his sections were firing MG's at the top of the ridge. Major Compton saw several of his soldiers lying on the drop zone. He grabbed the FAC and told him to bring in the

F-4s and eliminate the unit on the ridge. The FAC was on the radio and told the F-4s to come in and do their duty. Major Compton got on the units frequency and told his men to try to get to the boulders leading up to the ridge. Some of them made it but three more soldiers hit the ground. The medics were moving among them; one was hit but managed to get to one of the men.

Captain Hertzog was getting peppered with M-60 MG bullets from the paratroopers. He ordered his men to fire for effect. All of a sudden there was a roar over his head. Two of his tanks and one halftrack disappeared in flames. The roar kept coming; his unit further north was coming to his aide but was also hit. Where were these planes coming from, one of his tracks was firing at one of the planes but were soon engulfed in flames. Captain Hertzog jumped into a small gully, immediately his left leg went limp. His track had been hit and he had barely escaped. He crawled out of his gully and looked around. His entire recon unit was destroyed. Looking down at his left leg he saw a piece of metal sticking out he pulled it out and wound a bandage around his leg. This was a bad dream. He passed out.

Major Compton told the FAC to cancel the air drop and why. Even though there was no more firing coming from the ridge. He had injured and dead on his hands. He also told the FAC to contact the support airfield and get the choppers to their site. Captain Ryder was pale but OK. He walked to where the medics were working. One of the medics had a bandage around his thigh but was working on the wounded. It was the soldiers who had been on the far side of the field who were wounded and dead. Seven dead, 14 wounded said the medic as he looked up at Major Compton with tears in his eyes. Major Compton looked up to the ridge. There were soldiers moving around but appeared wounded. He asked the two medics who were not wounded if there was anything left for them to do. He was told all wounded had been treated. Major Compton looked up to the ridge again and told the two medics to gather all their supplies and follow him. They started climbing up to the ridge. As they approached a burning halftrack, a soldier pointed an automatic weapon at them,. There was a sharp order from somewhere and the soldier lowered his weapon. The one who had given the command was climbing out of a small gully hardly able to walk; one of his soldiers helped him.

"I'm Captain Hertzog" he said saluting Major Compton. Something very wrong has happened here today, I don't fully understand but maybe I was not meant to."

Major Compton asked if he had wounded that needed help. Captain Hertzog looked around and pointed to his own soldiers working on his wounded. Major Compton told his medics to go and help. They had worked about an hour when they heard choppers in the distance. Major Compton got on his radio and told Ryder to send one of the choppers up to the ridge. Three choppers CH-53s landed in the drop zone area one lifted off and landed on the ridge amongst the carnage.

"Do you want me to take the wounded back with me or to your headquarters?"

"I don't think you have fuel enough to take them to our headquarters?" Major Compton went over to the chopper and asked the pilot about his fuel situation.

"I have two external tanks; how far is this place to where you want me to go?" Major Compton turned to Captain Hertzog and asked him.

"About 30 kilometers NE they have a medical unit set up there."

"How many people are we talking about?" asked the pilot.

"About 32 wounded" answered Captain Hertzog. The dead will have to wait."

"Put them aboard and I'll come back and pick you up Major Compton." The chopper lowered the back access door and Captain Hertzog indicated to his still able troops to start loading the wounded. Captain Hertzog told his second in command that he would send vehicles back to pick up the dead and able soldiers in an hour or so. Captain Hertzog with the assistance of a soldier was the last man aboard the huge chopper. There was a dust storm as the chopper took off.

Major Compton walked around the smoldering tanks and half tracks he counted 34 dead. There were probably more inside the tanks. The second in command limped over to Major Compton and asked him what happened. Major Compton shook his head indicating he did not know.

Major Compton radioed Captain Ryder and asked for a final tally of dead and wounded. "Seven killed in action, 14 wounded - 15 if you included me," he said.

"Place as many as you can aboard the choppers and have one return. I sent the wounded Israelis back to their medical unit. He should return in an hour. Have the soldiers gather around that outcropping we used and have the FAC radio a sit-rep back to the support unit in Egypt. They should be able to get Task Force. Also have the F-4s rearm. I don't know what is going to happen here but it's a catastrophe. Better yet, have a couple of F-4s return here and circle the area, you never know."

"Roger," came the reply.

Major Compton sat down on a rock and one of his medics came over and wanted to know what had happened?

"I think its politics but that's between you and me. You guys did an outstanding job. I won't forget it nor will the Israelis.

They heard the chopper return. Major Compton tossed a green smoke grenade and the chopper settled down in a cloud of dust. The back door opened and Major Compton and the two medics walked aboard. Major Compton walked forward and told the pilot to land down below the ridge.

The pilot landed and shut down the chopper.

Major Compton and the two medics had just joined the rest of the soldiers by the outcropping when two F-4s screamed overhead. The FAC told them the situation and they gained altitude and circled overhead. They reported a truck convoy heading from the NE. Should they take them out? The FAC told them, no, they were friendly and coming to pick up the dead and the surviving Israelis.

"Roger," said one of the pilots. "We will just waggle our wings".

They heard a chopper coming. The chopper on the ground started up his engines.

Soon they were covered in sand swirling from the chopper landing. They split into two groups and boarded the choppers. A little over an hour they landed at the Egyptian Air Base. Major Compton was the first one out. He saw Colonel Lawson walking towards him. Major Compton saluted and asked about the dead and wounded.

"A C-141 is taking them to Ramstein Air Force base in Germany.

"Have their families been notified?"

"No one knows about this yet. I talked to the Army chief of Staff. He said to put a lid on it for now."

Major Compton looked into Colonel Lawson's eyes shook his head and walked over to where his men were gathering. It took all his will power to tell them this was a horrible mistake and not to say a word when they got back. They were still under the secrecy act which they had signed and it could have severe repercussions until the official version got out. This is being handled by the Chairman of the Joint Chief of Staff. His eyes filled with tears as he looked at the men and shook each one's hand. When he got to Captain Ryder he just looked at him and shook his head. He asked Ryder for the manifest and gave it to the medics and asked them to annotate by each man's name who was wounded and who was killed. They sat down on the tarmac and went down the list and handed it back to Major Compton who took it from them. He thanked the group for their professionalism and told them he had never worked with a finer group of soldiers. They all had their heads bowed.

Colonel Lawson came over and asked Major Compton to come with him. They headed for a small building and walked in. There was an Air Force One Star General there and the three of them sat down on chairs. Colonel Lawson introduced Major Compton to the General and then asked Major Compton to describe what happened.

Major Compton briefed the two officers on the entire operation. When he was through he looked at the Air Force General and told him that if it hadn't been for the F-4s no one would have survived.

"Where did you send my one chopper?" the General asked him.

"I got with the wounded Israeli Captain in charge and told him to load the wounded up in the chopper and they would fly them to their headquarters' hospital and for him to send trucks back for the dead and the few men he had left. He said he would and gave the order to his Sergeant. The Captain also told me he was very confused because he had received a message by a courier to let the Americans land and set up an air drop of food and medicine for the 3rd Army; it was signed by Dayan. About two hours later he received another message signed by one of Dayan's staff officers to pin the Americans down but not to hit the aircraft that dropped them. He said he had tried the radios but could not get through. He had started his halftrack to the NE where he knew he could get radio communication to verify the confused messages but then the aircraft appeared and he turned and implemented the last message. He was confused as to why they were firing on their friends, the Americans, but the last message had been signed by a General. So he obeyed."

"What did the aftermath of the recon unit look like?" asked Colonel Lawson.

"The tanks and half tracks were completely destroyed. I'm sure there were more dead soldiers in the tanks but I had other priorities, sending their wounded back to their hospital was about all I could handle. I had my own troops to take care of."

"Was the Captain badly wounded?" asked Colonel Lawson.

"Yes, he was bleeding through his bandaged thigh. He required the help of one of his soldiers to get around."

"I have sent a message to our boss the South Com. Commander. The C-141s at Liverno are being unloaded. There will be no air drop. I'll fly back with you and your men as soon as the General here releases a C-141 for the trip. The Air Force has set up a field kitchen in one of the hangers. Have your men get a meal or drink."

Major Compton walked out and told his men if they were hungry to go over to the hanger. He had one of the medics check Captain Ryder's wound which was redressed. Well let's go over and get a cup of coffee or something. The Air Force makes real food so let's take advantage of it.

A C-141 arrived and was refueled. Colonel Lawson got the men together and told them to get aboard.

Major Compton walked over to the Air Force General saluted him and thanked him for his support and to pass it on to the F-4 pilots and the helicopter crews.

"Your men did an outstanding job today - I don't understand the whole situation but then maybe I'm not supposed to."

"I'll see you in Brendisi tomorrow," said the Air Force General.

Major Compton boarded the C-141 and they took off for home. No one spoke on the way back; some of the soldiers appeared to be sleeping but Major Compton knew better. They had lost some of their friends and tried to shut out the situation by closing their eyes.

Chapter 3

Their arrival at Brendisi was quiet; no one was there to greet them. Trucks were there to take them to the base. When they had disembarked Colonel Lawson asked them to keep quiet what had taken place. They would all meet tomorrow. LTC Hays showed up his face was white and he didn't know what to say other then "good job" and shook each of the soldiers' hands. The South Com General came and saluted the troops. He said he had talked to Ramstein and the wounded would return to duty. The ones who had sacrificed their lives would be returned to the states. The three who had families here - he, Colonel Lawson, LTC Hays and Major Compton would go and visit the families in a few minutes. Their families would be taken care of. The ones who were not married their families would be notified. It had been a tragic mistake by the Israelis and messages of condolences had been received from Golda Meir, Moshe Dayan and their foreign minister Abba Eban. The families in Brendisi would also have friends staying with them the next few days.

The South Com. General and the designated representatives took off in jeeps and headed to the quarters of the first families to be notified. Major Compton rang the doorbell and a young woman with a child in her arms answered the door. When she saw who was standing on the stoop her face turned white! He told her there had been a tragic accident and that her husband had unfortunately not made it. He had been killed.

The words did not seem to sink in at first.

She looked at Major Compton who was still dirty with a torn and blooded uniform, her eyes glazed over and tears were running down her cheeks. She tightened the grip on her young boy in her arms and asked them to come in.

"Where is Tom and what happened?" She was addressing Major Compton.

"Sue, Tom was killed by friendly fire; he did not suffer that I can assure you. His body is at the Air Force Hospital at Ramstein Air Force base in Germany. Is there anyone we can call and have them come over and stay with you?"

Sue was crying now, wiping her tears she looked at Major Compton and asked if he wanted her to clean and bandage his wound. She was an RN and had supplies.

Major Compton was taken aback. He hadn't realized he had been wounded and looked down at his left side.

"Yes, please, if you don't mind."

"Tom always spoke highly of you, it's the least I can do." She placed her son in his play pen and disappeared into another room.

Major Compton looked at the three other officers just raised his hands as if he didn't know what to do.

"Let her fix you up" Colonel Lawson said. Sue came in carrying a large metal 1st aid kit.

Don't worry Major Compton, I'm not going to operate on you, just take off your shirt and tee shirt." Major Compton did as he was told. Sitting there without his shirt made him feel vulnerable.

"It's not bad, I'll just clean it and check to see if any foreign material is in there." She swabbed the wound with Iodine and gently probed the wound.

"You were lucky it's just a graze. I'll fix it up. She applied more iodine - this time Major Compton felt the sting. Sue put on latex gloves and sutured the wound. She bandaged it and looked at him.

"I didn't know I was hit, thank you. Is there someone we can call who can come over and stay with you?"

"Thank you for letting me do that" she said trying to smile but tears were welling up in her eyes. She rearranged the kit and took it into the other room.

"I just needed something to do; I really don't know what to do now. The 1st Sergeant's wife Emily and I are close, she doesn't have any kids; if you would call her for me I would really appreciate it. Her number is in the book by the phone." Major Compton who was now dressed went over to the phone and called the number in the book. The phone was answered by Emily herself. Major Compton introduced himself and asked if she could come over to Sue and Tom's place.

"What's the matter?" were her first words.

"Come over and we'll explain."

"I'll be there in two minutes" the phone went dead.

Emily walked in and saw the people sitting there. She went over to Sue and placed her arms around her.

"Tom has been killed!" was all Sue managed to get out.

Emily looked around and asked what happened.

The General explained there had been a terrible accident and Tom had died.

"Who else?" Emily asked.

"There are several more dead," said the General.

"From my husband's company?" she asked.

"No," said Major Compton.

"We will give you the details tomorrow" said the General. "Can you stay with Sue tonight?"

"Of course I can. What should I tell my husband?"

"Tell him Sue needs you and you'll be home tomorrow," said LTC Hays.

Emily looked at him in a strange way. "I'll be here as long as Sue can put up with me."

The officers all rose - Colonel Lawson placed a card with a phone number on it. "If you need anything day or night call this number. Do you need groceries or food?"

"No, we are fine," said Sue taking the card off the table. "This is your home number Colonel Lawson, I recognize it."

"I said day or night, Sue, and I mean it."

They left and headed for the other two families.

"That was nice of you, Major Compton, to let her fix up your wound. It got her mind off her sorrow for a few minutes," said the General.

They met with the two other wives and this time LTC Hays took over the announcement to the two grieving wives.

"Let's go over to the club and have a drink," said the General as they left the last wife. "And talk over tomorrow's plan."

They sat down in comfortable chairs away from the few customers already there. The bartender came over and took their orders and returned with their drinks. The General paid.

"I talked to the Army Chief of Staff; the shit has hit the fan in the Secretary of Defense's office. They are in touch with the Israelis. They got a thank you notice from Golda Meir and Dayan for transporting their wounded to their headquarters' hospital and want to know the name of the officer who authorized it. It seems that Dayan sent a message to the recon unit by messenger and the commander, a Captain Hertzog, signed the message indicating he understood. However one of Dayan's staff officers sent a second message telling the recon unit to pin down the American paratroopers. He had no authorization to send this message and is now confined to quarters awaiting court martial. The Israelis, even though they suffered a devastating blow, will do everything they can for the dead Americans' families and the wounded. Our President is being briefed as we speak."

"I talked to the Ramstein General in charge. Thank God our wounded will be able to return to duty. They are being treated. When asked what happened not one of them would talk and said it was a training accident. I will have my staff write up appropriate awards to everyone. It's the dead I worry about when they get back to the states and their families. I want you LTC Hays to be our representative. You will leave for the Pentagon tomorrow to report to the Army Chief of Staff. They will have representatives to notify the families and say the official words. You will visit the four families and stay for the funerals. Take your wife with you if you want. As of now, the Pentagon is formulating the official response. If you have any questions let me know. I will be in touch with the Army Chief of Staff."

"Sir, it will be my honor to do this and yes I would like to take my wife with me. Women seem to have a more sympathetic touch with words than we do."

"I want two meetings tomorrow one with the three widows and one with the wives of the wounded. How many of the wounded were married?"

"Sir, there are eight" said LTC Hays. "I want everything possible done for all of them. I have been authorized to fly them to Ramstein if they so desire. We also have a fund to take care of them and the widows, and the Army Chief of Staff will supplement it. I don't want any to be hindered for lack of funds. I'll brief them tomorrow."

"What about the troops that were not wounded, they deserve an explanation," said Major Compton.

"You're right," said the General. "I'll talk to them after the others; make sure they are available Major Compton. I know they are getting Israeli gold jump wings - everyone involved - what else I don't know."

Chapter 4

At the Pentagon there was a meeting with the Secretary of Defense. The Secretary was in a foul mood. All the services representatives were there.

"The first thing we have to do is keep a lid on this until I talk to the President. I have been briefed by the South Com Commander. The Israeli recon (who received two messages by courier) the first one was from Dayan telling him to pull back and not bother the American paratroopers and the resupply. The Recon Commander signed the message indicating he understood. Dayan has the message. The recon Commander then got a second message about an hour or so later from one of Dayan's staff officers telling him to pin down the American paratroopers and prevent the resupply. That staff officer is now under arrest. It seems the American officer in charge, after he airlifted the dead and wounded American soldiers to the Egyptian Air Base where they were loaded aboard a C-141 and transferred to Ramstein Air Base in Germany, diverted one of our C H 53 Choppers to take the Israelis wounded to their headquarters hospital. Golda and Dayan both expressed appreciation and wanted to know the officer's name. Let's find out who he is, this is the type of officers we want."

"Sir, his name is Major Peter Compton, he is the Executive Officer of the battalion in Brendisi. He has a good record not only from Viet Nam but Colonel Lawson the G-3 at South Com. Can't say enough about him."

"Let's make sure we follow his career and do the appropriate thing."

"Yes Sir, will do," said the Army Chief of Staff.

"Now what else do I need to know about this fiasco, I have the total dead and wounded, the ones with Families in Brendisi have all been taken care of and given a sponsor. The ones who are not married and whose parents are here in the States will be briefed by the Battalion Commander and his wife and a contingent from here. LTC Hays will arrive here this evening on a military flight carrying the bodies that will go to Walter Reed first. I want LTC Hays and wife put up in appropriate quarters, either military or hotel. I want LTC Hays and wife briefed when we have come up with the appropriate words, which I'm sure the White House is writing as we speak. The wounded I understand are not in serious condition and will return to duty at their request. When asked by the U.S. doctors what happened they all told them it was a training accident. Where in God's name do we get this caliber of soldiers from? Here we go again, it seems this Major Compton took extra ammo and 6 extra machine guns with him just in case and as a result kept the Israelis from killing and wounding more Americans. In the near future I want a low keyed meeting with this Major. Now where the hell did this second message originate? I hate to say what I'm thinking and I'm sure some of you have the same thoughts but until I talk to the President in an hour keep these thoughts to yourself. Air Force good job even though tragic;see that everyone involved are taken care of. Let's talk about compensation to the dead American families. I know there is a fund available but insufficient as far as I'm concerned. Their children should have some kind of free pass regarding their schools and let's not forget housing. There were 3 dead with families, wives and children. The other four leave parents behind. I'll check with the Staff Judge Adjutant (SJA) to see what our limits are. I will also discuss with the president what he can authorize. Army takes care of Hays and his wife; they should be arriving at Andrews Air Force base. The Air Force will know when the plane touches down; it will be a low key arrival but with honor guards, transport is laid on Walter Reed is expecting them. Is there anything I have left out? I have a meeting with the President in one hour. OK, everyone on the same page? This meeting is over; be prepared to meet later this afternoon or early in the morning. No leaks to the media."

The Secretary of Defense was ushered into the oval office along with his General Aide. The President looked tired. He indicated for them to take a seat.

"What the hell happened? I have seven young dead soldiers on my hands and God knows how many wounded. Who dropped the ball on this?"

The Secretary of Defense briefed the president on the entire episode including the wounded and that they had claimed it was a training accident.

"Promote those soldiers when they return to duty. Your telling me that Dayan sent a message by courier to the recon Captain telling him to leave the Americans alone and let the Air lift take place and this Recon commander signed the message that he understood and then some son-of-a-bitch on his staff sent a second message telling this same recon commander to pin down the Americans and prevent the air drop of supplies?"

"Yes Sir, the recon Commander told our officer in charge

he was confused but in the Israeli Army you obey your last command message."

"Had a call from Golda and she, of course, apologized but thanked us for sending their wounded in one of our helicopters to the headquarter hospital. They will all be OK but their losses were severe. Our Secretary of State is on his way to Egypt and then to Israel as we speak. The Egyptian and Israelis are to meet at marker 101, wherever that is. Hopefully some good will come of this."

The Secretary of Defense looked at his aide a little bit too long.

"What's going on?" the President wanted to know.

"Nothing we can prove but someone from the United States called Dayan's staff officer and told him to send that second message. Our Intel people are working to determine who called him."

"Shit, you're not suggesting what I think you're suggesting?"

"We have nothing yet. I'll let you know when we do." If I may, I want to discuss compensation to the families whose husband and sons were killed. We are checking with the SJA to determine our limits."

"We have latitude on an operation like this. I want the children taken care of through college. The widows will also be taken care of to include houses to raise their families. I want compensation to the parents of the unmarried and the appropriate awards to everyone involved.

Army & Air Force I'll leave the awards to you, Mr. Secretary. I want this kept low keyed - no media. I'm sure at some time this will leak out but it sounds like we sent in the right soldiers."

"Mr. President, are your people working up the appropriate words to the families?"

"Hell no, this place leaks like a sieve. If we did it the News

Media would be camped on the White House lawn now. Come up with the appropriate words and I'll sign it. No one here knows a thing about this fiasco, not even my Chief of Staff and I want it kept that way. I will see to it that funds are made available either through government channels i.e. a training accident or I'll get private funds which might be the way to go. I'll keep in touch with you. I want this handled quickly. Those who want the burial in Arlington arrange it. Otherwise we will fly the bodies to whatever state they want them interned."

The President indicated the meeting was over. They rose as the president left the room.

The Secretary of Defense told his aide to call the Pentagon and have everyone in his conference room when they got back. The aide borrowed a phone and made the call. When the Secretary of Defense got back to his briefing room, all the Secretaries and the Chiefs of Staff were present. He briefed them on his meeting with the President. When he told them that the Secretary of State was on his way to Egypt and Israel, there were murmurs amongst the people around the conference table.

"That son-of-a-bitch!" It was the Army Chief of Staff.

"My sentiments exactly but let's wait until the Intel boys get back to us. The Egyptians and Israelis are meeting at Marker 101 negotiating a truce/peace proposal."

It could in spite of all this mess lead to a peace between Egypt and Israel according to the President. He wants us to come up with an appropriate message to the next of kin. He will sign it. We have some in the files. He is looking into compensation. He wants all members involved Air Force and Army to receive awards and the once wounded promoted; also education through college for the children and housing for the families. I think we are on the same page here. Condolences were received from Golda Meir and her cabinet. She wants the name of the officer in charge who sent their wounded to the hospital - some would not have made it were it not for him.

"We have made arrangements for LTC Hays and his wife and they will stay at a hotel and will be present for tomorrow's meeting. I and my aide will accompany them to deliver the news to the next of kin," said the Army Chief of Staff.

"One more thing the President emphasized. No leaks on this. That's why he wouldn't let any of his people get involved. "The White House leaks like a sieve" to quote him. Let's get to work on the details and we will meet tomorrow at 12:00 hours."

The Secretary of the Army and the Chief of Staff stayed along with the Chairman of the Joint Chiefs of Staff.

"We have discussed the situation and we have come to the conclusion that all this talk is dead in the water," said the Admiral. If we start pulling funds some bean counter is going to question the reason for this amount of money and why not the standard sum handed out to others who have been in similar situation. We need to do this fast and hide it under some contract overrun or a new weapon system."

"I agree, it could leak out that way if someone follows the trail. I have some discretionary funds; if I have to I'll clean it out. The wives will receive a sum each month for the rest of their lives. That's not a problem if it comes out of the Department of Defense. However, that is certainly not enough to live on, buy a house and educate the children. The President has promised funds either government or private but he is walking on egg shells right now so it could take time. Any large sum will be scrutinized by someone that's for sure. We can't let this leak out; we will all be sacked one way or another."

The Secretary of Defense turned to his aide and asked how much they had in their fund.

"Almost two million that you could use and no one would raise an eyebrow."

"Well, that's a start. They all have insurance that will help some which will go to their wives and parents for those not married. We need more than has been discovered so far. Let's get the finance section to expedite the money they have coming and then I'll kick in my funds to the three wives. I'll call over to Jim Tabot and stir him up. In fact, give him a call and get him over here." His aide went into the outer office and made the call.

"He'll be here in 5 minutes" said the aide. The Chief of Finance walked in and took a seat. He knew nothing about what had taken place.

"Jim we have a problem on our hands and we need your help."

The Chief of Finance took out his wallet and placed $120 dollars on the table.

"That's all I've got; my wife and a couple of your wives are on a shopping trip today so this is all I have left."

There was a chuckle around the table.

"Put your money away, Jim, we need your cooperation not your personal money. Although, is my wife in that group? If she is, I just might borrow a few bucks. Actually we had a training accident and seven members were killed, three married with children. The Army has a list of their names, ID numbers. Is there any way we can expedite their pay and insurance plus the widow benefits?"

"Sure, I can have the paperwork and money in their bank accounts in two to three days. Was this an operational training accident or was it a case of a truck rolling over killing them, etc. If it was a rehearsal for an operation, they are entitled to a larger sum, say about $500 dollars more a month for the widows. You as Secretary of Defense would have to sign off on it."

That sounds good, Jim, get the list from the Army here and get it going ASAP and thanks for coming over."

The Army Chief of Staff gave the Finance officer the names and pertinent information and he departed the room.

The phone where the Secretary of Defense was sitting rang. He picked it up and listened to whoever was speaking. A frown appeared on his face.

"Thanks for the call and quick action." The Secretary of Defense hung up and looked around the table.

"That was the SJA. No funds, extra that can be authorized without the approval of Congress. It can be attached as a rider to a Defense appropriation bill but no funds can be handed out to any soldiers other than the normal benefits authorized. The President has the authority to hand out a onetime payment to the widows but even he is restricted in the amount. The children will be given preference to any of the Academies if they should so choose and a scholarship to other universities."

"I know some regulation would prevent us from doing what is right to those left behind. This operation came from the president, it was not covert operation from the Agency. Wait a minute, they were involved we have friends in high places at Langley and God knows they have funds." The Army Chief of Staff was fuming as he finished his tirade.

"I know how you feel Hal but let me explain. When we requested their help with the Egyptians and Israelis, George told me he would have to go directly to the Chief of Stations in those countries. It seems they have a mole or moles over there and he has requested help from the FBI. He has lost agents all over Eastern Europe and Russia. It's quite a mess and it's to be kept close hold. George wouldn't talk about it over the phone but came over to my house and we hashed it out exactly what he could do for us. I'm afraid if he pulls a large sum of money, someone else has to know about it and our circle gets larger. People talk even over there, either to impress their colleagues or pass it on to someone on the hill. I reiterate this has to be kept quiet. Let the news media find out about it and we probably won't get a penny for these good people. Let me work on it."

The meeting was adjourned.

LTC Hays and his wife arrived and were briefed and took off with the Army representatives to notify the next of kin. It was a taxing situation. Some of the parents couldn't understand how their son could be killed in a training accident. All of them requested that their son be buried locally. Arrangements were made to ship the caskets; an honor guard would be present when the funeral was to take place. It was to be sealed caskets and this in itself was difficult for the parents to understand.

LTC Hays and his wife headed back to Italy to be reunited with their family after the funerals.

True to his word, the Finance Chief of Staff had all insurance and money deposited in the individual bank accounts. All members of the battalion received automatic payments to a bank in the U.S. The days of the pay lines were history.

LTC Hays briefed the General, Colonel Lawson and the Chief of Staff and Major Compton on his briefing at the Pentagon and his travels.

"I'm not sure the widows will receive any extra living allowances except for the normal benefits. The children will get Academy or college educations. The President is adamant about keeping this secret or close hold. He is under a lot of pressure regarding the investigation going on in Congress. He promised funds but in order to get them he has to involve his White House people and he doesn't trust any of them. Even had the Secretary of Defense write the appropriate condolence messages to the people involved, didn't trust his staff. The only way to get money is for Congress to authorize it.

"Our widows are being packed up and want their husbands buried at Arlington. They are all headed home to their families for now but will require housing in the near future. I have talked to the Army chief of Staff and he has made arrangements for Arlington burials. The widows and their families will be flown in to Washington and put up at hotels. That part at least is taken care of. Is there anything else I have left out?" said the General looking around the table.

"From previous experience, which we all have witnessed, it's not now that the widows will suffer the most. It's a few weeks after they are on their own that it hits them that their husbands are not there. We need to keep in touch with them whenever they settle down and somehow organize a support group for them. I have a feeling most will settle near an Army base where they have commissary and hospital privileges. I'll tell you their husbands fought bravely and if this was a U.S. war zone they would get high medals for bravery. I personally think they are going to get screwed and get little help unless we do something. They can get VA benefits for housing but they have to pay the monthly mortgage which leaves them little money for living and don't think some shyster isn't going to find out about their insurance money they have received. It happens all the time! Once we know where they are planning on settling down we need to get them appointments with the SJA. I just don't like this whole setup. People are hiding behind their jobs both at the Pentagon and the White House. Don't tell me the President doesn't have money from his campaigns squirreled away somewhere or the Secretary of Defense doesn't have a slush fund. I for one will not rest until justice is done."

"Take it easy Pete" said Colonel Lawson. "We are all trying to make things right. Somehow those widows and kids will be taken care of."

"Major Compton, talk to the widows before they leave and make sure they contact us where they plan to settle and if they have any problems. Give them my phone number and as I told them before, they can call day or night. The Air Force is providing one of their upscale planes which are equivalent to a regular commercial plane to take them to their homes or relatives. I will also divvy up my funds into three envelops to be given to them upon their departure; it should keep them in good shape for a while. Is there anything else? I think we have covered everything and I don't disagree with you Major Compton, if nothing is done for them we can then formulate a plan. After all, we are the ones that sent them into harm's way."

The meeting broke up. Colonel Lawson, LTC Hays and Major Compton went into Colonel Lawson's office.

"I know what is going through your head Pete, don't act on it until all avenues are exhausted. That temper of yours needs to be kept under control. God knows I have warned you about it before. I feel sorry for you, Hays, to have him as an Executive officer; he probably drives you nuts the way he did me. Keep him under control and don't let him go out on a tangent."

"I personally like his attitude; he keeps the battalion in order and makes my job a lot easier, which I'm sure you have come to realize long ago. Not to change the subject, but I had a letter from one of the troops at Ramstein Hospital. They should all be released in a week or so. The Air Force is flying them back here."

"That is good news," said Colonel Lawson. "I know the General received a package from Dayan; he hasn't opened the inner package so we need to have a presentation. I assume they are Israeli gold parachute wings, what else I don't know. If there is nothing else, let's get back to work."

As LTC Hays and Major Compton walked back to the battalion headquarters, LTC Hays made a statement to no one in particular, almost like he was thinking out loud. "If I live to be a hundred, I'll never figure Colonel Lawson out. You are like a son to him Pete, he reads you like a book. You two are a lot alike."

"Are you saying I'm a bastard like him?" Pete said with a smile.

"No, but when you set your mind on something there is no changing it. By the way, I agree with you. I think we are going to get a lot of air and not much action. I have served in the Pentagon and I know the culture there. If anything does happen, it will be because of the Army Chief of Staff. He doesn't care who he has to take on. He has almost 40 years service and knows he will never get the Chairman of the Joint Chief of Staff slot. He has made a lot of enemies both at the Pentagon and in Congress. His problem is that he cares for the soldiers and their dependents. He was a one star General and a friend of the Senator from South Carolina who was Chairman of the Defense appropriation committee who together wrote the rider on to the Defense Bill back in the 60's where the Services got the same pay and raises as the Civil Service. No one thought about it until after the President had signed the bill and our pay almost tripled!"

"Well, I'm not optimistic about this but I'm not going to let it die. I picked those men and I will see to it that justice is done," said Major Compton.

"Oh, I have no doubt about that," said LTC Hays slapping Pete on the shoulder.

The package from Israel contained gold parachute wings for all the soldiers who participated. There was also an amount of money for the ones that had been killed. Combining that with the Generals fund, it was growing but not nearly enough to sustain them for any length of time.

The President asked one of his trusted friends from the Senate if there was any chance to get some money out of Congress for a training accident which had taken place. The Senator was candid with the president and told him his days as President were numbered and he would get nothing out of Congress.

He called his old friends in the private sector but was rebuffed by even those that had contributed generously to his election.

He reflected upon the Senator's words that his days were numbered. He told himself that he would not be impeached. He would resign before it came to that. He would make a deal with the Vice President who would do anything he was asked. Well he had tried; the Army or Pentagon would have to take care of the widows and their dependents.

The South Comm. General got a backdoor message saying there would be no additional funds for the widows from the President.

Major Compton got some messages from his friends in the Pentagon who were aides to the Generals and Secretary of the Army' also from the President's military attaché. They were all negative when it came to funding the fallen families.

Chapter 5

It had been months now and no more funds were forthcoming. He kept thinking he was missing something. His wife was growing concerned because he was not talking about whatever was troubling him. One night he came home late from work and had a stack of papers with him.

"Would you type these up for me on that new IBM Selective typewriter I bought you?"

"Sure, I'll do anything you want me to do, let me read what you want me to type."

Pete handed his wife five hand written pages he had finally decided upon after days of agonizing over every word he had written. It had to be professional and close hold. He had not even discussed it with LTC Hays or Lawson who was now a one star General.

Pete's wife read the five pages and looked at him. "Are you sure you want to send this without clearing it with your bosses?"

Pete's wife was the former Army's Chief of Staff daughter and knew the chain of command and knew the unwritten regulations when it came to going over someone's head.

"It could cost you a promotion."

"I don't care about promotions. I have enough friends who will back me if it comes to that. Will you type it in its correct format; two copies. One to go to Senator Clifton and one for me to show to my bosses after it's sent."

"I'll do it right now. The kids are asleep. Is this what has been troubling you all these weeks?"

"Yes, I guess. I have been in contact with the widows. They have settled close to their relatives and are receiving support from them. They seem OK but I know they are not. I'm just surprised that they didn't settle around an Army or other service post where they have more privileges, although the SJA has made it easy for them to utilize private hospitals should they need them. Yes, I want that letter to go to Senator Clifton. He and I got along great when he was here. I'm the one that notified his family when his nephew was killed in Viet Nam. He was part of the 5th Special Forces, so we have a bond there."

"OK, I'll get right on it, it's a good thing I have learned to read your writing. Did you know your spelling is atrocious not to mention some of your sentence structure?"

"Yes, but I do have my good points too, don't I?"

"Don't start that now or your letter will never get done," she said with a smile.

She went into the den and Pete could hear her typing. God he had been lucky, she never questioned him about anything, where he had gone or about Viet Nam. He had never said much about it, only the funny things. He got a beer out of the refrigerator and sipped slowly from it.

He had been lucky, he had met her, after getting an ass chewing from the Army Chief of Staff after being brought back to the States to write up a summary of an action he was involved in on the wrong side of the border, where hundreds of North Viet Nam troops had been killed with only four Americans wounded including Pete. He could tell after reading the summary that the Chief of Staff's heart was not into the ass chewing but it had been loud. As he departed and was about to walk into the corridor of the Pentagon, a woman's voice had reminded him that his green beret was still on her desk. He had turned around and there sitting behind a shiny wooden desk was the most beautiful woman he had ever laid eyes on. He apologized and went to retrieve his beret when she informed him that her father was normally not that vocal and that she was just filling in for his regular secretary who was sick that day.

"You mean that is your father?"

"Yes, he is and if you plan on taking me to dinner tonight you'd better behave!"

Pete had been speechless. He looked at her and said "What time should I pick you up?"

"Oh, shall we say 1930 and I'll make the reservation and your uniform is the correct dress. I live with my parents having just graduated from college. It's over in the Generals row #3. Don't be late."

Pete had mumbled something but walked out the door.

"Your beret, Captain."

Blushing he went back to her desk and retrieved his beret.

He had rented a car and arrived at 1930 hours and knocked on the door of #3.

A gruff man in uniform answered the door and looked at Pete. "Didn't I make myself clear earlier today, Captain Compton, or do you want some more?"

"Sir, I am here".....he never finished the sentence.

Betty came down the stairs and said: "Dad, this is Captain Compton. We are going out to dinner." She kissed her father on the check and said "Let's go Pete."

There was a "Humpf" sound behind the door as Betty closed it.

They had a nice dinner and Betty was an easy person to talk to. Pete could tell she liked him, God he had been out with real prudes where you had to practically drag a response out of them. The conversation flowed and it was time to take her home. He parked in front of her house and she invited him in. He was hesitant and she could sense it.

"My Father is either in bed or in his study. My Mother is visiting her sister in Roanoke, Virginia. We can go into the kitchen and have a cup of coffee or sit in the living room and my Father is a pussycat."

"A cup of coffee sounds good," the pussycat was not something Pete was ready to swallow yet.

Betty fixed them coffee and they were sitting at the kitchen table sipping the hot coffee.

"Did you make enough for another cup?" her Father walked into the kitchen in his robe.

Pete stood up.

"Sit down, Pete, I don't know if Betty has told you but I am a human being." The General took a chair and sat down. Betty poured him a cup of coffee.

"So what have you two been up to? You probably went up to Rock Creek Park and parked and God knows what!"

"No Dad, we had a nice dinner and came right home. It was our first date, the second date I'll take him up to my bedroom and make passionate love."

Pete almost slid under the table. He didn't know where to look so he sipped on his coffee.

"You have to excuse my daughter, Pete; she is headstrong like her Mother. God knows she didn't get it from me."

"Sir, I would like to write Betty when I get back to Viet Nam, with your permission, of course."

"I can't stop you from writing to her but anyone who is in Special Forces can't be quite right in his head; don't get me wrong. I and I alone are one of the few who think we need more Special Forces in the years to come but Viet Nam has taken a great toll of your comrades, which I don't have to tell you."

"Yes Sir, that's true but I still would like to write her."

"Write her, she doesn't listen to me anyway, so what can I do. You two will probably get married anyway and you are not even a West Pointer"

"Dad, Pete hasn't asked me yet but after I take him up to my bedroom tomorrow night, he'll ask."

"God, what have I raised here? I have tried to teach her right from wrong but as you can see I have failed."

The General got up and left the kitchen scratching his head. He stuck his head back in and said: "That was a good operation Pete, but I have to send you back day after tomorrow. Good night and behave."

"See I told you, he is a good Dad and whether he believes it or not I have been a good girl even in college. Oh, I have dated a bunch of officers but most of them have been jerks. The nice ones only dated me because who my Father is."

"Are you working tomorrow or can I take you out somewhere?"

"No, I'm free, I only filled in today."

"Do you like to sail? I know someone down at the Naval Academy who has a nice 36 foot sloop who would let us use it."

"Are you asking me out again?"

"I'm not sure but I don't think I asked you out tonight?"

"Hmm, Pete Compton, I think you are going to be trouble."

"I hope so."

He stood up and thanked her for a nice evening. He headed for the door and Betty reminded him his beret was still on the chair.

"I guess I'm a little confused."

Betty smiled and walked him to the door.

"How does 0830 sound?"

"It sounds good. I'll make some sandwiches and bring a thermos of coffee."

Pete gave her a peck on the check but she grabbed him and kissed him softly on the lips. Pete looked at her and said his goodnight.

"He is a good soldier Betty and has a good record," said her Dad.

"I know he is and I'm going to marry him when he finishes his tour in Viet Nam. He doesn't know it but I'm going to be his wife."

"Take it easy and take your time. There are plenty of nice officers out there."

"You are not listening, Dad, you and Mom married after knowing each other for two weeks. You have been lucky Dad."

"Yes, but there was a war at that time."

"You don't call Viet Nam a war? How many thousand have we lost not to mention the wounded? Pete spent 1 1/2 years in Walter Reed after one of his tours. That young man is going to be your son-in-law, Dad. Get used to it. You like him and you know it."

They went sailing on Chesapeake Bay and had a good time.

"When you get back from Viet Nam Pete, we are getting married."

"I think you Dad might have something to say about that."

"He likes you, Pete, and he doesn't like very many people."

When they got back home, Betty put the bag which had contained their lunch in the kitchen.

"Let's go, Pete Compton." She grabbed him by the hand and led him upstairs to her bedroom. "My Dad is at Ft. Bragg for two days and won't be home for two days. He is picking up my Mother in Roanoke on the way home."

Betty started unbuttoning her blouse and soon was standing naked before him. She removed his clothes and looked at him.

"Well someone is happy to see me", she said with a laugh. She pulled the bed spread back and then went into the bathroom and came back with a thin plastic sheet and some towels and placed them over the bed sheets. Pete looked at her.

"Just trust me Pete."

She got into the bed and he followed. They kissed and touched and Betty indicated she was ready.

"Go gently in at first, this is my first time."

"Are you sure you want to do this?"

"Surer than anything in my life." Pete entered her gently and hit a wall and pushed through. She dug her nails into his back and then joined him in their lovemaking. When they were through she curled up against him and told him she loved him. There was blood on the towels under them.

"Let's do it again" said Betty. This time it was more satisfying for both. When he returned from Viet Nam they were married. Betty's Mother wanted to know what the hurry was but told Pete she was not opposed to the marriage. They had a week's honeymoon and two months later Betty announced that she was pregnant.

Betty walked in and handed him the letter. It was three pages long.

"Word perfect sentence structure correct and military format." She sat down next to him and took a sip of his now warm beer.

Pete read the letter. It was good and to the point. He knew the shit would hit the fan at headquarters but he had tried everything as had his boss. Betty handed him a stamped envelope with Senator Clifton's address and marked confidential. Betty folded the sheets and placed them in the envelope and sealed it. The second copy Pete held in his hand. That's going to cost you Major Compton!

Pete placed the envelope and extra copy in the den. He came back and grabbed Betty's hand and led her into their bedroom. When he got to work the next morning he got a larger envelope, addressed it and placed the envelope Betty had addressed inside it, used the official military stamp on it and placed it in the outgoing mail.

Pete took the extra copy and walked into LTC Hays office and placed the copy of the letter on his desk. LTC Hays picked up the copies and read them. He looked at Pete and said, "I was expecting something like this. Let's go over and see General Lawson. They walked across the parade field and headed up to the General's office. They found him in with the Chief of Staff.

General Lawson looked up and LTC Hays handed him the letter. General Lawson read it twice and handed it to the Chief of Staff who read it.

"Has this gone out yet?"

"Sir, it's in the outgoing mail at our headquarters," said Pete.

"Call over to the S-1 and have him retrieve it and have someone bring it over here immediately. I am heading to the Pentagon tomorrow, I'll personally hand carry it and see that it gets to Senator Clifton. After all he is a good friend of the family," said the Chief of Staff.

You realize that this will require you to take a trip to the hill and brief him on the entire matter. I could do it but you were there and I know he thinks highly of you."

"Thank you Sir, I know it sounds like I'm going over your heads but we have tried everything to no avail. I have a copy of the after action report in my safe. I know it by heart and can give a good briefing on it."

"I'll take this letter in and show it to the boss" said the Chief of Staff and got up and walked into the South Com. General's office. After a while all of them were called into the General's office.

"Sit down, this is pretty serious. I hope we can back it up? I had a call from the Army Chief of Staff and he confirmed that the second message sent by Dayan's staff officer came from the State Department. The Secretary is shuttling back and forth between Cairo and Tel Aviv, Jerusalem. It looks like a permanent peace offering is in the works. Sadat is now in the United States' camp and the Secretary of State is probably going to receive the Nobel Peace prize. You got a tough row to hoe, Pete."

"So now you're here and what do you expect us to do?" asked Senator Rose with a frown on his face.

"Sir, I hope Congress can pass a bill or a rider and take care of the widows and their families. After all this was no ordinary mission, it came from the president who instructed the Secretary of State to coordinate with the Egyptians and the Israelis, which he didn't do. In fact he caused the death of seven Americans. He will probably get the Nobel Peace prize for not only killing Americans but also Israelis."

"That's a pretty strong statement coming from a Major who has an emotional attachment to this sordid affair. As for the Peace prize, the people in Oslo, Norway would have probably handed Hitler the peace prize had he won the war, a bunch of socialist near-do-wells!"

"We are getting off the track here gentlemen" said Senator Clifton. "Everything Major Compton has told us has been verified by the Secretary of Defense. It is an unusual request to be sure but it's been done before so we are not setting a precedent here. I suggest that we quietly contact our members in both houses that are on the Appropriation Committee and fast and get this taken care of. Major Compton, do you have anything to add?"

"No Sir, I know I have taken up a lot of your time when you should be home with your families and friends. I appreciate your tolerance and there will be no leaks from our soldiers who by the way know nothing about this. The members involved were given gold jump wings from the Israelis. We had a ceremony at our base. Not one soldier who was not part of this mission questioned why they were given these wings, which means a great deal to an airborne soldier.

They know that some of their comrades are gone but have not questioned it. They know their job as a quick reaction force is not without dangers and they accept it. I feel that should any of you have the occasion to visit our base in Italy, you will be proud of all of them. Again, I thank you for your time and for listening to me."

Major Compton got his papers together and placed them in his briefcase. He looked at Senator Clifton who nodded to him. He rose and left the room. Senator Clifton followed him to the outer office.

"It was a good presentation Pete. If the Army doesn't treat you well, consider running for Congress."

They shook hands and Pete thanked him again.

As Pete headed down the hall the gentleman who had led him in followed him and let him out.

"Good day, Sir," he said in his southern drawl.

Pete headed down the stairs and was lucky to flag down a cab.

"To the Pentagon E wing please," said Pete in a tired voice. He had received a message last night to report to the Army Chief of Staff. He was not looking forward to the meeting but then he had been chewed out by another Army Chief of Staff some years ago and that had turned out fine.

He showed his ID card to the guards and asked how to get to the Army Chief of Staff's office. One of the guards said he would take him there. Why had he asked directions? He knew the way. He had a lot on his mind and having someone show him the way made the walk easier. As they approached the various flags outside the Secretary of Defense's office, a LTC stepped out and asked if he was Major Compton.

"Yes Sir, I'm here to see the Army Chief of Staff" said Pete.

"He is in with the Secretary of Defense. They want you in here," said the LTC.

Oh shit, thought Pete. This is it. They are probably drumming me out of the Army. As he walked into the outer office, he took his green overcoat off and hung it on a coat rack, removed his beret and laid it on a table. He looked into a mirror and straightened his tie.

The LTC knocked on the door and ushered Pete into a large office with four men sitting around the desk of the Secretary of Defense. Pete saluted and stood at attention. The Secretary of Defense told him to take a seat.

"So you are Major Compton," said the Secretary of Defense. He introduced the others in the room: Secretary of the Army; the Army Chief of Staff; the Aide to the Secretary of Defense, a one star General.

"We have heard a lot about you Major Compton. Most of it good but what right have you got to go over our heads to Senator Clifton's committee? Have you not heard of the chain of command? Or do you think we just sit around drinking coffee all day? I suppose I can't blame you being in the outfit you're in but we were eager young officers at one time who thought that people in the Pentagon had no idea what was happening in the real world. I want you to know that the higher you get in the defense ladder the more your hands are tied in most circumstances. The bureaucracy here in Washington is unbelievable. I could not have done what you did today without half of Washington knowing about it. I have a copy of your letter. It is well thought out in which you have explained that the chain of command has done everything in their power to help. It's the sentence that saved your bacon Major Compton."

The Secretary of the Army stood up along with the Chief of Staff of the Army.

The one star General also stood up and started reading a citation even the Secretary of Defense stood and the Chief of Staff of the Army pinned the Distinguished Service Cross on the left pocket of Pete's uniform. The General read another order and the Secretary of Defense and Secretary of Army removed the gold Major leaves and replaced them with silver leaves of a LTC. They all congratulated Pete who was starting to get a little light headed.

"All the troops received awards including the ones that didn't make it; except for you, LTC Compton, so it was decided that you should be decorated accordingly. Your foresight in taking not only extra ammo but also extra machine guns saved many American lives and for that we are grateful."

"Sir, do you mind if I sit down. I came in here expecting an ass chewing and probably getting booted out of the Army and this happens!"

"By all means sit down," said the Secretary of Defense. They all took their seats after congratulating him.

"First, I would like to thank you all for this but I'm not the one who did the majority of the fighting. There is a Captain Ryder who deserves this more than I do."

"You mean Major Ryder" said the Army Chief of Staff. "Things have happened in Italy the few days you have been away. However, according to the after action report and the attachment LTC Hays wrote, your action was nothing short of outstanding including sending the wounded Israelis to their headquarters' hospital. The Secretary of Defense has received glowing reports from both Golda Meir and Dayan even though their casualties were severe."

"Well, LTC Compton, there is a plane waiting for you at Andrews Air Force Base to take you back home. A car is waiting for you down stairs. It will wait for you while you pack at your hotel. Have a safe journey and say hello to the troops from all of us."

Pete shook hands with all of them. The Army Chief of Staff walked with Pete down to the car slapped him on the shoulders and told him if he needed anything to contact him. Pete saluted him and got into the car.

On the way to the hotel, Pete removed the award and placed it in the blue flat case it came in. He packed his few things and they were on their way to Andrews Air Force base. There were perhaps a dozen other soldiers already aboard when he arrived. An Air Force E-7 grabbed Pete's bag and placed it in a separate room. He then led Pete to the front of the plane and showed him his seat. The engines started and the door was closed. They were taxing for takeoff. Pete snapped the seatbelt and leaned back in his seat. What a trip. He had not imagined that he would be received at the pentagon in such a manner. What would be his job when he returned to Italy? It could mean a transfer or some staff job at Task Force. They had been in Italy a year now, a hectic year at that. The Battalion was in good shape and they were starting to get replacements from the states. He had always gone down to the companies each morning to either run with them or just see them. One morning he had gone down to C Company. He always stood to the side while the company Commander took the report to show that all were present and accounted for. He had noticed a new young soldier in the 1st Platoon who looked like he had been in a fight. His face was cut and his one eye was black and blue. Pete had gone up to him and asked what had happened to him.

"I fell down the stairs, Sir," said the soldier.

"We don't have any stairs in our barracks," said Pete.

"I fell, Sir."

Pete let it go and asked the 1st Sergeant about him.

"His record is good but our troops found him smoking the wrong type of cigarette. At first he wouldn't listen but now he does. I must have overlooked that portion in my orientation when he reported in." The first Sergeant excused himself and disappeared in the door heading to the company headquarters.

Pete had discussed the situation with LTC Hays.

"I'll talk to the Company Commanders. It's good that the troops are taking care of these problems but I don't want it to go overboard. We need to make sure we cover the Italian laws and its consequences to the new replacements."

The plane stopped in the city of Milan where a few personnel got off and then preceded to Brendisi. It was still in the AM and the sun was shining. Pete was the last to leave the plane. As he got used to the bright sunlight he spotted Betty and what seemed to be half the battalion. General Lawson, LTC Hays, the South Com. General were all there to greet him. Betty ran towards him and threw her arms around his neck and kissed him.

"Welcome home soldier" she said with tears in her eyes. She kissed him again and held him close. The others were circling around him. "Hey, it's our turn!" It was Ryder.

"If you try to kiss me, Ryder, I'll have you drummed out of the Army," said Pete with a smile on his face. They all shook his hand and congratulated him.

The South Com. General shook his hand.

"I hear you met some high ranking people at the Pentagon. I see they treated you right, LTC, two years ahead of your contemporaries, not bad, not bad at all."

Pete thanked him. General Lawson grabbed him and said, "If it had been up to me you would have been demoted or kicked out of the Army. Someone must have made a mistake. Oh well, it happens. Congratulation, Pete, you deserve it. This is going to cost you a promotion party."

"Maybe we can split the cost since you didn't have one." Pete smiled at the General.

"God, Betty, he is as insubordinate as ever. How do you put up with this guy?"

"Oh, he has his good points. I just struggle along."

"Everyone laughed and applauded him.

"There is a staff car to take you and Betty home. Meeting tomorrow morning at 0800 TF Headquarters" said LTC Hays slapping Pete on the back.

They didn't talk on the way home. Betty kept squeezing his hand. As they entered their house, Pete asked where the girls were.

"They are at Sue Hays' house until later tonight. Right now you are going to have to put up with me, soldier." She kissed him softly on the lips.

Pete placed his bag on the couch and opened it, took out the medal case and opened it.

"What do you think about this?" he looked at her. Betty took it out and held it.

"My God, no one knows about this around here or I would have heard about it."

"I was surprised; the Secretary of Defense placed it on me along with the Army Chief of Staff. I thought I was getting an ass chewing which usually happens to me when I go to the Pentagon or I get a wife, I don't know which is worst."

"Don't press your luck, Pete Compton, just because they promoted and decorated you doesn't mean you run this house and I won't tolerate any insubordination. Come with me." She grabbed his hand and led him into their bedroom which contained a bottle of champagne in an ice bucket and two glasses. Betty undressed him, hanging up his uniform. Pete removed the rest of his clothes.

"Well, someone has missed me" she said looking at him and getting undressed.

"The champagne will have to wait. I have first priority, you know, I have never made love to a LTC."

Pete slapped her on her butt and pulled her onto the bed.

It was 1730 and they were both exhausted.

"I need to call Sue and have her bring the girls home. They miss you an awful lot Pete. They are definitely Dad's girls. Go and take a shower and get into something comfortable. I showered while you slept."

It was nice to be home even though he had been gone only four days. The shower rejuvenated him. He had just gotten dressed when he heard a commotion in the living room. He walked out and the girls jumped at him. God, they were a good looking pair, two years apart. They hugged him and he kissed them. He noticed Sue and walked over and thanked her.

"I expect you to reciprocate in the near future" she said smiling.

"No problem" said Betty, "anytime."

"Help me bring the food in" Sue said to Betty. They brought in covered dishes and placed them on their dining room table. Sue gave Pete a kiss on the cheek and congratulated him and departed.

"This looks great!"

"Yes, we picked it up from the restaurant downtown," said

the oldest girl now six years old. They had a nice dinner and the girls talked about what they had been up to the last few days.

Chapter 6

The 0800 meeting at Task Force headquarters brought some surprising news. General Lawson briefed everyone. He had talked to the aide to the Army Chief of Staff and he along with now LTC Compton was being transferred to the Ft. Bragg, North Carolina to the JFK Center for Special Warfare. They were both being assigned to a team that would join the Secretary of State in Paris to negotiate the peace in Viet Nam. Senator Clifton and his committee had promised to get the money for the widows one way or another but it would take about two months. This was good news. General Lawson and LTC Compton would leave for Fort Bragg in early January. LTC Hays would keep the battalion until General Lawson left in January and would then move to Task Force as the G-3 taking General Lawson's place. LTC Hayes was on the promotion list to full colonel which he had not known about and which made him happy. The results of the meeting was to be kept close hold until the Task Force General announced it in a few weeks. The Chief of Staff was on his way back and would arrive in two days.

After the meeting General Lawson motioned for LTC Hays and Compton to follow him into his office. The three of them sat down and General Lawson buzzed his secretary for three coffees.

"You are going to find Hays, that you are getting a frustrating job. Basically 80% revolves around the battalion. It's going to take all your will power to not go over there and run it as you see fit. Having been the Battalion Commander "you" know the ins and outs of what is going on and you want to jump feet first into its operation. You have done an outstanding job and the battalion is probably the finest outfit in the Army. The new battalion commander is a boot licker who I have been told will never make more rank than a Colonel if he is lucky. He has some friends but he has burnt some bridges behind him and I think this is his swan song. He is airborne qualified but has never been with an airborne unit. I'm telling you this Hays, not to degrade him, but to inform you so that you know what lays ahead of you. You Hays will become the bastard."

"I knew it would happen someday but not so soon. I was hoping that Pete here could take the battalion but I guess that was too much to hope for."

"Believe me you don't want Pete in that job. He will give you ulcers within weeks. Besides he was picked by the Secretary of Defense for this job he is getting and it won't be pleasant. We both have to leave our families at Ft. Bragg and that's not going to go over too well with Nancy or Betty. I know Pete has a nice home in Fayetteville at Cottenade right outside Ft. Bragg. I hope to buy a home there, also. I know Nancy is not going to be far away from Betty."

"I don't know what Pete and I are going to be doing at the JFK Center until we go to Paris but I hope it's something less stressful than here. Who knows, I might get to swing a golf club once in a while."

"That's all I know for now. I don't know who is replacing Pete as Executive officer. If you have someone in mind Hays start working on it. There is a Major coming in around February. I don't know anything about him. You might want to check with some of your friends in personnel in D.C. since you worked there but to save you a lot of grief make sure you put the right person in that slot. That's it, there is a lot to think over for both of you."

Pete went home and told Betty about the news. She said she was ready to go back to the States but could they spend Christmas at Cortina and ski? The girls were getting good at it having spent the last two winters in ski school for three months each winter chaperoned by her. Pete was a ski bum as was Betty, so they had decided that the girls were going to learn early in life like they had.

"I don't see why not. I'll talk to our Italian Liaison Officer. I know he and his family skis. Would you do me a favor and write or call our real estate agent in Fayetteville and tell him to make sure our house is in good order. The Air Force Colonel and his wife, our renters, are moving to Arizona or have moved at the end of November. I know they have taken care of it, but I don't like surprises nor do you. If painting is required have him get someone to paint it the way you want it."

"I'll do it tomorrow. I hope Nancy and General Lawson get a house close to ours. It's so peaceful and nice out there. I'm looking forward to being in our home again."

The Christmas was great! They had rented a condo apartment in the Dolomite Mountains at Cortina. The price was stiff but the skiing was great. The girls were starting to show off. They would both yell at Pete and Betty to ski faster because they thought they were skiing too slowly.

"I guess we are raising a couple of ski bums" said Betty out of breath.

"Yes, did you see how they handled the moguls? It looks like their bones bend with each mogul. Ah, to be kids again!"

"You will always be a kid when it comes to skiing" said Betty laughing, "You're not saying they tire a Special Forces LTC out are you?"

"No, they don't tire me out but I hope we can take a trip out to Colorado before I'm off to Europe. We spent a lot of money on their new skis and boots not to mention their outfits. I'd hate to see them grow out of them before we ski again."

"You know my parents have a place in Vail. God knows... they have asked us to use the place enough. But I was either pregnant or you were gone."

"Oh God, Vail. I skied there when I was a Lieutenant. I almost died out there after ski hours. At least this time I'm married with kids so I have to behave myself."

"Oh! Is this a confession or a bachelor's bravado?"

"Neither. I was just horney, which reminds me isn't it getting too dark for another run?"

"Do you have horns, Dad?" It was the almost 7 year old daughter.

"No, he doesn't have horns" said the 5 years old. "We would have noticed it with his hair so short."

"Your Dad has different kinds of horns which don't show" said their Mother flipping some snow at Pete.

"Let's go in and get warm and go and have our supper," said Pete.

"You have to be careful what you say Colonel. There are little ears that are getting big and before you know it you are going to have to explain certain things to your teenage daughters."

"Let's go and get something to eat. I'm starving!" said Pete and skied toward the condo.

Their two weeks at Cortina were great but it was time to start organizing things for the packers who were coming in a week's time. They had only bought a few pieces of furniture since their house furniture back at Ft. Bragg was in storage, so things went smooth.

Pete had called a couple of friends and neighbors and asked if they would get their things out of storage. When they arrived home everything was in place including beds made and food in the fridge.

"Oh, those wonderful people; we will have to throw a party," said Betty, when she saw her house. It was late and the five year old was asleep in Pete's arms as he walked towards her room with her. He placed her on her bed and Betty got her clothes off. The seven year old was dragging and was sent to lie down on her bed.

Pete brought their suitcases in and placed them in the spare bedroom. Betty came into the family room wearing a robe as Pete started a fire in the fireplace. He went into the pantry and found a bottle of cognac and poured two tumblers 1/3 full.

"I'll be right back."

When he reappeared, he was wearing a robe and sat down next to Betty. They toasted to being home again.

"Hmm this hits the spot," said Betty taking another sip.

Pete looked at Betty's robe which had opened at the top.

"Why you hussy," he said pulling her robe apart and started kissing her.

"I was wondering how long it would take you to notice. I'm naked underneath."

"It's great to be home soldier. Let's go to bed."

General Lawson bought a house less than a block away. Nancy and Betty went on a buying spree to furnish the new home.

The kids were in school and Nancy and Betty played golf and tennis. Ft. Bragg had all the facilities and the weather was good.

Chapter 7

General Lawson and Pete got their orders for Paris. They were to report to the American Embassy.

Their suitcases packed, they headed for Paris. There was no indication as to how long they would be there.

They arrived and reported in. A Member of the Embassy staff took them to a hotel about a half a block away. Their rooms were adequate nothing fancy. They were to report to the Embassy the next morning in civilian clothes at 0900 hours. They unpacked and decided to get some rest.

Pete woke up at 6 PM and was hungry. He got dressed and knocked gently at General's door, no answer. He walked down stairs and asked about a restaurant. The woman behind the desk explained that it was a little early for a good restaurant to be serving but recommended a bistro around the corner. Pete found the bistro and General Lawson having a meal. He was asked to take a seat at his table.

"You would think these people spoke English with all the Embassies around here," the General was not in a good mood. A waiter brought Pete a menu and he ordered a meal in French and a cup of coffee. General Lawson looked at him and shook his head.

"I guess I should have known you'd speak the lingo, where did you learn?"

"High school, college and Ft. Bragg," Pete replied with a smile.

"Why French, you're Norwegian; I know you were born over there."

"When we did our area study at Ft. Bragg prior to deployment to Viet Nam, the Montagnard tribe we were assigned to had only 1100 words in their language and no written language except for a few words; but some of them spoke French as did many Vietnamese, so I took a refresher course in French."

Pete's meal arrived and it was good. General Lawson ordered a cup of coffee and waited for Pete to finish his meal.

They arrived at the Embassy and were shown into a conference room. They were briefed on the procedures along with about seven other people. The Secretary of State was the spokesman and negotiator. The other people were from the State Department. The negotiations got off to a rocky start. The South Vietnam delegation would not go along with some of the demands from the North Vietnamese. The South Vietnamese wanted a neutral Cambodia without any North Vietnamese in that country which they had been using as a sanctuary. The North Vietnamese wanted South Vietnam to pull back from the 17th parallel and make that a buffer zone.

In one of the sessions, the Americans still missing were brought up. The North Vietnamese denied they had American prisoners. As for the missing in action they admitted there could be Americans who had been killed, i.e. in air planes shot down and were hidden in the jungle and mountains in North Vietnam. But as far as prisoners, they had been returned.

One day after leaving an unfruitful session regarding MIA's from both North Vietnam and U.S., Pete was walking down the hall to the bathroom. As he opened the door to the bathroom, a person behind him came in and slipped a piece of paper in Pete's jacket pocket. The person was a North Vietnamese who shook his head when Pete went to reach in his pocket.

"Read later," was all he said and went into one of the stalls.

As Pete and General Lawson went to get something to eat before their evening sessions with the other U.S. Representative s, Pete took the paper from his pocket and read it. He handed the note to General Lawson who read the short note twice.

"The North Vietnamese sent over 1500 U.S. prisoners to Laos? Where did you get this?"

Pete explained.

"How do we handle this? The Laotians are not willing participants and have sent only a few observers who haven't even been formally recognized. They want nothing to do with these negotiations. The Communist's will end up controlling Laos. We need to give this info with an explanation to the Secretary of State's "second man tonight".

"That's what I was thinking. Pete replied," I just hope he gives it to the Secretary of State. These negotiations are dragging on and people are getting tired and frayed. I know the Secretary of State wants to come up with some sort of peace deal even if the South Vietnamese are not happy with it. I heard he is meeting with the head negotiator from North Vietnam, Politburo Member, Le Duc Tho, although from what I understand they are not making much headway. The North Vietnamese are not happy with the U.S. refusal to help restore North Vietnam with all the damage that the bombing raids have done. They want compensation in the billions of dollars."

"Where are you getting this from Pete? I have heard nothing about his and now this note?"

"I listen to the lower echelon North Vietnamese talking. I understand a little Vietnamese although the North Vietnamese or should I say some have a little different dialect, than the South Vietnamese. A few are giving me a little gossip. I sort through the bullshit and try to determine what is real and what is bull. Some of these South Vietnamese want to come to the U.S. and live. They see the handwriting on the wall."

"Be careful. However this note is a bombshell and could set this negotiation back years if the politicians in Washington and the President choose to press it. I wish I had access to a secure phone. I know I can't use our Embassy communication?"

"May I ask who you are trying to get in touch with?"

"Yes, I only trust one and that's Colonel Hammond. I talked to him before we left the States."

"I might know someone at the Canadian Embassy. Let me go over right now and see what I can do."

"Be careful, Pete, this could blow back in our faces if we handle it the wrong way."

Pete went to the Canadian Embassy and asked if Colonel York was available. The guard looked at him. Pete showed his military I.D. and the guard had Pete ushered into the building where another military, a captain, sat behind a desk. Pete asked for Colonel York. Pete showed him his I.D. and explained that they were old friends. The Captain behind the desk lifted his phone and pressed a button. He explained that LTC Compton was in the lobby and requested to see Colonel York. Pete stood there and looked around. The Embassy building was a lot better appointed than their own Embassy. An elevator opened and Colonel York came out of it with an extended arm.

"Good to see you, Peter. I saw in our memo that you were in town. I have been wanting to get in touch but I know it's dicey for you over there."

"Not so dicey that two old friends can't have a talk." Pete shook his hand.

"Let's go up to my office."

The elevator took them up to the third floor. Colonel York preceded him down the hall to a half opened door. There was a woman secretary sitting behind a desk.

"I don't want to be disturbed." Colonel York informed her, as he opened the door to his office. He ushered Pete in and told him to sit down and joined him across a small table.

"What have you been up to since our school days at that wonderful institution at Ft. Leavenworth, Kansas? Or shouldn't I ask? I know you had a problem with the Israelis."

Pete was taken aback. He tried to smile but didn't think he was successful at it.

"I'm afraid I don't follow you?"

"This section is the equivalent to your Cultural Affairs Section in your embassy so very little happens to our neighbor to the South that we don't know about."

"Well, it was a fiasco with yours truly in charge but it was a case of lack of communication. Or, should I say counter communication by a certain person in our State Department who has his sights set on bigger and better things. All is well now except for a few minor details."

"Politics are the same all over, Peter, but we soldiers have to clean up their messes one way or another."

"How are Pam and the family?"

"Fine, thank you, and I hope Betty and the girls are happy and in good health."

"Yes, thanks, not happy about being left alone back at Fort Bragg but that's the life of an Army wife.

"Ok. You didn't come over here to say hello and chit chat. What can I do for you, Peter?"

"We, and a comrade of mine, have a serious problem that has developed as a result of our quote "Peace Negotiations" and I need some help. My comrade is General Lawson, a good friend. We need a secure line to the Pentagon and can't use our own Embassy communications."

"How serious is this problem?"

"Extremely."

Colonel York looked at Pete for a moment and went to his desk and picked up a pad of paper writing down something and handed it to Pete.

"Come to this address tonight with your friend and you'll have a secure line."

"There is a time difference so give me a time when we can reach a certain person."

"How about 1800 hours? That will give you time to make a call and make sure that person is in his office."

"Thanks. I appreciate this and I won't forget."

Pete stood up shook hands with Colonel York who escorted him downstairs.

When Pete got back to his hotel he knocked on General Lawson's door. The door opened immediately.

"Come in."

Pete, brief General Lawson on what had happened.

"General Lawson picked up his phone and told the hotel operator he wished to make a long distance call to the United States. He gave the number and in a few seconds he had his wife, Nancy, on the phone. He made pleasant comments.

"I want you to call my best friend and classmate and tell him to be in his bosses office at 1800 hours our time over here. I will call you back in 1/2 hour to confirm. Tell him Oxbow, yes Oxbow."

Hanging up he looked at Pete. "I hope Hammond is in. I don't trust anyone else. Let's have a beer." He went to the small refrigerator and got two cans of Heinekens.

"I don't know what Hammond can do other than to tell his boss."

"Well, they can start sending a blackbird over Laos. It shouldn't take long to pick something up."

"Yes, I suppose that's one way to verify this message. It's time to call again. He called Nancy and was told that his friend would be waiting for him. She also had someone who wanted to talk to Pete. General Lawson handed the phone to Pete. It was Betty.

"I miss you Pete. How are things going?"

"Oh, I miss you too. Things are going just wonderful, just wonderful. Give the girls a hug from me. I have to go. Love you." Pete handed the phone to General Lawson. He made small talk with Nancy and hung up.

"Well, we are set. We have 45 minutes to get to that address. Let's go."

Back at Ft. Bragg, Nancy looked at Betty.

"What's wrong?"

"Pete and I have this code word, when something is wrong. He used it twice which means something is really wrong."

"Let's have a glass of wine and hope for the best," said Nancy.

They arrived at the address Colonel York had given Pete. A guard asked for identification. He then let them into a courtyard and opened a door for them. Colonel York was there to greet them.

"Welcome to my home away from home."

Pete introduced General Lawson to Colonel York, who took them into an almost barren room with a desk and four chairs. On the desk were two phones, one red and the other blue.

"The blue phone is at your disposal, General Lawson. You can dial direct to Washington D.C. I'll leave you alone. Oh, press the #2 button and dial your number." Colonel York departed the room.

General Lawson took out his small book and sat down in the desk chair and dialed the number. He waited a few seconds and started talking to Colonel Hammond. Colonel Hammond informed General Lawson his boss was listening in on the call.

General Lawson briefed them on the situation.

"Yes, I'm one hundred percent sure it's true. No, I have not briefed anyone else on this. The Laotians want nothing to do with these talks and no one else knows about it. I don't know what you can do with this but then that's why you people get the big bucks. I don't know what I can do with this information. I'm calling on a secure line courtesy of our neighbors to the North. I couldn't use our own Embassy - too many ears and questions. If you want me to give this information to our glorious leader here, let me know. You can use our own Embassy for a yes or no answer to me personally. In the mean time I'll keep this close, unless you have an answer now."

"I got this from my partner whom you know and recently decorated. He feels the same as I do. If we do the math, the numbers correspond close to what we are looking for."

"OK, I'll keep it close for now. Have a good day."

General Lawson hung up and looked at Pete.

Colonel Hammond looked at the Chairman of the Joint Chief of Staff.

"I don't think our Secretary of State has this information or even if he did he would ignore it in order to speed up this treaty with the North Vietnamese."

The Chairman leaned back in his chair and stared at his fingers.

"When I went through Ranger school in the 50's we learned "leave no man behind". Here we are talking about over 1500 U.S. Prisoners of War. What as a nation are we coming to?

The President won't lift a finger that we know. He needs this Treaty badly. We don't want this to leak. We need to get the Agency to start flying their bird over Laos as soon as this treaty is signed which I think will be soon. We will give away a lot and screw South Vietnam!"

"The CIA Chief is in with the Secretary of Defense. Let's see if we can grab him and bend his ear for a few minutes." The Chairman of the Joint Chiefs of Staff pushed a button on his phone and asked them to give a note to the CIA Chief and have him stop by his office. In less than five minutes there was a knock on the door.

Colonel Hammond opened it and let the CIA Chief in.

"Got your note. What can I do for you?"

"We have a situation and we need your help."

"This is not my day, the Secretary of State is giving the store away over in Paris and according to the Secretary of Defense, the President won't lift a finger as long as we get a peace treaty.

The Chairman of the Joint Chiefs of Staff briefed the CIA Director on the latest intel.

"We know that the North Vietnam were sending some prisoners of war to Laos but we didn't know how many. Where did you get this information or shouldn't I ask?"

"It comes from a very reliable source. We just got it about an hour ago. Can you use one of your Blackbirds to start making runs over Laos? I know you have that new system that can just about pick up an ant pissing."

"You know we are not supposed to be doing anything to upset the peace process and the withdrawal of U.S. troops from Vietnam. You know and I know that there will be no peace until North Vietnam has conquered the south and it will happen. It's a civil war for Christ sake. We had our civil war. The domino effect will not happen. If it does, it will not last. Will there be bloodletting, you bet, but Vietnam has too many resources and will someday become an economic factor. Well this little speech will give you two credit hours in international relations should you choose to go back to school. What can we do? Yes, I can authorize some flyovers but it has to be a silk purse operation. It can't be advertised in my section. I have a man on station that can put it in motion and if anyone finds out about it "we are doing it to make sure the North Vietnam are complying with the ongoing peace treaty." We will start unobtrusively and go from there. Was there anything else?"

The CIA Chief departed.

"You know what we need to do Hammond. We need to start drawing up plans for a new special ops force. One that is secret and draw people from all the services and establish a new Joint Task Force down at Ft. Bragg. Ease the command section down there over a period of months. They have the facilities down there. The Green Berets can run the school, training and interviewing. I don't want a bunch of knuckle draggers. I want an elite unit that can think. If they pass the training, I want them to go before a board of officers and senior NCOs to determine if they are fit mentally. I know it will take some time to get a force together, probably a couple of years. I don't want the men recruited for this force to know anything about it other than if they pass they are part of something special. We draw people from SEALS, Green Berets, Rangers and Marine Force Recon. It has to be voluntary. The Air Force can start or keep doing the special flying down in Florida only ratchet it up a notch or two. Call a meeting for the Chiefs of Staff for day after tomorrow.

The Paris peace accords were coming to a conclusion. There were last minute changes or disagreements but North Vietnam knew they had what they wanted. The South Vietnamese were not happy. The United States would back them should the North Vietnam attack. The world was told that there was peace in Vietnam. In the United States, the President declared peace with honor. The Secretary of State was declared a hero. The troops were coming home only to be met with hecklers and demonstrations.

General Lawson and Pete arrived in Washington on their way back to Ft. Bragg. They had received a message while in Paris to report to the Army Chief of Staff. They entered the Pentagon and walked into the Chief of Staff's outer office. Colonel Hammond was there to greet them. He briefed them on what was going on. They were to see the Army Chief of Staff and then come down to Colonel Hammond's boss, the Chairman's office.

"I'll see both of you in a few minutes. Go in and see your boss and get briefed.'

They knocked on the door and entered. "Good to see both of you. I haven't seen you, Lawson since Vietnam. Congratulations on your promotion. Get comfortable. I have something to discuss with both of you. Help yourselves to a cup of coffee." They both got a cup and sat down in comfortable chairs.

"How was Paris or shouldn't I ask?"

"We gave away the store, I'm afraid."

"Well, we all know that but I want to tell you both about a new force we are about to organize at Ft. Bragg. It's strictly a secret force where we get volunteers from all the services. There will be a unified command located at Ft. Bragg. You, Lawson will be the Army representative. You, Compton, will work with an old friend of yours, "Charging" Charlie Beckwith. Pete put down his cup and was about to say something when General Lawson placed his hand on his arm.

"I know how you feel about him but I need someone to keep me informed and see that he doesn't wander too far off his target and stack the force with his old buddies from the Delta Force in Vietnam. By the way, the new unit will be called the Delta Force. Its objective is to be our force for anti-hijacking of passenger planes and a few other missions. It will be an extremely high caliber unit and no one who tries out for it will get a free pass. We are getting volunteers from the Green Berets, Rangers, SEALS and Force Recon. Each class will start with about 75 men. If we can get 25 to 30 graduates per class, we will be lucky. It will take us about one year to get the force we need but the training will continue. There is no ceiling on the total force but only a few people will know the exact strength. Let's head down to the Chief of Staff's office and get some more information."

They both rose and followed the Chief of Staff out and into the corridor. A short walk and the Chief of Staff opened the door to the Joint Chief of Staff outer office. There were the Chiefs of Staff of all the military branches waiting. Introductions were made. Colonel Hammond came out and ushered them into the conference room. They all took a seat. The Joint Chief of Staff walked in and they all stood up.

"I have just talked to the Secretary of Defense and he is in complete agreement with our plan. Before I start, I want to say to General Lawson and LTC Compton, "That problem we had has been taken care of by the Budget Committee in Congress and it has passed. The President signed the bill three days ago. Good work Compton."

General Lawson poked Pete in the ribs with his elbow.

"Now when I tell you this: it's classified - I mean its classified! The name of the unit will be Delta Force. Each of you will designate a Colonel or General to be your representative at the Unified Command to be established at Ft. Bragg, N.C. It will be a PCS (permanent change of station). You will put out to your respective services that a new unit is being formed and it will be strictly voluntary. However, I want the best people you have. Each class will consist of about 75 people of which according to the initial training program I have read, about 25-30 men will graduate. This is not a confidence course. This is serious. It is physical but mostly mental. Your men have to have the right mental attitude or your men will not make it. At the end of the basic training, they have to appear before a board to determine if they are mentally qualified. This board will have on it qualified Military Psychologists as well as CSM and senior officers who have been associated with the type of operations this unit will perform. I would leave it to your Sergeant Majors in case of enlisted personnel and Company or Battalion Commanders for officers. There is no rank when a person goes through this course. This will be stressed at Ft. Bragg's unused old walled prison when they get there. Put out to your commands that I don't want anyone who volunteers to be turned down if he is an exceptional soldier that they can't do without. Believe me, you want to send the best damn soldiers you have when I'm authorized to tell you the missions they will have."

"Air Force, I want you to up your training with your Special Ops units. You have been issued the new guidance/radar systems available. If something new comes up, you won't have to ask for it. Your planes for the next two years will take a lot of abuse, don't worry about it. New or refurbished planes will be available to you and your training budget is unlimited. You will have your authorization tomorrow. If someone comes up with a new concept, try it. When I was a young lieutenant, I used to think "what are those old generals thinking? We can accomplish the task or mission in a more efficient and easier way." If someone has a better idea, try it.

"Are you saying that out of 75 men only 25-30 will make it? What's to keep us from stacking our quota so that a few of our men make it?" It was the Navy Chief of Staff.

"Fist of all, there is no quota. Second, if I see a service

sending only a few men, we will have a talk. I have discussed this exact problem with the Secretary of Defense and I have his blessing. The class can be 76 or 80 but the optimum would be 75. Talk to your senior officers. I can guarantee you that if the right message is conveyed to your men, you will have no problem with volunteers. If they don't make it, it is no stigma on their careers. They can go back to the unit they had been part of before volunteering."

"Who will be running this school or who is in charge?" It was the Chief of Staff of the Marines.

"It will be Colonel Beckwith with a cadre of officers and SGM both on active duty and retired; people who have been involved in covert operations in Vietnam. Some are ex-MACV-SOG personnel. The school will run two test groups through to iron out any problems or unforeseen situations. You can start sending volunteers in a month and start sending your joint staff within the same time. Ft. Bragg has already allocated office space and some housing. There is BOQ for any single lower grade officers or aids. Any more questions?"

There were none and the Chiefs of Staff started leaving.

"General Lawson and LTC Compton, please stay a moment."

When everyone had left except for Colonel Hammond, General Lawson and Pete, the Chief of Staff leaned forward in chair and starred at General Lawson and Pete.

"You have probably guessed why or one of the reasons why we are forming this unit. Your intel better be right because we are spending huge sums of money to get this force trained and continue this course. When the Secretary of Defense asked how certain I was on the intel, I staked my career and reputation on it. Is there any doubt in your minds about this info?"

They both answered "No".

"I would not have called Colonel Hammond had I not

been sure. The only problem I have is that I wish we could go in tomorrow and free those poor bastards. However, I see your point in delaying this operation until we have trained personnel and know exactly where they are. The Green Berets have suffered heavy casualties of the highly trained personnel in Vietnam. We have highly motivated people but lacking training. There will be casualties among the POW's if they have to wait more years; either by working them to death or dying from starvation. I can tell you that the Laotians, the Paet Loas are not friendly towards the U.S. or the Army we trained and equipped over there. It's only a matter of time before they have the entire country under their control."

"Don't think we haven't brain stormed this situation but we need a cohesive well trained smart unit to go in there and get them all out. Blackbird flights are starting next week. One thing I want to tell you is that I'm under great pressure to reduce the Special Forces (Green Berets) units and there are factions who want to do away with them completely. We have abandoned the Montagnard in South Vietnam. The Special Forces are training Cambodians and South Vietnamese regular forces as we speak. However, their future is in jeopardy. They have been tasked to death by Generals who are still fighting WWII. I foresee a day coming and not too long off when the need for Special Forces will be paramount. I want you, Compton, to go out on test runs of this course. See where improvements are needed. I don't want this course to be a Paris Island basic training course. We treat the people with dignity and we don't degrade the ones who don't make it. There will be officers and enlisted, all ranks come off the uniforms when starting the course. Officers don't pull rank on enlisted soldiers. If I hear of it, that officer or commander will have a one on one with me. You go through General Lawson and report on the course. Do either of you have any questions? This meeting is over."

Colonel Hammond walked them out into the corridor. "The old man is very serious about this. I hope Beckwith has calmed down a bit. Keep us informed on the commander and training. Have a good flight home."

General Lawson and Pete collected their luggage in the Army Chief of Staff's outer office and headed down to a staff car waiting to take them to Andrews Air Force Base. The ride home was quick. They took a taxi to Cottonade where they lived.

"We have two weeks off. Enjoy yourself, Pete, and my best to Betty."

"Same to Nancy, you know she could have done a lot better than picking you for a husband."

"Why you insolent pup; I'm going to tell her exactly what you said. No, I better not. She will probably agree with you. Have a good one."

Pete rang the door bell and was greeted by Betty and two beautiful girls. It was great to be home. There was a chorus of "Did you bring us anything from Paris?"

"You'll have to wait until I unpack my bags."

Betty put on her usual sultry act.

"Hey soldier, have you got plans for tonight?"

"Yes, as a matter of fact I have. If I don't get more hugs and kisses from all of you, I'm going to a motel for the night."

"You always say that Dad when you come home. How many do you want this time?" It was the oldest girl.

"At least a thousand from each of you"

"We don't have that many but we will give you all we have."

Pete sat down in a comfortable chair and took his jacket off. The two girls hugged and kissed him until they said they had run out.

"OK, open that small bag; there is a package for each of you. Your names are on them."

The girls grabbed the bag and unzipped it in record time

finding their packages and ran to their respective rooms.

"Now then soldier, how about their Mother? Do you have something for her?"

"I have several things for you."

Betty sat on his lap and gave him a nice homecoming kiss.

"I have missed you, Betty" he said between kisses.

"Are you saying those French women aren't as good as I have heard?"

"Naw, they are way overrated."

"Be careful soldier. Talk like that could get you a dry spell. No I take that back I'm tired of dry spells. Good to see you home. I do think you have lost some weight and you look tired. Was it that tough over there?"

"It wasn't tough physically but mentally it was a disaster in spite of what you read in the newspapers. The whole thing is or was a disaster. The only good thing is we are going to be in our home here for quite a while, meaning years. Lawson and I have both been assigned to a new task force here."

"Oh, God, our prayers have been answered. Nancy and I were just talking girl talk today and saying how nice it would be if we finally had a states side tour. Not moving for at least two or five years."

"We'll be here. I just hope you don't get bored?"

"Not as long as you're here I won't be bored."

Chapter 8

The new assignment was not without its bumps. The staff was in the process of being assembled and had no idea what was being planned. Colonel Beckwith was busy contacting old friends and getting his inner circle together. The exact starting date had not been determined and there was confusion to say the least. Pete found Colonel Beckwith in his temporary office and reported to him. To say Colonel Beckwith was less than happy to see him was an understatement. Colonel Beckwith informed Pete that he had just gotten a memo assigning Pete to his staff/cadre signed by the Army Chief of Staff. Pete had been standing in front of Beckwith's desk. He looked around and saw a folding chair leaning against the wall. He went over and got it and sat down in front of Beckwith who was somewhat taken aback by this unauthorized gesture which he had not offered.

"I see you haven't changed much since the last time I saw you in Vietnam and you are now a LTC. Let's see the last time I saw you, you were a Captain. That's a pretty fast promotion and the Distinguished Service Cross. I heard a rumor you were in Italy. I didn't know we had a war going there? What happened?"

Pete was wearing his class A green uniform with the Gold Israeli's parachute wings and his decorations.

"It's all classified, Colonel Beckwith, but you can check with the Secretary of Defense or the Army Chief of Staff. I'm sure they will inform you sir."

Colonel Beckwith's face turned red and Pete was sure he was about to get one of his famous outbursts but he just sat there and looked at Pete.

"Well, I guess I'm stuck with you."

"No, we are stuck with each other. I can assure you that I will be loyal to you and carry out your orders. I can further assure you that I want this project to work more than anyone. A lot of people depend on it. I'm sure you have been briefed on it."

"I haven't been told a fucking thing about anything other than there is a taskforce forming here at Bragg and I'm supposed to be in charge of training some volunteers. I think it's a Joint Task Force: Army, Navy, Marines and Rangers, of course. No one has briefed me."

"General Lawson is in his office in the main JFK Building, he might have the authority to brief you."

"Are you saying that Colonel, er... I mean General Lawson is here? Holy shit, I think I'll retire. He is the biggest bastard I know. I don't know if I can work for him."

"He is a lot like you" said Pete with a smile on his face.

"I'm going to take that as a complement even though I don't like him. Talk about a hard ass! Do you know him?"

"I have worked for him and I have worked for you and you are a lot alike. I'll tell you one thing, he is very intelligent. He doesn't miss a thing. If I were you, I'd go and see him."

"Yeah, I guess I'd better. Do you know what this is all about and why the big secrecy?"

"I do, but Sir, I'm not the one who should tell you with all due respect. I'd go and see General Lawson."

"Here is a list of staff personnel I have come up with. Some you know and some you don't. You will be my second in command. Look at the list and see what you think at least about the people you know. I'll be back in an hour."

Pete sat there looking over the typed list of personnel. Beckwith had stacked it with his old buddies. Pete crossed off about eight individuals; one a Major who was an ass kisser and Beckwith's errand boy. There were some names he did not know. He had an SF book with him in his briefcase. He looked some of them up in the index. They were all there. He cross referenced them and eliminated four more. That brought the staff down to seventeen. That should be enough. If they needed more they might utilize some of the people who washed out because of injuries or some unforeseen incident.

Beckwith came back looking like a whipped puppy. He sat down behind his desk and looked at the list of staff members. He was about to say something but changed his mind.

"General Lawson hasn't changed a bit. He informed me I was completely in charge and he would not interfere in anything including the selection process. Tomorrow when you come in, wear fatigues. We will go over to the old Jail which has walls all around it and see what we have to do to get it in shape for training and establishing a shooting range. I have identified a lot of ammo that no one wants. We need guards 24/7. What do you think about hiring some retired SGM who are wasting valuable talents sitting around their homes or drinking beer at the NCO club?"

"That sounds good but they have to be briefed and sign the secrecy act. There can be no leaks about this to their friends."

"I agree. After listening to Lawson, I'm kind of surprised they gave me this project. I'm not particularly popular with a lot of high ranking officers. Lawson promised to support me 100% which almost floored me. He has a lot of clout. I see you have crossed off some people. You would have gotten an argument from me had you done it before I saw Lawson. I'll see you tomorrow. I'll get the people left on the list. They will go with us to the Jail. Come up with some basic ideas, just jot them down and be prepared to brief the people over at the Jail tomorrow."

Beckwith held out his hand and Pete shook it.

They started fixing the old jail complex. It needed some work. A shooting range was completed and guards were posted. The retired SGM were happy to be part of the organization and earn some extra money. Pete had come up with a training schedule and Beckwith had added some of his ideas. The finished schedule was submitted to General Lawson and the rest of the Joint Task Force. It came back with changes, some of which were incorporated. The volunteers were starting to show up and helped with modernizing the jail. Living facilities had been set up along with a first class mess hall. All training gear which had been requested showed up. Nothing was denied them. The volunteers brought their own uniforms and gear and they were confined to the Jail. Nearby Camp McCall was also available to them and when not at the jail, Camp McCall was their home. The cadre had gone through a rehearsal and Pete had gone with them. It was tough! The 48 hours map and navigation up in the North Carolina mountains was a ball buster. It was timed and checkpoints were established where a volunteer had to be at a certain point by a certain time. The course was laid out like the Star of David (the Israeli symbol), As a result of the first rehearsals by the staff, it was decided to increase the staff with eight more people. The second trial went smoother and they were ready to start.

The first class of 77 students was formed up for a group picture. CSMG Mays took the picture and told the group to look around at their fellow classmates. The next picture he informed them would be of the graduating class and most of them would not be present for the picture. The volunteers all laughed because they were not ordinary volunteers. They had proven themselves time and time again and no course would keep them from making it. CSMG Mays just smiled at them and walked away.

Although the hours were long and some days and nights he was gone, Pete was home most evenings. It was a good assignment and Betty and the girls were happy.

The first class graduated: 26 of the original 77. CSGM Mays took their picture and congratulated them. They had all passed the selection board. Those that were not HALO (High Altitude Low Opening) parachutists were sent to the course. The others started marksmanship and other training. There was a one week break between classes giving the cadre a chance to go over changes to the course, adding or fine tuning it. Colonel Beckwith was back to his old self. He was enjoying his role and the fact that he got every piece of equipment he asked for. At one of the meetings with his cadre, he admitted this was the toughest course he had ever seen and he was proud of the work the staff was doing.

When Pete got home one evening, Betty told him the Secretary of State had received the Peace Prize. Pete looked at her and shook his head.

The phone rang. It was General Lawson. "Have you heard who got the Peace Prize?"

"Yes, Betty just told me. You and I talked about it - we knew it would happen."

"Yes, but the North Vietnamese Le Duc Tho refused by

saying there was no peace and he is right but our politicians are happy. See you tomorrow." The General hung up.

The training was going great. Colonel Beckwith amazed Pete. He was really into it and kept the staff on a short leash and Pete was enjoying working for him. Some of the early graduates had performed missions both in the Middle East and Africa. They were getting up to strength where they could start planning for the POW mission. The Joint Task Force was pleased with what they saw.

There was a new President in the White House who was very controversial. He had placed a Navy Admiral in charge of the CIA and people/agents were being cut in favor of satellite imagery. The morale at the Agency was low. The Blackbird program had continued and the POWs were located. However, an unforeseen incident happened that changed the focus of the POWs. The American Embassy in Tehran, Iran was taken over by students at first and then the new regime in Iran took over and the embassy staff became prisoners. The Embassy was looted. There was a lot of diplomatic effort spent on freeing the prisoners but to no avail. A few managed to escape and some were killed. It was a presidential election year and the American prisoners in Iran became a major issue. They had been prisoners for over four hundred days and the President decided to do something. The Delta Force was assigned the mission to free them, however, all the branches of service wanted a part of the action and it became confused. The Air Force Special Ops Unit was put on alert. They had the large helicopters available with the latest navigational equipment and were well trained. However, the Navy insisted that they had helicopters on Air Craft Carriers in the region and wanted to use them. The President was a Naval Academy graduate and his CIA Chief was Navy, so it was decided to use the Navy choppers whose maintenance was iffy and its pilots less trained than the Air Force Special Ops pilots. The Navy was betting that the operation would not happen so no special training occurred. When the order to go was given the Navy was surprised. One chopper on the way to a rendezvous point in Iran had mechanical problems and turned around. Colonel Beckwith was put in charge of the Delta Force which was prepared. They landed at the rendezvous point in C-130s. However, the mission turned into a fiasco during a refueling mission for the choppers and a fire broke out causing severe damage to the choppers, C-130s and personnel. The rescue was a disaster. Pete had stayed at Ft. Bragg and continued the training. The news of the disaster made the headlines both in the newspapers and TV. Each Service claimed the other service was in charge of the overall operation.

A new President was elected and the prisoners were released by Iran. There was a reshuffling of the CIA and other agencies. Agents were placed back on the ground again and the morale and intel was reestablished. The Joint Task Force at Ft. Bragg was reshuffled. It became bigger and more cohesive. The new Chairman of the Joint Chief of Staff and the Secretary of Defense kept a closer eye on their operations. General Lawson was now a two star general and was in charge of the Army Section. Colonel Beckwith retired. He had too many Generals gunning for him and with the old President out of office, a fellow Georgian native, Colonel Beckwith, was hung out to dry.

Pete had a talk with him before he retired and Beckwith said he hoped Pete would take his place but he had not recommended him or anyone else because his word meant nothing anymore. Pete was sorry to see him go. They had gotten close over the last year. There were people who hated Beckwith and then there were the ones that really liked his bravado and tough stance on things.

Pete was at Camp McCall in his office when the door

opened and in walked General Lawson.

"Got something for you, Pete" General Lawson said with a smile on his face. Pete had come to attention when General Lawson walked in.

"Sit down and take a look at these." Pete opened a large envelope and took out aerial photos which had been enhanced. They showed new pictures of the POWs. They had scratched a huge POW sign in the dirt in their compound with their feet.

"There are at least 1500 prisoners here. We need to rehearse fast. This time there will be no fuckup. Get back to Bragg and report to the Joint Staff headquarters. I'll see you there in an hour." General Lawson grabbed the photos and departed.

Pete drove back to Bragg and walked into the Joint Staff headquarters. He headed for General Lawson's office but was diverted by a Captain to the Conference Room. As he walked in a large crowd including Betty and Nancy were there. He didn't know what was going on. General Lawson told a Major to read the orders. LTC Compton was promoted to full Colonel. General Lawson pinned the Eagle on his collar. Betty and Nancy each gave him a kiss. Colonel Compton was also told he was now in charge of the training of the new force. There was coffee and cake and everyone congratulated him. Someone yelled "speech".

"I don't know what to say."

"Don't say anything. Just cut the cake. I'm hungry!" said General Lawson.

Pete cut the cake, someone else took over the cake cutting and Betty and Nancy served coffee.

"Well Colonel, how does it feel?" It was Command Sergeant Major Mays.

"I still don't know what to say. It's a complete surprise. You're the one that deserves this Eagle. You have been the backbone of the entire operation.

131

"Naw, I wouldn't be in your shoes much less an Officer. You people are too much like politicians."

"You're right and we have a lot to do in the next weeks."

We're going to the club tonight." Betty informed him when they got home. The General and Nancy arrived and they all had a drink and toasted Pete again.

General Lawson confided in Pete of the events preceding his promotion to full colonel. "You know you are three years ahead of your contemporaries now. I got a call from the Army chief of Staff. He is about to retire. He asked if there was anything he could do for me before he left. I told him there was an LTC who should be promoted immediately. He got angry and asked if you were still an LTC and I said "yes". You will have his orders tomorrow and I want him taken care of. He should be wearing your stars. He is working his ass off and if Beckwith tells me that, I know it's true. Give him my regards. I have put a letter in his file and the previous Secretary of the Army endorsed it."

"So you see you are not forgotten."

"I appreciate it, believe me. Betty will probably go on a shopping spree again. It happens each time I get promoted."

"I have to look like a Colonel's wife. What do you expect?"

"We'll pick you up in two and a half hours. Civilian dress." The General and Nancy departed.

"The girls won't be home for at least an hour. It's tennis lessons today and I have never been to bed with a full Colonel. How about it soldier? He grabbed her arm and took her into the bedroom.

"General Lawson and Nancy picked them up and they went to the main Officer's Club. When the General and Pete went over to another table to say "hello", Nancy looked at Betty.

"You look like a newly plucked chicken tonight, eyes sparkling and a glow in your face. Is it the Colonel?"

"You mean it really shows? I don't know what the SF put in the coffee but Pete is unbelievable! You would think he would slow down but he is as good as ever. I have to be careful and not smile at him so much it triggers something."

"I'll have to remember that, although I'm not complaining. Generals can be brutes and I love it."

The training continued and all rehearsals for the freeing of the POWs increased. The Air Force had gotten new and refurbished planes with the new GPS systems and was ready to go. Choppers were stationed in Thailand with full support crews. Pete came home late one night and tired and went in and kissed the girls goodnight. He went out and sat down next to Betty who had fixed him a cocktail.

"You look like you could use one tonight" she said kissing him softly on the lips. "I suppose you have heard the news?"

"What news?"

"A retired Colonel Gritz and a team of men are on their way or are in Thailand and are going after some American POW in Laos."

Pete almost spilled his drink. Gritz had done some good work in Vietnam in '67 or '68, covert action in Cambodia but he was not in shape. Pete had seen him not too long ago and it was apparent that he had let himself go. He had been living up in Idaho, Coeur d'Alene, or some such place with a bunch of ex Green Berets, loose cannons. Where the hell had he gotten the intel and funds to stage a raid at his age?

"Excuse me, I have to call General Lawson."

Pete got him on the second ring.

"A little late isn't it, Pete?"

Pete explained what Betty had just told him.

"If this is a joke, it's not funny. I'm going to make a call and I'll be right over."

Betty had been looking at Pete all this time. She had never

seen him so upset.

"Did I say anything wrong? What is the matter?"

"Turn on the TV and see if there is anything on the news?"

Betty turned the TV on and sure enough the TV news anchor was explaining that a Green Beret Colonel and a team of men had located American POWs in Laos and were on the way to free them. There would be more news about them once they came back to Thailand.

The doorbell rang and General Lawson walked in.

"Betty, I'll have whatever Pete is drinking." I just talked to the new Army Chief of Staff. They are in a meeting with the Secretary of Defense as we speak. To say the shit has hit the fan is an understatement. It seems this Gritz had been contacted some time ago by the State Department and asked if he was up to a mission and was briefed on what it would entail. Of course, Gritz jumped at it and said he would furnish the men but he needed equipment. It seems a rich Texan and a conservative movie star had come up with the money for just about everything they needed. The State Department had authorized a hefty sum to pay these raiders as they were referred to. They are in Thailand as we speak and Gritz is being interviewed by a local Thai TV station. They have been over there close to a week now and are getting ready to cross the border into Laos."

Sure enough the TV anchor informed them they had a News Alert. Betty turned the TV up.

There was Gritz, in all his glory overweight and in tiger camouflage suit, telling the Thai TV station about their mission. It was unbelievable! He practically told them when and where they were crossing and that he had the full backing of the U.S. State Department. The news anchor informed them that was all but was sure there would be some updates in the next few days. After all this was a classified mission.

General Lawson looked at Pete.

"How the hell did anyone find out about this? The State Department again! I'll lay you odds that our old friend who screwed up the Israeli operation is behind this. He doesn't want any POWs freed. It would make him look like a fool. After all the hoopla about the peace Treaty, he still has his friends. We will have a meeting tomorrow morning and get the latest. Doesn't Gritz realize that the Laotians watch TV also? Someone is paying a lot of dollars for this. The contributors probably don't know about our program. Well, I'll see you tomorrow morning in the conference room. Thanks for the drink, Betty."

After the General left, Betty looked at Pete and frowned.

"Is this what you have been working so hard and long hours on?"

"Yes. It's been held real close. We knew over a year ago where the POWs were but we didn't have the force to go in and get them. Now we do and now this fiasco. They won't get a half a mile into Laos before they are hit, if they get that far."

At the meeting at Ft. Bragg, the Joint Task Force was told by the Army Chief of Staff via a secure line, that the operation was cancelled. New photos from Laos showed the POWs were being split up and taken to different locations by trucks. The Blackbird recon would continue.

Pete sat next to General Lawson and knew who was behind this fiasco. Gritz and his team had been ambushed as soon as they hit Laotian territory and they had escaped by boats back to Thailand.

General Lawson stated that the Delta Force had many more missions to perform and the training would continue. The force would continue to grow but its classification and mission was to remain secret and that the troops who had been training for this mission would receive other missions.

After the meeting, Pete went back to Camp McCall where CSMG Mayes had gathered the force which was to go in and get the POWs.

Pete informed them what had happened. Most of them knew already but to hear it officially was a letdown to say the least. He described new missions by groups of two or more and nothing had changed as far as classification.

"Continue to hone your marksmanship for you are going to need it. Some of you will take refresher foreign language courses. We have more missions than we can fulfill at this time. Hence, new people will continue to expand the force. Nothing changes as far as Delta Force is concerned. It will remain a highly trained elite force and few people will know about it. OK, that's it. Get back to training. In the next few days you will check with me for your next mission. Nothing will be written down."

Pete returned to his office. General Lawson and a man in civilian clothes were waiting for him.

"Pete this is Bob Miller."

Pete looked at Miller and at General Lawson.

"Did I say something wrong," quipped the general. "Both of you look like you are about to laugh."

"General Lawson, let me explain," said Miller. "Pete, here, rescued me and my partner in Cambodia in '69 right before we were about to lose our heads, literally. We were young, just out of training, and Vietnam was our first posting. We wanted to impress our boss and fell for an old trick. Pete here briefed our boss afterwards and made us look like heroes."

"Why am I not surprised; I have worked with this young Colonel for years. In fact, he was my adjutant when I was a Colonel in the 82nd Airborne Division. He caused me more headaches than you would believe. He still hasn't changed. Is there more I should know?"

"No, there is no more, although this is the first time I have heard an agency person tell the truth" said Pete.

"Well, what I was going to say is that Mr. Miller here is our agency liaison officer at JFK Center now and he will be working closely with you and the Joint Staff. I have work to do." The General left.

"I'm sorry to hear about the POWs, Pete. We have been following closely your training here and the events in Laos. We think we know where the leak was but unfortunately it's over and until we locate some of them again, we have been told to hold it close as I'm sure you have also.

Chapter 9

Pete was sitting in his office at the JFK Center for Special Warfare at Fort Bragg, North Carolina, thinking about the disaster regarding the POW rescue in Laos. How had the State Department found out about the Delta Force plan to rescue the POWs and then subvert it by using old retired Green Berets who hadn't stepped a kilometer into Laos before they were ambushed and sent running for the border and back into Thailand? He would have to sit down with Bob Miller who was the CIA representative now at JFK Center. After all, Bob owed his life and career to him after the Agency's fiasco in Cambodia in 1969. Oh well! That was history and the North Vietnamese had taken over South Vietnam after the Secretary of State had negotiated a peace with North Vietnam in 1973. "Peace with Honor" the President had told the nation, but forgetting to mention that over 1500 United States prisoners were sent from North Vietnam to Laos during the peace talks. When the Nobel Peace Prize had been awarded to the Secretary of State and to Le Duc Tho, North Vietnam's negotiator, Le Duc Tho had refused his half of the award saying "There was no Peace" and subsequently North Vietnam had overrun South Vietnam.

Pete's boss, General Lawson, had been in a foul mood for over 2 months now and had left for the Pentagon 2 days ago, for what Pete didn't know. His last words to Pete had been to keep the Delta Force training going and had given him a phone number where Pete could reach him if any new intel developed and for Pete to talk only to him.

There was a knock on Pete's door and Bob Miller walked in. "I was just about to call you," said Pete, standing up and shaking Bob's hand. "Well, I thought I would come over and chit chat a little," said Bob closing the door. "I guess I have to be a little more polite and respectful towards you now that you have been promoted and have an eagle on your collar."

"Shit, it's about time you spooks show a little respect and start telling the truth; what's going on?"

"Well, not much that you can hang your hat on, but the Black Bird (reconnaissance plane) has picked up some things around Pakxe in Laos which is close to the Thailand border and one about 70km northeast of Vientiane, the capital of Laos. It's one of the last places we expected anything. We have been looking north towards the Burmese border thinking they wanted to get as far away as possible; anyway, three camps have been located. I guess the old axiom is being followed, "keep them hidden in plain sight.""

"Is this info worth telling my boss about or do you think he has been briefed at the Pentagon?"

"I don't know, Pete, but we have kept the info compartmentalized – not even the President has been briefed. As you know, we have a mole or moles in the Agency, so it's been held close. I got the info by courier yesterday; the word is no electronic transfer of the information. Anyway, that is not the purpose of my visit; although it could be incorporated into what I came over to talk or should I say pick your brain about. Can you enlighten me about the 3 numerical projects you helped write up in 69 and 70, where we send in small units of Special Forces (SF), the Green Berets, into the Highlands of what used to be South Vietnam?"

"Jesus, Bob, what are you people thinking about now? Have you contacts in the Highlands of Vietnam, say between Pleiku and south of Ban Me Thuot?"

"Let's just say we are in contact with an old friend, Ibaham in Cambodia. He is getting old and his son has now taken over the FULRO (Unified Front for the Liberation of Oppressed Peoples) force and has received many recruits since the unification of Vietnam; they now have modern arms and plenty of potential."

"Bob, you are going to have to go to someone higher than me to get the information on that. If General Lawson was here maybe he could brief you and those of your people who are involved in this, but I think he has to get an okay from higher up."

"I don't want specifics; I just want a general outline on how it works."

"Okay, you know about the SF force we had in Cambodia the last years when the war got bigger and better; hell, those SF soldiers were so dedicated that when wounded they refused evacuation and the Purple Heart because they knew they would never get back to Cambodia. They had medics and a Doctor who would fix them up and unless it was life threatening, would keep them there. It was during the latter part of the war that Montagnards from South Vietnam contacted the leader of the US Force there and asked for help after North Vietnam took over. They are maybe behind us and the modern world, but they are not stupid; they saw the handwriting on the wall and knew they would need help. We came up with a program and

I think it's ongoing but not many are aware of it. Our people go in usually in civilian clothes, but always with a green beret in their rucksack. The program has been so successful that the Vietnamese have declared the area from south of Ban Me Thuot to the north of Pleiku a non-pacified area and are inclined to let the Montagnards run it as a semi-autonomous area. As you know, that area and over into Cambodia is almost like the prairie in Nebraska with clumps of jungle interspersed. Ibaham has been operating across the border in Cambodia since early 1965 or maybe late '64. When I was involved in '65 he had a force of over 10,000 soldiers and their families which made a hell of a logistic problem for him. He ended up dividing his people into sub groups, grew some of their own vegetables, i.e. corn and started going over to Vietnam's SF camps for arms and hijacking food trucks."

"I know the Agency was generous with both money and advice, hell you guys were running and supporting the operation; what happened?"

"Well, you remember we had a peanut farmer from Georgia as President and along with the CIA Director, a fellow Annapolis graduate, cut us out of the loop. We lost control but want to get back in. My boss has identified a lot of funds for this project so we need to coordinate with you folks and help where we can."

"I have given you the overview but I'm sure the people who are running it will be happy to have you aboard. I can tell you that there is no electronic transmission about this operation; all information is written and there are high-ranking officers here at the JFK Center who are not aware of this project. We learned our lesson when we planned the POW rescue."

"Well, I'll tell you something, the State Department got a back channel message from Hanoi asking the US to stop supporting the Montagnards, so the State Department came to us thinking we were running it, but of course we told them that we had at one time helped but not any longer, and as far as we knew the project had been terminated. That's when my boss located dormant funds and here I am."

The phone on Pete's desk rang and he picked it up. He listened but didn't say anything other than "yes, Sir" then hung up. Pete looked at Bob but didn't say anything for a few minutes.

"Do you remember when you first started at the Agency and your boss walks in and says "we have a problem/situation" that needs to be taken care of right away? It usually meant you had a problem/situation which you had to handle immediately. I just got a warning order from my boss."

"Anything I can do to help?" asked Bob with a frown on his face.

"He didn't say but requested you be in his office tomorrow at 0800 hours along with yours truly. Why do I have a feeling that he has been talking to your boss?"

"This may be speculation, but get your map out of SE Asia and I'll show you the three POW camps we found and also where Ibaham is currently located."

Pete went to the far wall of his office and pulled down the map; Bob circled the three sites he had mentioned. "Hell, Ibaham is over a 100 kilometers from the nearest POW camp. I think we are in the right church, but the wrong pew," said Pete looking at the map.

Chapter 10

The meeting next morning in General Lawson's office brought a few surprises. Along with Pete and Bob was a man in civilian clothes whom Pete had not seen in years, a Colonel Lindor, now retired. General Lawson introduced the Colonel to Pete and Bob as the head of JFK Center's 3 numerical projects. Col. Lindor shook Bob and Pete's hands and stated that he hadn't seen Pete since meeting him at Fort Bragg in 1967; whereas he had subsequently hand-carried Pete's application for an RA commission at the request of Pete's boss at the time, Colonel Warmbrod and the 18th Airborne Corps C.G. "I always wondered how I got that RA commission in such a short time," said Pete. "You were part of a Department of Army briefing team at the time – your friend and mine Major Lindsey introduced us."

General Lawson had been sitting behind his desk looking from Pete to Col. Lindor while this verbal exchange took place. "Is there anyone in the US Army or the Agency that you don't know or haven't met before?" The General was directing his comment to Pete. "I have had the unfortunate pleasure of working with this young Col. both as my adjutant when I was a Brigade Commander in the 82nd Airborne, and later in Italy, Paris, and now back here at the JFK Center. I can't seem to get away from him. Can we get on with this meeting which I feel is paramount to freeing some good American POWs who should have been rescued years ago?"

"Colonel Lindor has been working on and directing a project which few people are aware of from his office in the basement of this building and his office or Headquarters at Ubon Ratchathani Air Field in Thailand. What I'm telling you is beyond Top Secret and not to be discussed with anyone outside this room. You, Bob, have been designated by your boss at Langley to work with us and be the liaison officer for your Agency; your orders or assignment will arrive by courier in the next 2 days. You, Pete, will be our representative and will continue to train the Delta Force until a replacement has been designated. In your next class which starts next week, there will be four candidates who speak fluent Thai and Lao. They have worked for Col. Lindor at his Headquarters in Thailand and have been part of his project the last 2 years. They are all Captains in the US Army Special Forces and have volunteered to go through your Delta training. They are not to be given a free pass, but the experience and training should rejuvenate their skills. You might say they are being retrained. If some do not pass, they will continue to work with four of your people to hone their skills; that goes for all four – pass or no pass. The people who they work with will become part of an expanded team of eight."

"You, Pete, will be in charge of this group and go to Thailand on a TDY (Temporary Change of Duty) along with Bob; make contact with Ibaham's people in Cambodia and determine if they can be of some help in freeing the POWs. It can be a diversion in the vicinity of the three camps located in Laos. Colonel Lindor will have a Delta Force at his Airfield and do the actual rescuing of the prisoners. Col. Lindor can give you the details of what is going on in the area where the three camps are located. You, Bob, will cover Pete and his groups' back with your assets in the area. Nothing will be written down, but both of you will be given TDY orders for Thailand. You have 2 months to get your people trained and oriented and pick Col. Lindor's brain on his operation. Cambodia should not be a problem; you will parachute into Ibaham's area; you will have Burst communication with Col. Lindor back in Thailand. I know there are a lot of questions but I think after working with Col. Lindor, most will be answered. You, Bob, will get a refresher course at our airborne school and wear a uniform with Captain Bars on it. Gradually inform your wives on this, but be vague on the details. The Agency is being generous with their TDY pay, so that could be a silver lining regarding your absence; the exact amount will be made available to you in the next few days. I would wait a month or so before you tell them about your new adventure. I'm just going to say this once – no leaks to anyone other than your wives and that will only be that you are going to Thailand. *It's classified beyond Top Secret.*"

The next Delta class had 75 trainees including the four Captains from Col. Lindor's outfit. Only one graduated. Pete had picked four Captains who had been in one of the initial classes and had performed at least one mission each. These eight Captains trained together along with Pete and Bob. The physical training was conducted by the Captains on a rotational basis which Pete noticed they enjoyed, especially when he and Bob had trouble keeping up or were soaked with sweat.

One evening when Pete came home and was having a drink with Betty, she commented that he looked great and was getting in great shape. "When are you leaving" had been her comment. Pete was taken aback for he had not said anything to her yet. "Probably in about a month; TDY to Thailand." When were you going to tell me?" asked Betty. "Truthfully, in the next couple of days. We haven't been officially told yet; all we have received is a warning order. I will be going over with nine other guys; what we are going to do we haven't been told yet."

"I have never asked you about anything you have been involved with and I'm not going to start now. However, I will just say that you have three girls here that love you very much, so be careful."

"They don't ask Colonels to do crazy things, so you have nothing to worry about. I will ask you one thing though; don't mention anything to your folks when they come down to take the girls to Disney World or to Nancy. When I know something definite, I will tell you."

"I love you, Pete Compton," said Betty raising her glass gently touching Pete's glass.

Chapter 11

Their time with Col. Lindor lasted maybe an hour each day. By the second month, they were all in tune as to what was going on and what their mission would entail. At the end of 2 months Pete was sitting in his office going over some new Intel with Bob. A LTC Smith had taken over the Delta Force training, so everything now centered around their mission. "Have you told Jean about your TDY to Thailand?" Pete asked Bob. "Yes, well… she noticed my new body and endurance. At first she was enjoying it but after a few weeks she asked if I was taking something, a new pill or did the SF put something in their coffee. She was not complaining, in fact she was enjoying the new revitalized me. I then told her about our training and our upcoming TDY to Thailand and that it was a close hold assignment. She understood but told me to continue my physical training. We put our wives through a lot, Pete; it's a wonder that they haven't left us long ago."

Pete informed Betty that he was leaving in about a week and would be working with Col. Lindor at this base in Thailand.

His best estimated timeframe for being gone would be 60-70 days. "Can we just go in and lay on the bed; the girls are asleep so you and I can have some quality time?" Betty said kissing the top of his head. "Lead the way, Mrs. Compton, and clothes are not required," said Pete giving her a gentle slap on her butt.

New equipment was issued to the 10-man team from uniforms (tiger suits) to harnesses and weapons. They were also given a 2 day course on the new updated Burst communication. Two days were spent at Camp McCall on briefings about the latest Intel and then on individual basis brief back to a board consisting of Gen. Lawson, Col. Lindor and a representative from Langley (the Agency); this entailed the entire mission consisting of map coordinates of Ibaham's village, and radio frequency key words, i.e. be alert – weapons – something is wrong – get ready for extraction, etc. At the end of the second day, Gen. Lawson was happy with the brief backs and preparations. "I want to emphasize that Col. Lindor will have a sufficient Delta Force available to him to hit all three camps; the men have been departing in groups of eight for the last month and are being briefed and trained on the layout of the camps. Planes and helicopters are available at his airfields; it's the Air Force Special Ops. They have not been briefed on the location yet but Col. Lindor will handle that when the time comes; right now they are pulling preventative maintenance on their planes. I know that you have all been POR'd (records, checks, wills brought up to date and shots given) and your rucksacks and duffel bags packed. Does anyone have any questions?"

Pete stood up "Where is the money for Ibaham's force?" The man from the Agency leaned forward in his chair and told them that the money was at Col. Lindor's base in Thailand where one of the Agency's men was in charge of it. Pete said okay, "I have one other question – who besides us knows about our team going to Thailand?" Gen. Lawson looked at

Col. Lindor and the Agency man and answered, "The three of us, your wives, and you. If this statement is not accurate, then someone correct me. The Air Force crew that's flying you there in a C-141 only knows that they are transporting 10 or so passengers plus their equipment; you will not land at Col. Lindor's Air Base; the C-141s attract too much attention, hence they will land outside of Bangkok where C141s are a norm. A C-123 will transport you on your arrival to Col. Lindor's base. Your departure will be 2 days from today at 0600 hours from Pope Air Base here, stops at Travis in California and Hickam AB in Hawaii, and then into Thailand. Unless you have any questions, you are free to go. If something happens between now and our departure, you all have my phone number."

Pete stayed and waited for Gen. Lawson as he had gotten a funny feeling when Gen. Lawson was briefing them. "Do you have a question, Pete?"

"Have you told Nancy that you are going to Thailand?" The General looked at Pete and smiled, "Nothing escapes you, does it? Yes, I have told her and she is talking to Betty on their shopping trip today spending the TDY money."

"I haven't told Betty about the TDY money, so I'm safe."

"Ha! She is the daughter of the former Chief of Staff of the Army; are you kidding – your money is gone along with mine."

"I guess you're right, wives are devious and bear watching; but I'm glad she and Nancy are on the same page and live near each other. They can talk to each other and compare notes."

"I have only told Nancy that I'll be gone for a few months to Thailand, nothing specific."

"Same here, but they will read between the lines; dumb they are not."

Pete saluted the General saying, "I'll see you at Pope." He drove home and parked in the garage. Betty's car was gone. He let himself in and headed for his den. He was glad Gen.

Lawson was going; it meant Betty and Nancy could lean on each other. Betty made the most of their last 2 days together. The girls were not told that their father would be gone and where. Betty would tell them when they got back from Disney World in Florida. Her parents had picked them up a week earlier for their much anticipated trip. Pete had told them to bring him back a tee shirt.

"They are going to miss you, Pete; they are definitely Dad's girls."

"How about their Mom, is she going to miss me also?"

"I'm going to tell you something, Pete," Betty shared. "The first time I saw you at the Pentagon, I knew I was going to be your wife. I have loved you since that first moment. I know you thought I was pushy, but you had no chance and it's been a great and exciting life. We have many years to go, so don't do anything foolish; you are my life." Pete reached for her hand and took her into their bedroom.

Chapter 12

Everyone showed up at Pope Air Force Base and their equipment was loaded aboard the C-141. Betty had driven Pete to the base and Nancy had brought the General. Goodbyes were said and the men boarded; the clamshell doors in the back of the plane closed. They were the only ones departing and were soon headed down the runway with the powerful engines coming to a high pitch whine as they took off.

Nancy suggested they head over to Pope Officer's Club and have breakfast. As they were sipping their coffee, Nancy mentioned that her husband and Pete made a good team and told Betty (on the QT) that Pete would make General in little over 5 months. "Are you certain, Pete knows nothing about this?" said Betty. "I know my tight lipped husband said he had a surprise when he came back from his trip to the Pentagon. We were in bed when he told me and I kept asking what the surprise was and he wouldn't tell me, so I did what any red blooded wife would do; I grabbed him by his most vulnerable parts and squeezed a little; he begged me to stop and said okay, he would talk, which he did. He made me promise not to tell Pete but didn't say anything about you, so there you have it. His parts were not damaged as they worked just fine afterwards. We wives have to maintain control – after all, they go on their adventures and leave us back here to carry on doing the administrative jobs, caring for their homes, banking, etc. Which reminds me, did Pete tell you what their daily TDY pay is on this trip?"

"No, Pete doesn't say anything about extra pay; he just puts it in our savings account when he gets back from his trips."

"Well, my dear, the Agency is picking up the tab for this little adventure and I can tell you it's going to pay for the new car I have been telling you about." Betty was looking at Nancy with a blank look on her face. "You know, I have to get more involved in our finances. Pete is generous and has never denied me anything. We talk about investments and my Father has steered him to a newly formed tech stock which is doing well; we have diversified our portfolio, but I could use a new car. The girls are into sports and the car is definitely getting tired and showing its age. You are right, Nancy, we deserve to drive cars that start on the first try in the mornings; after all, we are the wives of senior officers. Pete has this idea that when he gets home from one of his trips, the first night we are in bed we are caught up on our intimacy. Not true, as you and I well know; that thinking is locker room talk with no substance. Of course, he doesn't get away with it, but that's how they think."

"Oh, I know" responded Nancy. "I think I'm married to Pete's older brother."

When they touched down at Hickam AFB in Hawaii, the pilot came back and told Gen. Lawson that they were experiencing problems with engine #4, and it would take a few days to repair it. Col. Lindor went into the Base Ops Center and made two calls, one to his office in Thailand and one to the

Moana Hotel in Honolulu. He then informed them that they all had rooms at the Moana; their gear was transferred to the Base Ops Center and locked up.

Pete and Gen. Lawson were sitting under the famous Banyan Tree at the Moana sipping a beer. "So you have been at this hotel before; was it in conjunction with R&R from Vietnam?" Gen. Lawson was looking at Pete. "No, I wasn't married during my tours in Vietnam so I didn't take R&R. We always had mechanical problems with our C-130s when we got to Hawaii, both coming and going home; all prearranged with the Air Force crew, of course. We got a slip of no availability from Fort DeRussy here and Uncle Sam picked up the tab at this hotel. There were only two hotels on the beach when we first started going over to V.N. on 6 month deployments and then PCS (Permanent Change of Station – 1 year tours), the Royal Hawaiian and this hotel. The Royal Hawaiian was bright pink in color, so we chose this white colored Moana."

"Wait, are you saying you arranged it with the Air Force crew?"

"Yes, sir, they needed a little rest and we had been sitting on those webbed nylon strap seats which get to you after a long flight." Did you arrange this mechanical problem also?"

"No, sir, I had nothing to do with it, but Col. Lindor sure made some quick arrangements, maybe he did, but I doubt it." Gen. Lawson smiled at Pete and said, "The seats in the C-141s are not that great; we used to stay the Royal Hawaiian." Pete laughed and sipped his beer. "What are you going to do with the TDY money the Agency is giving us?"

"Well, Betty hasn't complained, but I'm going to buy her a new car; the one she's driving is old and tired."

"It's funny you said that, Nancy has been hinting at a car she has been looking at; I'm going to buy it for her."

"God, they put up with a lot of crap and never complain;

it's the least we can do for them. It takes a special woman to put up with the life of a soldier and they deserve everything we can give them. You and I have been very lucky in our marriages. Isn't it time for super, I'm starving?"

Chapter 13

They landed at a Thai Air Force Base outside of Bangkok and immediately transferred their equipment to a C-123 painted a dull gray without any markings. The trip to Col. Lindor's Air Base lasted about 1 hr. 30 minutes. The C-123 taxied into a huge hanger, shut down, and the main doors of the hanger closed. Sleeping quarters were available next door along with a mess hall staffed with Air Force cooks. The team secured their gear and was told food was available if they were hungry, which they were. Pete noticed a few DF (Delta Force) people were sitting at tables eating and went over to talk to them. He joined Gen. Lawson, Col. Lindor and Bob Miller at their table as they were digging into steaks and baked potatoes. "Thank God for the Air Force mess," said Gen. Lawson between bites. "Amen," said Pete cutting into a medium rare steak.

The next morning they were briefed by Col. Lindor on the latest Intel. The team wore their new tiger-striped fatigues with no name tags or markings. Pete and his team would parachute into Ibaham's area the next day with an Agency man that controlled the money - U.S. dollars along with the local Cambodian currency called "Riel." The Agency man estimated that they would be at Ibaham's village about a week negotiating with Ibaham's son about possible diversionary raids in the area around the town of Pakxe in Laos where two of the camps were located. The other camp was at Ban Don (northeast of Vientiane), which according to recent photos from the Black Bird showed almost an open camp with little or no activity as far as guards, but with four guard towers, one located in each corner of the camp. The camp was too far for Ibaham to get there undetected and get extracted. It would have to be an assault by the DF. The area around Ban Don was flat and would lend itself for both C-123s or helicopters.

The Air Force Special Ops planes that were to be used at the two southern camps at Pakxe arrived that afternoon. The other planes and helicopters for the Ban Don camp were already at Loei Air Force Base in Thailand, about 20 km (kilometers), approximately 12.4 miles, from the Laotian border, along with a large Delta Force who had been studying recent Black Bird photos and had Col. Lindor's 2nd in command with them. Based on the latest Intel, it had been decided to hit all three camps at the same time.

Pete's team got ready for their insertion taking prior agreed-upon equipment. He had the new Burst radio in his rucksack; Bob carried the back-up radio. Gen. Lawson sat down with Pete 2 hrs. prior to boarding the plane. "As in any operation, let's remember Murphy's Law, what can go wrong will go wrong. I have talked to the Air Force CO (Commanding Officer) and I have a special radio frequency where I can contact him or his subordinate in case of trouble. I want you to write these two frequencies on the inside flap of your survival packet on your web harness. The first 1st one is mine and the 2nd is the Air Force CO. When at Ibaham's place and you detect anything suspicious, contact me. These Burst radios are secure and dependable. Any questions?"

"No, Sir."

The team boarded the plane in the dark, but sunrise should be about the time they exited. The flight was smooth and after 1 hr. and 15 minutes, the red light came on. It was time for the last equipment check, i.e. the parachutes. The door was opened with the Agency man in the position to exit first. The sudden dive by the plane to the 400 ft. jump altitude caused Pete's stomach to react as it always did no matter how many jumps he made. The green light came on and the 11 men exited the plane. Pete was #2 and looked up and saw Bob's chute blossom over his head.

They were all on the ground and saw headlights heading their way. Ibaham had trucks? Pete gathered his chute and placed it in a bag that each man carried. It was getting light and Pete could see the trucks; they were not American models left over from the VN (Vietnam) war. He took his rifle and chambered a round placing it on full automatic. He looked around and the other team members, except for the Agency man, were also cocked and loaded. The two trucks pulled up; one had about a dozen men with weapons and the other was empty except for the driver. The trucks were 1½ tons and stopped about a 100 ft. from the team. The front door of the occupied truck opened and a Yard (Montagnard) came out and said something; the Agency man answered and walked towards the Yard saying something to him. The two spoke and the Agency man directed Pete and his team to get on the 2nd truck. He then lifted up the large duffel bag which contained the money up into the 1st truck which contained the armed men. He then got in the front of the truck with the Yard he had spoken to. As Pete and his team settled into their truck, he told them to keep their weapons ready.

They followed the 1st truck and were soon at a large village. The sun was up and Pete looked around as they drove slowly through the village which contained long houses built on the ground and not on stilts as he had expected. There was a good size forest or jungle on the north side of the village. Smoke hung low over the village and people were coming out looking at the two trucks which had stopped at a large long house. Pete and his team were told to unload their gear by the Agency man who was now talking to an older Yard and a middle-aged man. They were speaking French; Pete pretended he did not understand but bowed his head slightly at the introduction. The French they spoke was scattered with Rhade words. Rhade was the tribe Ibaham belonged to and the one Pete had worked with during his time in VN. There were a total of 28 major tribes in Thailand, Laos, and Cambodia.

The Agency man told Pete and his team to hand their weapons to two Yards which had been standing by the side of the older man. Pete answered that the weapons stayed with the team along with the rest of their gear. By now a group of armed men, not Yards but Vietnamese had assembled about 50 ft. from them, not appearing to be hostile but still a force to be reckoned with. Pete spoke in French to the old man who was called Ibaham and his son explaining that they were here as their friends and in old Rhade custom were expected to be treated as guests with their weapons and gear remaining with his team. He also informed them that his leader was waiting for a radio message from him to say that they had been well received and that he, Pete, was the spokesman for his team and to include this gentleman, indicating the Agency man. Pete had noticed the reaction by the Agency man, not only at his words but at his fluency in the French language. He went on and explained that he had worked for many years not only with the Rhade tribes in the area during the war in South Vietnam, but also the five other large tribes. He was honored to finally meet the great Ibaham and his son and looked forward to a great and long partnership with them. To show their sincerity, he told the Agency man to retrieve the duffel bag containing the money and to present it to Ibaham who slightly bowed his head.

Pete then asked if there was a house he and his team might utilize and relax a little and transmit a message to his leader. Ibaham's son said a house had been prepared for them and to follow him. Pete and his team gathered their rucksacks and started to follow the son, with the exception of the Agency man. Pete told him to grab his gear and come with them; he reluctantly did as he was told. They walked to the northern end of the village where there was a motor pool, or truck park. As they approached a house sitting by itself adjacent to the motor pool, Pete saw a Cambodian who quickly looked at Pete and placed his finger over his lips indicating for Pete not to say or recognize him. The Cambodian along with a younger man walked over to a truck and lifted its hood. Pete was stunned at the recognition of his old friend but did not let on at the chance meeting. The house had recently been built and was clean with new straw mats covering the floor. They arranged their gear along the walls leaving the center of the house open. Ibaham's son said to make themselves comfortable and would see them later. Pete thanked him for his generous hospitality and the son departed.

Pete told his team to take a seat including the Agency man. He explained that there could only be one spokesman and that he had worked with the Rhades for many years and that Ibaham and his family were part of that tribe; although he had also spotted other tribes in the village. "The village is in close proximity to Ba Kev not far from the VN town of Pleiku. This is an Army operation and will remain as such.

The Agency role is to facilitate introductions and smooth the way for an expedient agreement with the Yards so they could get on with and complete their mission. No one is to wander around this village alone. Any personal friendship between any Yards, male or female, is not allowed. We covered this back at Fort Bragg. Meetings with Ibaham or his son will be with a minimum of four people on a rotational basis. The rest of you will guard our equipment; don't be surprised if Ibaham places armed guards in the vicinity of this house. This is not to imprison us, but to protect us and them. I'm going to make radio contact with our boss back in Thailand. Oh, do not try and curry favors from these people, or become too helpful to them; they will take advantage of you."

Pete got his radio and ran a check procedure; the power was in the green and ready to transmit. He was set up in the far end of the long house and was far enough away from his team to speak into the cartridge using key words for their safe arrival, but also a cautioning word for "everything is not what it seems to be." He placed the cartridge into the transmit slot and pressed "send" – 15 seconds later he received a "roger – understand." Placing his radio back into his rucksack Pete made eye contact with Bob who was sitting about 10 ft. away from him. Bob got to his feet and sat down next to him. The other team members were resting with their eyes closed including the Agency man. "Something is not right here," Pete whispered to Bob. "Send a message to your boss at Col. Lindor's HQ (Headquarters) and have him review your colleagues' actions and background regarding Ibaham's village. He is not our friend; request possible extraction. I noticed an airstrip less than a quarter mile to the east of the village as we descended by parachute earlier. Why did we jump in when we could have landed in a C-123? The nearest village of Ba Kev is far enough away where the landing of the plane would have been less obtrusive than have it remain in the air for the drop. And why didn't your man brief us at Col. Lindor's' HQ about the airstrip? Right now he is pissed at me for taking over. I have to take him with me to all the meetings with Ibaham. The trucks that picked us up are Russian or Chinese, the type used by the North Vietnamese to ferry supplies during the war. Ibaham could have stolen them when making raids into Pleiku or other areas in the Highlands. I counted about 30 some trucks and they are in good shape. The major thing is what the hell are Vietnamese soldiers doing in a Montagnard village? This whole thing stinks! Your Agency must know something about the Vietnamese; there weren't many of them but one is too many as far as I am concerned. I didn't transmit their presence to Gen. Lawson cause he would have sent the entire Delta Force in here. I don't want to start an incident here until I know the whole story." Bob nodded his head.

Pete went over to the Agency man and spoke to him. "I'm not here to usurp your authority, but you must admit that the presence of armed Vietnamese soldiers raises a red flag; were they here when you were here last time?"

"No, I was about to ask Ibaham when we met him earlier; as you well know there is no love between the Yards and the Vietnamese."

"I think we should speak to Ibaham's son as soon as you think it's proper. Let's not bring up the Vietnamese issue yet; let's see if he can be some help in freeing our POWs." The Agency man indicated okay and got to his feet. The other team members had been listening and Pete indicated for two of them to come with them. "Side arms only," said Pete as they walked out of the long house.

The Agency man led the way to Ibaham's long house. The son was sitting on the ground outside the house with a woman combing and picking lice out of his long hair. He motioned for

Pete and his men to be seated in the shade of his house where he was sitting. The woman was dismissed and introductions were made to each of the team members, as was the Rhades' custom. Ibaham's son made casual conversation asking about their accommodations and if they suited them. Pete thanked him for his generosity and said it was much too good for them, but thanked him again. "I'm not sure how I can be of assistance to you; you already have people in the Highlands of VN working and helping our people there. What can we do that will help with any problems you have?"

"We have located a few Americans who are being held by the Laotians across the border and would like to rescue them."

"Ah, yes, we know about them; they are being starved by the Laotians and are very weak. You want my soldiers to rescue them? Is that the reason for your visit? I can tell you that there are three camps near Pakxe where they are being held. It will take many soldiers to rescue them and also money when inside Laos to bribe the border guards at crossing points; they like American dollars. They will take Thai Bath, but not Riel."

"It's good to hear that you know where the Americans are located – that will make our job much easier. Have you seen these places yourself?" Pete was looking hard at Ibaham's son who was smiling at the Agency man and gave him a slight wink. "Yes, of course I have seen these places; how else could I know that the Americans are being starved? We trade with the Laos people and hear many stories."

"Would it be difficult to rescue the Americans and how many soldiers would it take?"

"I will send some people to Laos and they can look and see what has to be done. It will require some American dollars to let us look at the places."

"We gave you American dollars this morning so for now you are fine!" Ibaham's son looked at the Agency man but didn't say anything. Pete continued, "How long do you think it will take your people to get back here?"

"Maybe 3-4 days if they don't have problems."

"That sounds good; let me know when you hear from them or they are back. Thank you for all your information and all you are doing. I will let my leader know how helpful you have been. I'm sure he will show his appreciation. Thank you again and we will talk later." The Agency man seemed to want to linger but Pete told him and the others they would head back to their long house.

When Pete and the others walked into their house, Bob looked at Pete. "Let's eat some food; we have plenty of rations and there is water in the large jar by the entrance." Pete went over to his rucksack and Bob joined him. "I talked to Col. Lindor who now has secure contact with my boss at Langley. Our man has been here off and on for 2 years; he replaced the regular man who got sick while here and was sent back to the States; he passed away before he could be debriefed. Our current person was eager to return here. They are running a background check as we speak. Col. Lindor said to be careful and that he and his boss want updates 3 times a day. I told him about the airstrip and the VN soldiers which he asked me to retransmit."

"Let's eat and then formulate a plan A and a plan B. I have an old Cambodian friend here who maintains their trucks; we exchanged nods when we came in this morning."

"I agree with your boss, Pete; is there anywhere you do not know someone?"

"I will tell you, and only you; his name is "Andy," just "Andy." And we go way back."

"Let's eat, I'm hungry."

They joined the others and talked in general terms about their situation. Pete brought everyone up to date about what

Ibaham's son said about the American prisoners and that there were three camps in the Pakxe area. One of the Captains that Pete hand-picked out of his Delta group said to no one in particular that he felt that they were wasting their time here, especially after what he had heard at their last meeting with Ibaham's son. They seemed to have their own agenda here and seemed well organized from looking at their motor pool; those are new or fairly new trucks. Pete agreed that a lot had changed over the years and that Ibaham had at least nine other villages this size. "Did your Agency purchase or pay for these trucks, they look like Russian or Chinese models?"

"If we paid for them, it had to be before my time here; the trucks have been here since my first time here about 2 years ago; my predecessor got sick and here I am back to this God forsaken area. It's Nebraska with a gentler climate and jungle here and there."

Pete was surprised at the Agency man's casual demeanor and willingness to impart his information. He was smart and had to be watched more carefully. "Well, it's time for my next transmission to the old man (Gen. Lawson). Does anyone have anything or have heard or seen anything worth passing on besides the Vietnamese in the village?" No one said anything. When Pete went over to this rucksack at the back of the house, the Captain who had voiced his concern came over to him and whispered that he would like to take one other Captain with him and take a quick look at the jungle next to their long house. He said he had a gut feeling that there was more going on here than they were aware of. "Excuse yourself and take your friend that you did the mission with along; use a toilet break as an excuse to the others."

The Captain went back to the team and announced so everyone could hear that Colonel Compton had given him special permission to go to the bathroom as long he took someone with him. "I guess we have to raise our hand from now on." There was laughter among the team. The Captain pointed at his friend to come with him and they both picked up their rifles and went out. "That's not what I said." Pete looked at his team and used the code word. "You can use the bathroom whenever, but go in "pairs." The men recognized the code word which meant "be extra alert," but the Agency man just smiled.

The two Captains went out, looked around, and a man who looked like a mechanic came over to them and asked in English if he could be of some help. The Captains looked at each other and told him they were looking for a place to relieve themselves. The mechanic looked at them and said in a low voice. "The two of you should not go into the jungle. If you really need to use the toilet, we have one by the motor park; come with me." They followed him to a small hut with a thatched roof and woven straw mats around its sides. When he pushed aside the door, there sat a wooden toilet raised about 2 ft. off the ground. "Captain Compton taught us how to dig down and make toilets and to keep it clean. Whisper to Capt. Compton what I have told you. He has a friend here." The mechanic left and went over and raised the hood of a truck. They used the facility and returned to their long house. One of the Captains went over to Col. Compton and whispered what the mechanic had said. Pete smiled and announced that there was a modern toilet by the motor pool. Pete transmitted the noon report including seeing an old friend who said not to enter the jungle adjacent to the village where they were staying, and also the conversation with Ibaham's son. "If the camps the Black Bird has discovered are in fact POW camps, why two and not three in the Pakxe area like Ibaham's son says? Are they POW camps? Are they a ruse to embarrass us again? I have little faith in the leaders of this village and the so-called Agency man who is supposed to be an expert but wanted us to hand our weapons and equipment over to Ibaham on our arrival. What did his predecessor die from?" Pete pushed "send".

Was he getting paranoid? He needed to talk to Andy. It was time for him and Bob to use the toilet. Pete still had his harness on; he looked over at Bob and pointed to his harness and picked up his rifle. Bob had a smaller version of the Burst radio contained in a pouch on his harness which only Pete was aware of. Bob put his harness on and joined Pete as he walked out the opening of the long house. One of the Captains who had talked to Andy went over and sat by Pete's rucksack. The rest of the team was stretched out on the reed mats using their rucksacks as pillows, including the Agency man.

Pete and Bob walked over to the motor pool. Andy walked towards them pointing towards the toilet. Pete looked at him and nodded his head. Bob went into the toilet area and closed the door. Andy informed Pete that Ibaham's son was planning on capturing his team tonight when they were asleep and transporting them into Laos. Andy had been told to have four trucks ready and fueled tonight and that their long house was being watched. Pete and his men should move out through the far end of their long house and make their way along the north end of the jungle where they would come to a shallow river, cross it, and follow the north bank of the river. There is an elephant trail which would lead them within a half a kilometer of an airstrip. "Why not go into the jungle directly behind our long house; it would be shorter?"

"No, there are traps and it leads to a small prison where there are dead American prisoners; they were old when brought here and starved to death. You will smell them when you get to the river; don't go near them as they have not been buried; you can come back and get them some other time. I have to go and will see you again." Andy walked among the trucks and disappeared.

Bob came out and Pete went into the toilet hut. He talked through the door which he had left open. When he was finished he came out and looked at Bob. "What do we do with our friend from the Agency?" were Bob's first words. "I know what I should do, but let's wait; we have about 4 hours of daylight. I need to call the old man (Gen. Lawson) on a different frequency." Bob started to pull his radio out of the pouch. "No, let's use the radio in my rucksack; it's more powerful." As they walked into the long house, Pete announced that should anyone need to use the facility (toilet) to do so now cause he wanted to have a meeting in ½ hour. The people departed in two's and returned; that left the Agency man and one Captain – they walked out.

Pete went to the far end of the long house and cut a large hole in the wall but left enough of the wall intact so it wouldn't fall down. He then got on the radio's emergency frequency and informed Gen. Lawson that they were leaving and taking a hostage with them. They would be waiting ½ kilometer at the north end of the airstrip and when they heard the planes, they would mark their location with a green smoke grenade; be at the strip in 2 hours or less. He pressed "send." A "roger" was received ending the transmission.

Pete had just put away the radio when the Agency man and Captain returned. "We saw Ibaham's son and another man heading this way," said the Agency man. Pete was surprised at his statement and announced the code word for hostage-taking and be prepared to leave. The team started getting their equipment ready, including the Agency man. Pete looked at Bob; nothing was said. Ibaham's son walked through the door to the long house followed by a man wearing a pistol. Pete greeted them and introduced them to the rest of the team. "Ah, your house is better than mine; maybe we should change houses, it would make my women very happy."

"It is an old Rhade custom that once you have given your guests something, you cannot take it back," said Pete smiling. "You know too much about our customs," said the son laughing. The man he had brought with him walked over to one of the Captains and looked at his rifle. As his back was turned, the Agency man stuck a syringe into the man's upper arm; the man was about to turn but fell to the floor. Ibaham's son had been talking to Pete and was momentarily stunned by this development. The Agency man stuck the son with another syringe. "He'll be able to walk but will be a little groggy." Directing his attention to two of the Captains he said, "Tie his friend's feet and hands with tape if you have it." The two Captains went to work and also placed tape across his mouth. "Let's get out of here," said Pete placing his rucksack on his back.

The Agency man took Ibaham's son by the hand and exited the opening Pete had cut earlier. "We need to skirt the jungle until we get to the river, cross it, and hit a trail that will take us to the airstrip. When we hit the trail, place a short rope around our friend's neck; use a loop that can be tightened." No alarm was heard from the village. After about 20 minutes, they hit the river and found the trail; there was a sweet stench coming from somewhere in the jungle. "You and I need to talk later," Pete said to the Agency man who just nodded his head. They saw light up ahead meaning they were approaching the airstrip. Ibaham's son with a rope around his neck was starting to cough but didn't say anything; his eyes looked red and wild. There was the sound of aircraft. Pete told one of the Captains to throw a green smoke grenade. There were now gun shots in the distance and the sound of trucks. Pete got on his small radio and informed the planes that enemy was on the way. They heard someone running down the trail toward them. It was Andy; he was out of breath and it took him a few minutes to tell them the trucks would not be a problem. There was only enough gas in them to start-up. He asked if he could come with them. Pete informed him he was more than welcome. "Check Ibaham's son's boots – he has a gun in them." A Captain patted him down and found a .380 Sig Sauer (single-action pistol) in his left boot and a K-bar knife in the other boot.

Two C-123s were coming in and turned around in front of the now expanded team. They all ran for the open back of the first plane. The loadmaster yelled at them to hang on; they would use the jet engines to help them get airborne. Rounds were now peppering the planes as they sped down the runways. The 2nd plane had a Gatling gun and was hosing down the attackers. When they were airborne and heading back to Col. Lindor's HQ, Pete sat down next to the Agency man. "By the way, my name is Jack Martin; I don't think anyone has mentioned that before." Pete shook Jack's hand. "What I wanted to tell you before is that it was *not* Ibaham back there and this is *not* his son. I don't know what happened back there, but we used to have a good relationship with Ibaham when I was here about 2 years ago. My predecessor was either poisoned or came down with something strange; he was practically dead when they took him off the plane at Andrews; he was on a stretcher and I had a hard time understanding him. He told me to get back and contact Andy who would show me the alternate route to the airstrip they had built which Andy and I did while the village was holding a sacrifice and most had drunk too much Nam Pei (rice wine). I pretended all was okay when I got in the truck with Ibaham's so-called son."

"I thought we were walking into a trap back there and didn't want to say anything until I was sure we could extract ourselves. I knew you were suspicious so I radioed my boss back at Col. Lindor's place and told him the situation and for him to play along with Col. Lindor and Gen. Lawson and not blow my cover. Those people back there have no idea where the prisoner camps are. Andy told me they had picked up some prisoners from a village outside of Pakxe at the request of the leader of the village; they had found them in the jungle. The prisoners were in bad shape and some had died in route to Ibaham's village. They were placed in the jungle behind where we stayed today and not given food or water; they died within a few days and left unburied. We think that the camps around Pakxe are POW camps but that has not been verified yet. There is a definite camp outside or I should say NE of Vientiane, according to the photos from the Black Bird. I brought this guy along to see what information we could get from him."

"Well, I feel a lot better after this talk, but our friend here mentioned a 3rd camp near Pakxe; is that also bogus?"

"I don't know," answered Jack, "We have several sources in Pakxe and we need to verify this info before we say too much. When the initial fiasco about the POWs went south, we knew that the prisoners were transferred out in smaller groups. Andy said he thought there were about 15 POWs that they picked up in that village in Laos, but that's a small group."

"Were they dumped there or somehow escaped and the villagers found them?"

"I don't know - my predecessor mentioned something about American prisoners but he was hard to understand before the medics took him away; I never saw him again."

They arrived at Col. Lindor's airfield. Gen. Lawson along with the Agency Chief of Station was there to greet them along with about 15 Delta Force ops who had been brought down from Loei Air Field. Bob Miller and Jack Martin took their now blindfolded prisoner over to Col. Lindor's makeshift jail. Gen. Lawson announced that he wanted everyone in Col. Lindor's briefing room in ½ hr. Pete briefed Gen. Lawson on the way to the briefing room. The Agency man, Jack Martin, joined them along with Andy. Jack stated that he had looked up the Bio on

Pete and knew when they first met the supposed Ibaham and he himself had told Pete to hand over their weapons to the Yards, that Pete would no way comply. He also stated that he had to play his role with this Ibaham fake Yard. The briefing room was filled to capacity and Pete asked Andy to tell them everything he knew about this "new" Ibaham and his son. Pete could tell that Andy was nervous, so he started out by telling everyone who Andy was and how he had gotten to know him.

Chapter 14

"Back in '65, Andy was just a young man, originally from Cambodia, who could repair any vehicle to include old chain-driven French trucks. Andy was working for the Special Forces "B" Detachment in Ban Me Thuot. Each time me or some of my men came into the "B" Detachment from our "A" Team location to get a shower and clean up, we had to wade through mud up to our ankles. One day I asked Andy if there was any chance of getting some grass sod and gravel to stabilize the area; Andy of course had the answer. He said he would need some help from me."

"What do I have to do, I asked him? His answer almost floored me. According to Andy, the Darlac Provence Chief in Ban Me Thuot has a beautiful lawn behind his house and a large pile of gravel next to the lawn. "You and I go over and tell the Province Chief that the Navy C-Bees are coming to build a huge bunker in the back of his house where the lawn and gravel are located, but they need the area cleared and ready for them when they get here in a few weeks." Andy also told me the Province Chief is a nervous man and wants to have a safe bunker. I couldn't believe what this young man was implying, no, not implying, but telling me what I had to do. Long story short, I was tired of wading through the mud and the "B" Detachment wasn't doing anything about it. Andy and I went to the Province Chief and told him this fantastic lie. In a little over a week, the "B" Detachment had a beautiful green sod and stable gravel-covered area. No bunker was ever built. "That my friends, is how I got to know this fine young man; I mean old man now." Everyone laughed and Andy was smiling and came up to where Pete was standing and shook his hand. "Just tell us how you came to the village and what you know about it."

Andy started talking and went back to when South Vietnam was overrun. At first there was no retaliation but as the North Vietnamese leaders took over, some people were rounded up. Andy's wife had been killed in the fighting, but his two sons and a daughter and their families had been left alone. One day a jeep stopped in front of his house and three soldiers came and took him away. He thought they had found out about the American dollars he had hidden, but they took him to a motor park and asked if he could fix some of their vehicles, mostly trucks. They had treated him nice and he asked if he could get his two sons and his son-in-law, who were also good mechanics. He was told to take a vehicle and get them; they would get food as pay. He and his sons repaired the vehicles and within a month the vehicles were in good shape. There were problems in the area with bands of Yards conducting raids on VN units and convoys. The VN military left the Highlands area, most going to Nha Trang. Andy's sons and families were moved to Nha Trang and given housing; they continued working as mechanics.

Andy was told to take a truck convoy of eight vehicles to

Pleiku where he picked up another 26 trucks and was then told to go to Ba Kev in Cambodia. In Ba Kev they picked up about a 100 Montagnards and drove to Ibaham's village. The drivers, who were armed Vietnamese, stayed in the village and mingled in with the Yards. They were given women and houses and for the most part stayed out of sight. One night Ibaham and his family were put on a truck guarded by five of the Vietnamese and headed south; the truck and the guards returned to the village. The next day a newly arrived elderly Rhade and a younger man with family were declared to be the new leaders. The American Agency man wanted to know where Ibaham and his family were. He was told by the Vietnamese drivers/soldiers that Ibaham was sick and wanted to go to one of his other villages. The American got sick and was driven to Pakxe in Laos and taken into Thailand.

On the return trip from Pakxe, the trucks brought 15 American prisoners who were placed in a recently built prison in the jungle to the north of the village where they died and were left unburied. Andy and a helper kept maintaining the trucks. About 6 months ago, Jack Martin arrived and Andy had gotten to know him. The man they called Ibaham and his son had come to the village right after the original Ibaham had left. Andy did not think the new Ibaham or his son/family were Rhades, at least not from the Highlands; but they spoke the Rhade and French languages. He had a feeling they had lived in a town or city because they were not good at making fires or cooking in the traditional way. Andy looked at Pete and said that was all he knew.

"Thanks, Andy," said Pete. "If you think of anything else, let me know."

"There is one thing more, the prisoner has a funny heel on his boot; I think the left one; he can open it by twisting it – I have seen him fiddling with it." Two Delta Force men left the conference room and returned a few minutes later with a pair of black US Army boots. One of them twisted the heel of the left boot and it revealed a small plastic container with two pills in it which he gave to Pete. "These are cyanide pills," said Pete. "Our prisoner had a plan. From what Andy and Jack Martin have told us, we need to verify what exactly is in Pakxe and northeast of Vientiane. The next step is to talk to our prisoner."

Chapter 15

General Lawson took over the meeting. "Col. Lindor has two men talking to our prisoner who seems willing to talk but wants to make a deal. It's been a hectic day so let's go over to the mess hall and get some chow." Gen. Lawson, the Agency Chief of Station, Col. Lindor, Pete, Bob, and Jack Martin were all sitting at the table eating. Pete looked around the table and made a statement, to no one in particular, that if the prisoner did not talk or answer their questions that he had a man that could make him talk. "Let's hold up on that Pete until we evaluate what we have learned from him so far. That village has no doubt been in contact with whoever is running the show back there. My question would be whether the entire village is onboard with this new Ibaham and also the few Vietnamese who are solders that Andy mentioned?"

"What do you think, Jack?"

"I don't think they are happy with these new people; remember the Yards dislike for the Vietnamese is universal, at least among the tribes in the Highlands. I have talked to

Andy about this and he thinks the people in the village are waiting for someone to come in and get the village back to normal, or like it used to be. Andy said the Vietnamese have been given houses and women and the fact that they are living with them is strange since the Vietnamese consider the Yards to be "Moi" or savages. The Vietnamese are living adjacent to the rest of the village, not isolated but separate. I don't know what kind of relationship they have with the women. I haven't seen any children or pregnant women and the Yard women are definitely fertile."

"Let's start with Pakxe and find out what is there or what is not there. Can you make contact with your sources there and based on what we learn, do a recon in the area? I would like the information in the next few days if at all possible." General Lawson was addressing the Agency Chief of Station who looked at Jack Martin and told him to take care of it first thing in the morning. Pete related to them that when he first arrived in the village, he was surprised that the village was not built on stilts; the houses were on the ground. This was supposed to be a Rhade village; other tribes built their long houses on the ground and were subject to vermin, mice and rats which they used for food. With what he had read from Professor Robert Anderson's writing in area studies at Fort Bragg, and having lived with the Rhade, he didn't like what he saw. The village was not old, maybe 10 years. The jungle next to the village had plenty of timber, so it was not for the lack of building materials. The other people left the table with Gen. Lawson and Pete sitting there sipping coffee. "I know I have nothing to base my idea on, but I have a feeling there is something in the area of Pakxe that is worth checking into. The supposed Ibaham's son seemed very familiar with Pakxe, which he said they traded with, and Andy stated they got the 15 American POWs from there. I would like to look at the enhanced photos of the area; I think we have overlooked something."

"I know better than to argue with you once you get an idea into that head of years. Col. Lindor has given me an office and I have the latest photos there; let's go over and have a look." Gen. Lawson and Pete left the mess hall and went over to the office where a large makeshift table had been placed in front of a metal desk. "Let's spread the photos on the table and see what we have," said Gen. Lawson handing Pete a stack of 12" x 12" photos. They were numbered running from north to south covering an area about 15 km (kilometers) north of Pakxe. The pictures showed two camps which looked like they could be POW camps. Pete was looking at the terrain north of the camps, and at a long ridge line which connected to the higher hills or low mountains. He kept going back to the ridge which was about 1 km long. "Can we get some more photos of this ridge line or enhanced pictures; there is something here which reminds me of something I got involved with back in '69."

"Let me see what you are talking about," said Gen. Lawson using the large magnifier sitting on the table."

"I don't see anything unusual about this ridge. It looks to be about 1.5 km long and 150-200 ft. high, maybe a little higher; what am I not seeing?" Pete replied, "Look at the vegetation, the trees towards the bottom of the ridge, and follow it to the top of the ridge." Gen. Lawson spent about 5 min. scrutinizing the ridge. "It looks like some of the vegetation is dying or maybe some sort of beetle infestation like we have back in the mountains of North Carolina – why?"

"Could that ridge have been tunneled out like the North Vietnamese and Vietcong did in South Vietnam, hence dying vegetation?" Gen. Lawson looked at Pete. "Are you thinking that it could be a holding place for our POWs?"

"Not necessarily, but it could be a storage place for some ammunition or a command bunker, reception area; I don't know but I think it's worth a closer look. The ones I got familiar with both in Vietnam and Cambodia had ventilation holes or grids on top which are hard to find; but if you know what to look for, they can be found. Also, look at the ridge where it meets the higher terrain; there is a path and an old excavation there with shadows or two guards there."

"You know that's a stretch, but I'll see what I can do. I'll get with Lindor and the Chief of Station and get another run by the Black Bird or enhanced photos. Good work; maybe there is hope for you yet. I know you are not going to let this go, so to save me a lot of grief and work, I'll get with them tonight. Go and get some rest."

The next morning as Pete was going through the mess line, Gen. Lawson motioned for him to join Col. Lindor, the Chief of Station, and himself. As Pete was sitting down, Jack Martin came over to their table with a stack of photos. "Are these the ones you wanted?" He asked the Chief of Station. "I think we have something here but I don't think it's a POW holding area; however it's worth a look as it could be something related." Gen. Lawson was looking at the pictures handing two to Pete. "What do you think, Pete?" Pete was looking at them; they were taken at a different angle. He looked at Jack Martin. "You said we had resources in Pakxe; can you get in touch with them and have them recon the supposed POW camps? Either verify or determine if in fact they are bogus; also look around the area for newly or recently dug graves. We need the info in the next 3 days if at all possible. They can contact your HQ here. I want to take a group across and up to that ridge; I would like Bob and Jack here plus the eight other team members to go with me."

"Hold on here, we have not sanctioned any foray into Laos

on a wild goose chase; we need to plan this," said Gen. Lawson looking hard at Pete. "We can plan all we want, but all we need is someone who has been in there before and knows how to avoid built-up areas. These photos were taken yesterday and there are three guards at the north end of the ridge. Can we meet in the conference room, say in ½ hour and hash this out? I want to go in today. Col. Lindor, can you get me at least four spools of Detonating Cord, 20 lbs. of C-4, four spools of Det. Wire, and a hand held generator; oh, and a couple wooden boxes of blasting caps?"

The conference room was packed again. Pete placed four pictures on the cork board in front of the room. "Andy, do you recognize this area?" Andy went up and looked at the pictures. "Yes, I took our prisoner up at the bottom of and along this ridge. If you look closely, you can see a little used wide path from the south going almost up where the ridge meets the higher hills. I drove him up there and turned the truck around and waited for him. He was gone for about 2 hours."

"Are there any built-up areas or houses in the vicinity?"

"No, but close to Pakxe there are rice fields and houses. Also, along the border with Thailand north of Pakxe there are no houses, but the Lao troops patrol the border."

"Thanks, Andy." Pete looked around the room; no one said anything. "Besides the people I have already identified, I would like a reaction force of Delta personnel not only with the helicopters but with the C-123s that came in and extracted us, to be on standby. I also need to know the best crossing point. It is now 0900 and I would like to leave in 3 hours." Col. Lindor rose and said the equipment he had requested was ready and available. Gen. Lawson stood and looked at Pete. "When I see that look on Col. Compton's face, I know not to argue with him or try to change his mind. The only addition I have to this mission is to make sure the radios you are taking are in good working condition. I would also recommend the small new individual radios which you can use as a signaling device among yourselves. They fit in the palm of your hand. In addition, the Agency has those tiny microphones that you can let out on a wire with the hearing portion which fits in your ear; take a few of these with you."

Jack Martin stood up and went to the front wall and pulled down an area map. "The best place to cross is north of Pakxe. There is a peninsula there that sticks into the river with no houses, and maybe a patrol once in a while; here we only have to cross one body of water. We have these small boats whose motors you can't hear; two boats should take care of the entire force. There are a couple of hills we have to traverse, but nothing extreme. Compass reading about 25° NE. I would recommend that we are taken across and the boats returned to the Thai side, and that we go over this evening as the area is open and a daylight crossing would be easy to spot." Pete got up and took a look at the map. "Okay, change of plans, we go in at 0400 tomorrow; that should get us across in darkness and give us a chance to move out in semi-darkness with less chance of anyone getting hurt, sprain an ankle, etc. Col. Lindor, can you coordinate with the Air Force and have them on standby at 0400 until we get back? Reaction Force per SOP (Standing Operating Procedures) counting on you guys. Gen. Lawson, do you have any other suggestions or advice besides what you have already told us?"

"Yes, weapons on full automatic, safety on. Remember Murphy's Law – What can go wrong will go wrong. Good luck; you have the best man I have ever worked with leading you. That's all."

Pete asked the people going with him to stay, also Andy. "Okay, let's get the demo from Col. Lindor and divide it up; bring your rucksacks in here and we'll pack them here; also the small radios and listening devices."

"Andy, is there anything else you can remember about the ridge?"

"There is small game roaming the ridge, deer and honey bears, which means there are no booby traps on the ridge. The sides going up the ridge are not very steep, no problem walking up; that's all I can think of."

"Thanks, Andy."

"Col. Compton, do you want me to go with you?"

"Andy I trust you with my life, but I think we can handle it."

"I think you look at me as an old man, but you, Colonel, are older than me. I'm used to walking and haven't been with a woman in over a year so my body is not tired." The rest of the team laughed and some suggested that Andy was in better shape than any of them. "The patrols are usually 4-6 soldiers and are used to Cambodians since many of them fled to Laos during the purge. I am not in uniform and if a patrol comes along and is blocking our way, I can always say I'm trying to find a way into Thailand to make purchases for Ibaham in Cambodia. Everyone knows about Ibaham and the FULRO force. The only thing I need is some American dollars (currency of choice) strapped to my body and some to give to the patrol. What do you think?"

Pete smiled at him. "Andy, I think you are about to have an adventure. I'll get you a local rucksack to carry your food in; what about your boots, are they in good shape?"

"Yes," Andy replied, "they are almost new and I have my old Vietnamese rucksack so the only thing I need is some food which I would like to pick out from the mess hall kitchen myself. We Cambodians eat a little differently than you people, as you well know, Col. Compton."

"Okay, I'll get you into the kitchen, no problem. Let's get

our gear and some rations and meet here at 1500 hours to make sure we have everything."

Chapter 16

The men dispersed each doing his own planning and getting the demolition from Col. Lindor. Pete went into Gen. Lawson's office and found him studying some maps. "Pete, I agree with the crossing point, the only thing that bothers me is that I talked to Col. Lindor about sending someone who has been in that area and he doesn't have anyone nor does the Chief of Station, they usually cross south of Pakxe."

"I have a man that volunteered to go with us ....Andy."

"Isn't he a little old and can he keep up with your team?"

"He pointed out to me and the team that he is younger than me and is used to walking, speaks the language, and hasn't been with a woman in over a year, so his body is not tired."

"The more I get to know him the more I like him; he doesn't miss much – that boot heel catch was good."

Pete explained to Gen. Lawson what Andy needed and the General said he would personally take care of it. "You are going to blow that ridge; don't you think it could attract a lot of attention and maybe disrupt our real mission here?"

"The way it has worked in the past is that it creates a rumble within the ridge, the ridge collapses in on itself, and buries anyone in it. If we are lucky, we will get the Lao military leaders in Pakxe and create confusion and maybe make our mission easier. It will take a while for the Lao to reestablish a command structure."

"That's a lot ifs so I hope you're right! The mikes I suggested taking with you are state of the art and you should be able to hear any conversation within the ridge by lowering them into the air vents. You have the guards to contend with; use your sniper weapons with the silencers and don't get into any pissing contest with the Laos, you are getting far too old for fun and games."

"Yes, Dad, I'll be careful," said Pete smiling. At the 1500 hr. meeting each man went over his mission. Pete had designated four demo men and two snipers. He explained what the air vents could look like. Weapons were checked along with the ammo and by 1630 hours everyone was on the same page. The prisoner had told the investigators that he could lead them to the prison camps, but Pete had recommended that they wait for the Agency contact reports. Pete reported to Gen. Lawson that they were ready to go. Gen. Lawson looked at Pete and informed him the Chief of Station had received an initial report regarding one of the camps they had surveyed. The camp was a burial place with at least 30 shallow graves.

"I contacted my friend Hammond who by the way got his first star, he talked to his boss and a graves registration/forensic team is being sent from Hawaii and should be here in a week."

"That fucking State Department should be plowed under and strewn with salt. If we had gone in, we could have saved at least some of those poor bastards. The culture there stinks; it's the same at the Pentagon when we were trying to get some funds for those widows. Is the Chief of Station using his resources to check out the camp northeast of Vientiane?"

"As we speak. Don't let that temper of yours cloud your mind, Pete. We are here to make the best of a sorry situation, so keep a cool head cause you are going to need it the next 2 days. I don't want you to linger in there; do the job as you see fit and get back here, we have a lot of work ahead of us. I have talked to Col. Lindor and the Chief of Station and we are going to clean out that village you were in using Yard forces from some of Ibaham's other villages. So you see, we have a lot to do. Let's go over to the mess hall and have our evening meal. I'll make sure Andy gets what he needs."

The meals in the mess hall were not limited to one entrée, but steak and baked potatoes had become the meal of choice. Pete had asked Gen. Lawson where Col. Lindor got his supplies from. "Don't ask," had been the short answer. The food and its preparation was another thing that surprised Pete; it compared favorably to an upscale restaurant.

At 1800 hrs., Pete had his final inspection of not only the men going in, but also the standby reaction force and its' helicopters of which there were two CH-53s recently refurbished (Jolly Green Giants) and two C-123s, one with heavy fire power. The helicopters and plane crews were briefed on the beacon locators which the team would carry and radio frequencies. Pete also briefed them on potential landing areas close to the ridge.

By 1930 hrs. everyone was on the same page. Jack Martin told them the travel time to the boats would take 1 hour by truck and the boats and crews were already on station and waiting. "Does anyone have any questions? No one is confused? I estimate that we should be back here tomorrow night. One more thing, Col Lindor – have your entire medical section on standby, emergency personnel, etc. We don't know what we will encounter or bring back." Pete looked around the briefing room. "Okay, let's get some rest; our next meeting will be at 0230 hrs. here with everyone ready to go. This meeting is over with unless there are some last minute questions or foreseen problems which we haven't covered."

Gen. Lawson, the Chief of Station, Col. Lindor, Jack Martin, and Bob remained as the briefing emptied. Jack placed eight photos on the table. Pete looked at them and asked, "What are these and what am I looking at?"

"We got these half an hour go," said Col. Lindor. "I moved some assets from Vietnam to watch the village in Cambodia that you were in. Two 1½ ton trucks moved towards the Laotian border and according to these photos are in Pakxe as we speak. A driver and a person riding shotgun are the only occupants of the trucks. According to Andy, the village received a supply run from Pakxe the day before you jumped in there and supply runs consist of 10+ trucks once a month. A 2nd convoy of two to five trucks goes up to Ba Kev in Cambodia on emergency runs depending on the needs of the village."

"So these two trucks are in Pakxe to do what? Could it be a prisoner run?"

"This last photo shows two covered ¾ ton vehicles going north along the ridge road," Andy briefed on. "It could be a meeting of the command section from Pakxe according to our sources. There are only guards left at their HQ in Pakxe. One more thing our sources informed us on – there is an access point to the ridge at its southern point; no guards are posted there, so I think, Pete, your theory that the ridge is tunneled out is valid," said the Chief of Station.

Gen. Lawson looked at Pete. "Based on what you have heard, are you satisfied with the number of personnel you are taking in?"

"Yes, but have the two helicopter crews remain close to their ships and add gas masks to their equipment and portable oxygen breathing apparatus, which I know they have but probably have not tested them; something to do while waiting for our signal. Thanks for the info on the access point on the southern tip of the ridge. I overlooked that once in Cambodia and hence the souvenir on my upper left chest. Anything else? Let's get some rest."

Chapter 17

One of Col. Lindor's guards woke Pete and his team at 0200 hours; it was time to get ready. The trip to the boats took about 1 hour. There was no one awake in the villages they passed through except for a few dogs that let them know their trucks were not welcome at this early hour. The boats and crew members were ready for them. Jack Martin split the men into the groups and they boarded the two olive drab fiberglass boats. Jack briefed the men handling his boat that he wanted to go ashore on the north side of the peninsula as far in as possible. Pete was surprised when the boat he was in started moving and there was no noise. There was a large air scoop in the middle of the boat which they were told not to lean against; this was the source of the engine intake. They were fast approaching the far shore and the boats skirted the peninsula going into a grass covered inlet. The boats halted once grounded on the grassy shore and the men jumped out onto dry land. The boats returned to the opposite shore.

Pete and Jack led the men into a small clearing. Pete briefed the men they would be heading on an azimuth of 20° (N.E.). As long as the visibility was limited, they would walk slowly and try to go in a column of two's. Pete and Bob Miller would lead them with Jack Martin bringing up the rear. If any of them had a problem, they were to key their miniature radios. The vegetation was dense for the first hour and then opened up a little. They took their first break after 2 hours; it was now 0600 hrs. and was light. Pete checked his map and conferred with the men; they were halted on top of a ridge. If he was correct, they had one more ridge or hill and then would be able to see their objective. Each man checked his gear and ate an energy bar; no one had a problem and after 15 minutes, resumed their march.

They reached an outcropping and could look down into the small valley below. To the left up the valley was smoke rising in the early mist. Pete looked through his binoculars and saw five armed men squatting around a fire heating their breakfast in what looked like American aluminum canteen cups. Each team member looked at the men by the fire. "Those are Laotian soldiers," said Andy after he had looked through Pete's binoculars. The men were moved a little further south and crossed the valley. They headed up what should have been the last ridge before arriving at their target. The going was slow with vegetation dense and the ridge steep; when Pete reached the top, he motioned for his men to crouch down and spread out along the top of the ridge. The view of their target ridge was unobstructed. They were approximately 200 meters from the bottom of their target ridge. Andy looked through the binoculars for a few minutes. "If you look closely towards the bottom of the ridge, you can see the path I told you about. We are looking at the southern part of the ridge where there is supposedly an entrance. Look what's coming up the path," said Andy as he handed the binoculars back to Pete. Two 1½ ton trucks were moving slowly up the path. They stopped at the beginning of the ridge. One of trucks started moving again; the other remained and one of the occupants jumped out and guided the driver as he turned around and backed up towards the end of the ridge. The driver shut the vehicle down and got out with two machetes, handing one to the other man. Together they started chopping down small vegetation and low branches making a path further in where the ridge ended. The driver backed the truck further in then shut it down; he got out and joined the other man squatting down and lighting up a cigarette.

Pete signaled for his men to move further south. Fifteen minutes later they were less than 200 feet from the two men, one of which was urinating against a tree. Pete indicated for the two snipers to take the men out. The snipers moved to where they had a clear field of fire; there was barely any audible sound and the two men by the truck toppled over. Pete then signaled for the men to move forward. "Search those two men and drag their bodies so they are hidden from view." Pete told two of his men and Jack to search for the entrance to the ridge; the rest of the men he told to follow him up the ridge. Jack and the two Captains started moving up the ridge but had gone only a short distance when they saw dead vegetation intertwined forming a barrier about 10'x 8'. The three men pulled on the barrier and it came lose. As they pulled it to the side, it showed a large gaping hole with an unmistakable foul odor. Their flashlights revealed a room about 30'x 40' in size. They shone their flashlights around and gasped at what they saw. There were about 40 bodies, some of which were alive and who shaded their eyes from the bright lights.

"Radio Pete on your small hand-held radio and inform him what we have found," Jack told one of the Captains. Pete had just gone over to a ventilation hole one of the men had found when the radio in his pocket buzzed. He listened to the transmission and cursed. "Start taking them out, but wear your breathing masks and gloves; I'll send some help; place them in the back of the truck…out." One of his men had lowered a mike into the ventilation hole. "Nothing, I think I hit metal or steel."

"Rig it to blow and lead the wire down the ridge to where the truck is, then you and your partner help load the prisoners onto the truck. Use your breathing masks and gloves. Good work! Andy, go with the Captains and help."

Pete found two ventilation holes next to each other. A mike was lowered into one of them; the Captain who was listening said it was definitely a meeting with some men arguing. "Rig it and lead the wire back to the truck and splice into the other wire that's already there. Help load the prisoners wearing your breathing masks and gloves." As they moved up to the ridge, Pete found another hole. There was no sound coming from the mike. "I'll rig this one. Snipers, you go forward and take out the guards and anyone else you can see. Bob, get a spool of wire out of my rucksack and tie one end around the small tree next to me and start spooling the wire back to the truck. Radio back to base using your Burst radio and tell them what we have found. I want one helicopter to take off immediately and head for the open area 200 meters south of the ridge; turn on the beacon for them, it should take less than an hour. Then have the other chopper leave 15 minutes later. You should have the POWs down there by then."

Pete rigged the ventilation hole and spliced the wire Bob had left him into the demo. The two snipers came back and reported five kills. Pete told them to follow him down the ridge; when they got to the truck, Andy had driven one load of POWs down to the open field and left men to guard them. Andy backed the truck up the path to where the men waited with the rest of the POWs. They were loaded and along with four men drove down to where the rest of the POWs were. One of the Captains spliced the three wires together and inserted them into the hand-held generator. Pete took the generator from the Captain and told the men to head down the path. Pete waited until the men had disappeared and then twisted the handle on the generator sending electric current towards the demo. It seemed like a long time before he heard anything, then there was a low rumble coming from the ridge, then another and a third one. The first vent hole must have contained ammunition because the ridge above him exploded sending trees and vegetation hurdling into the air. Pete grabbed his rucksack and ran down the path with the now disconnected generator; when he got to the clearing, he could hear the first helicopter coming in. Green smoke was thrown and the helicopter landed. The rear door dropped down and the loading of the POWs began. The crew chief had a gas mask on; he lifted it and was talking to the pilots and then replaced the mask.

Pete got on the Burst radio and told whoever was listening that very fragile cargo was on the way and for all medical personnel to stand by wearing breathing masks and gloves. The helicopter took all the POWs and closed the door taking off. The second helicopter was inbound and received a green smoke and landed. Pete was satisfied after taking a head count and told the team to get aboard. He went forward and asked the pilot to gain altitude and fly over the ridge they had blown. Pete went back and asked the crew chief to open the rear door as he needed to take some pictures. The crew chief strapped a safety harness on Pete and anchored it to a "D" ring in the floor of the helicopter and then opened the door. Pete crawled out on the door which now became an extension of the floor and took a dozen pictures of their handiwork. The first vent hole was still smoking and small explosions were going off. The rest of the ridge had folded in on itself; anyone who could have been inside would not have survived. Pete gave the thumbs up sign and crawled back into the helicopter with the crew chief closing the door behind him.

No one was talking; the entire team sat with their heads bowed. Andy had tears running down his cheeks. Bob Miller had collected all the breathing masks and gloves and had them in a large plastic bag.

They landed a distance from the other helicopter. The medical personnel were unloading the POWs onto stretchers while at the same time cutting their clothes off and placing them in large plastic bags. They were then covered with sheets and moved into the decontamination area where their hair was cut close to the scalp as well as in their groin area. They were then cleaned with surgical soap and taken into the hospital area where IVs were started in their arms followed by examinations. Out of the total 42 POWs, 9 were deceased, 12 were in critical condition, and 21 were relatively stable.

Gen. Lawson called his friend General Hammond at the Pentagon and requested a mobile hospital with staff be sent to their location as soon as possible (ASAP) explaining what had transpired and the need for supplies, facilities, and secrecy. Gen. Hammond explained to the Chairman of the Joint Chief of Staff the situation. "Get the Service Chiefs in here now and let's get this taken care of." When the Service Chiefs were assembled, the Chairman briefed them. "We have a situation in Thailand where we have just brought in 42 U.S. POWs from the Vietnam War. They are being treated at a small U.S. hospital in Thailand with insufficient staff and supplies. The exact location will be provided to you later. These POWs are too fragile to be flown to a large U.S. hospital at this time. Who has mobile hospitals that can be there hours from now?" The Marine Chief stated that he had two mobile hospitals at

Kadena Air Base in Okinawa, one fully staffed that could be there within 24 hours. "Alert them now – Gen. Hammond will give you the location. I want this to be a Top Secret operation, no pillow talk. No one outside this room is to know about it; no aids, no staff members; you will make the call. Go and alert them. Anyone else have anything close? Hammond, have our Graves/Forensic people in Hawaii leave today."

The Army Chief stated that he had a hospital in Seoul, Korea that can send personnel and supplies that can be there in hours. "We are expecting more POWs in the next few days and weeks; some did not survive hence the forensic teams. These poor bastards have been through hell and those who survive will be given the best care we can offer. Those that didn't make it will be buried in the States with full honors. Any communication will be on secure lines outside the tentacles of our security agencies. If I hear of a leak, that Service Chief will be fired per conversation with the Secretary of Defense."

"Army – send your personnel and supplies; Hammond will give you the location. Navy – where are your hospital ships located? I know they are attention-getters, but alert them that they may be needed; move one to a base close to Thailand using a cover of humanitarian nature. Some of you are probably wondering how we are getting the POWs, "don't."

"After the fiasco we had, not even the President knows. That's all I have. Air Force – make planes available to the Marine and Army; use C-130's not C-141 attention-getters. Coordinate directly with the Chief of Marines and Army, not their staffs. If this leaks out, it can jeopardize our operation; right now American lives are at stake – *go do your thing*." Gen. Hammond contacted Gen. Lawson and told him what was coming in the next 24 hours. "If you need more support, contact me only."

After cleaning up, Pete and his team met with Gen. Lawson, the Chief of Station, and Col. Lindor. The Agency had developed Pete's photos which were being passed around. Pete was chairing the meeting. "First, I would like to thank the team that went in; have never worked with more professional people – thanks again. The boat personnel were pros; I didn't realize we had boats like that. Jack Martin, your briefing and guidance was impeccable. Nothing went wrong; the only thing we need to find out is what Andy eats in his diet; had a hard time keeping up with him; great advice, Andy – thank you. Now we have had our first taste. I know the POWs we brought back are getting the best care, but I have a feeling we will need a larger capacity to handle them. Is there anything new on the POW locations?"

"We have confirmation on the camp NE of Vientiane as housing POWs; a rough estimate is 200 personnel plus or minus a few. The camps in Pakxe had no live personnel observed. We know the one camp is a graveyard with 35 shallow graves counted." The Chief of Station said, leaning back in his chair, "Our prisoner – has he given us anything worthwhile? I'm not second guessing anyone, but I think his vacation is over after seeing the people we brought back, both dead and alive. I think it's time to get his undivided attention."

"Pete, he is dead," said Gen. Lawson. "He must have had another cyanide pill hidden somewhere."

"Okay, so what is our priority, the POWs NE of Vientiane? If what we brought back is an indicator, we are going to need more medical personnel both here and at Loei." Gen. Lawson explained what was coming in the next 24 hrs. "Col. Lindor has expanded the mess facilities and living facilities, so we are ahead of the curve there. I do want to say job well done, Pete, by you and your team. From the looks of these photos, should the Army not treat you right, you can always start a demolition Company. The Black Bird photos show the southern half of the ridge still smoking with no sign of life. As for priorities, we need to get the POWs northeast of Vientiane. We moved some Delta personnel 2 hrs. ago up to Loei, so we have a good force to go in; air assets are available to them. Let's get some chow unless someone has a question or suggestion? No one - okay let's eat."

Chapter 18

Gen. Lawson motioned for Pete to stay. When they were alone, he looked at Pete and told him one of the POWs wanted to talk to him. "Go over to the medical section and see him; his name is Wallo, first name Larry." Pete grabbed a table to steady himself. "Are you alright?" Gen. Lawson grabbed Pete by the shoulders and held him. "Holly shit, Larry was lost in the tri border area (where South Vietnam, Cambodia and Laos all meet) back in the spring of '65. I better go and see him."

Pete went into the medical facility and got a breathing mask and gloves before asking where Wallo was located. A doctor took Pete to Wallo's bed and left. Wallo was skin and bones and hooked up to an IV. He smiled when he saw Pete. "Thanks, Lieutenant," he whispered. "Come closer but keep your mask on. I know you want to ask me a lot of questions, but I need to tell you something before I go. We were all injected with a slow type of virus/poison. The ones you brought out that didn't make it died from the injection and not from starvation; they were the first in our group to die. I think they died about five days ago. I was in the last 10 to get injected. Tell the doc to draw blood from me and have it analyzed. I think I have a week or 10 days; another 10 should die any day. I don't care if I die, but there are people north of Vientiane who will get injected any day now. I heard our guards talking, understand Vietnamese, and they are Vietnamese and not Laotians. I'm tired, thanks again Lieutenant, we will talk again."

Pete had tears in his eyes as he left Wallo's bed. He walked over to the mess hall and motioned Gen. Lawson, Col. Lindor, and the Chief of Station over to an empty table. "What's the problem, Pete, you look upset?" Pete related what Wallo had told him. "Was he lucid; was he in a good frame of mind?"

"Hell yes, he says he and the last 10 men have about a week to 10 days. He speaks and understands Vietnamese. We need lab people fast. Walter Reed Hospital has that research facility; I know they have a team that can leave within hours."

"Christ, I'll get my friend on the horn. Come with me, Pete. Col. Lindor – have the doctors draw blood from Wallo and let us four meet in the conference room in a ½ hour. Let's go, Pete. Can I use your secure line?" Gen. Lawson was directing his question to the Chief of Station. "Yes, of course you can, but I'd use Col. Lindor's phone – he has that new high tech system." Col. Lindor got up and told them to come with him. Gen. Lawson pressed the buttons and got a voice he didn't recognize; he looked at Col. Lindor who took the phone from him. "Bob, is that you? Good, I need the Chairman of the JCS office, a General Hammond; if he's not there, get him at his home, thanks." He handed the phone to Gen. Lawson. "Hammond, are you in your office? Good, I need a lab team here ASAP; I know Walter Reed Research has a team. This is very important; right now 33 American lives depend on it and about 200 more in the next few days. Yes, I'm positive, same source as before; I'll hang on.

"Yes, sir thanks – but we need help right now – I'm sure Gen. Hammond briefed you."

"If I divert a "Romeo" to your site, say in an hour, can you get some vials of blood packaged and they can take it to Kadena. They have an upscale lab there; I'll alert Walter Reed and get them on their way. Kadena can have the results in a few hours; that way we know what we are looking for."

"That sounds good; I'll have our runways clear. Thanks." There was a click and the phone was dead. "They are sending one of their "Romeos" (Recon plane also referred to as a Black Bird) so our air strip needs to be cleared." Col. Lindor stated he would personally take care of it. The black plane landed 40 minutes later; it never shut down; a padded package was handed to one of the pilots and the plane took off and was gone.

"Well, I think we are on the right track," said Gen. Lawson as he looked at Pete, the Chief of Station, and Col. Lindor. "Wallo said there were Vietnamese at the camp north of Vientiane. I didn't say anything to Hammond about that. I think we are going to need a "SPECTER" (C-130 gun ship) when we go in at the next camp. I don't want my next statement to be misunderstood, but I don't want any guards, Laotians, or Vietnamese left alive at that camp. If we take a Vietnamese prisoner, I don't think he will know or tell us what they are injecting our POWs with. I better give Hammond a call, or do either of you have a source who can deliver such a plane by tomorrow?" The Chief of Station informed them he could have one at Loei Airfield early in the morning ready to go. They were sitting in Col. Lindor's office when his phone rang; he picked it up and listened. "Tell them good work and I'll send a C-123 in to pick up the bodies first thing in the morning, ETA 0700 hrs." He hung up the phone.

"That was my radio section. They just got a message that the problem at Ibaham's village has been taken care of. I figured you had enough on your plate, General, so I had my resources take care of that problem. The Vietnamese in the village have been taken care of by the Yards. The old man and his family asked to stay, but were sent to one of the other villages. Ibaham and his family are back. Hell, they are going to need body bags for those poor people; I better go and take care of some things. You are welcome to stay in my office as long as you want." Col. Lindor left closing the door. "Well, good to know we won't have to go back in there. We have people in Pakxe we have to dig up. Is there any way to contact the Laotians Government and see if they will cooperate in Pakxe?" Pete was addressing the Chief of Station. "I'll see what our sources in Vientiane can come up with; after all, we just want some dead bodies. There is that ridge you collapsed and the POWs you rescued. However, from the last photos we got the section where the POWs were is also gone or smoking. We can deny we were there and that somehow the ammo or whatever they had there caused the ridge to collapse. Let me go and make contact; see you later."

Gen. Lawson looked at Pete. "How well did you know Wallo?"

"He came from Finland and the Russians had a price on his head. He was an officer in the Finish Army and as you know, they joined the Germans in fighting the Russians. He did some covert work against the Russians when they reached the Fin border; caused Russia severe headaches. Then he escaped to the U.S. and got a commission as a Captain, I think. I was a 1st Lieutenant when I met him at Fort Bragg in the early 1960's. I ended up doing some work with him in Vietnam; he got me out of a major jam over there – saved my life if truth be told. He disappeared in the tri border area in the spring of '65. I liked him, still do; couldn't believe he somehow wouldn't show up somewhere, so here he is. When I saw him today I

201

hardly recognized him, he is skin and bone. He still calls me Lieutenant."

"Pete, if we ask the Laotians' permission to dig up the POWs at Pakxe, we have to delay our rescue of the POWs north of Vientiane because that's going to get the attention of a lot of people, not to mention our politicians back in the States."

"I know, I have been thinking the same thing. There has to be a lot more POWs somewhere in Laos; hell, they have to feed them or maybe the Vietnamese are feeding them; what can they gain by keeping them?"

"Well, you remember Paris - the North Vietnamese wanted billions from us to repair their cities and port facilities. They may be waiting for us to make a move diplomatically, I don't know; then we would have a lot of people mudding the water."

"Hell, let's get the POWs north of Vientiane; we are ready to go; these people are alive, the poor bastards at Pakxe are dead. We can't do any more for the people we have here and the medical team will arrive tomorrow. We can fly up to Loei Air Base in the morning."

"Pete, you are not going in on the POW rescue up there. We have people who have been rehearsing for weeks, let them do their job. There will most likely be other camps according to the Chief of Station. They are diverting the Black Bird to another area where you were some years ago. Go over and see how Wallo is doing and see if he can shed some light on other camps; don't press him too hard, let him do the talking."

Pete left and went over to the medical section, grabbed a mask and gloves, and headed over to Wallo's bed. "How are you doing; you're looking better?" Wallo looked at Pete, closed his eyes and opened them again. "Heard about our blood going to the lab at Kadena, good work, Lieutenant," Wallo smiled. "I'm having a hard time believing I'm in friendly hands. I don't know what they are feeding me in this IV, but I feel better than

I have in a long time. I know you want to ask me about other camps, but I have to tell you something. There is a doctor here, the one with the mustache; he is the one that injected us in the last camp I was in. I couldn't believe he was here."

"Are you certain - there are only American doctors here?"

"I saw him yesterday and asked the doctor taking care of me what that doctor's name was; he told me Zink, and that he was new here. There is something else, there was a lot of noise and commotion in the room next to me; Americans were yelling. I think you should check this out, Lieutenant."

Pete checked his side arm and knife. He walked to the door about 20 ft. from Wallo's bed. Opening the door he looked in. There was a medic checking the IVs on about 25 patients lying on cots; they had white sheets over them but Pete saw OD tee-shirts on them; some had kicked off their sheets and had tiger suit pants on and boots. He walked in locking the door. The medic saw him and told him he couldn't be in here. "Is that far door locked?" Pete asked the medic. "Yes, sir, this is a restricted area."

"Why aren't you wearing protective clothing and a mask?"

"Dr. Zink said I didn't need it because I had been vaccinated."

"Come here." The medic was hesitant but came over to where Pete was standing by a bed. Pete had been looking at the patient and recognized him. "Is he getting a regular IV or is there something else in the IV bag?"

"It's a regular IV; they were given something yesterday to make them drowsy, but they should be okay now. Dr. Zink is coming in about ½ hr. from now to administer something to them."

"Do you have band aids?"

"Yes, sir, in this cabinet."

"Get them and follow me."

Pete started pulling the IVs out and the medic placed a band aid over the area in the patient's arm. They were about half done when some of the patients started talking and sitting up, placing their feet on the floor. They all had Delta Force uniforms on minus their shirts which were hanging on the end of their cots. "Put your shirts on and help your buddies that are not awake yet; don't make any noise." Pete and the medic had pulled the IVs out of the rest of them and most were dressed; some were a little groggy but were coming around. Pete counted 31 Delta Force personnel. They were helping each other as some were a little unsteady on their feet. "How long have they been here?" Pete asked the medic. "They were sedated yesterday."

"Can they eat or what should I do with them?"

"They can eat if they are hungry, but some fresh air would help them; this door leads outside and it's not far to the mess hall."

"You open the door and then stay close to me." The men walked outside, took deep breaths and started moving and exercising their arms. Pete asked them how they felt and got a thumbs-up from them. "I will lead you into the mess hall; don't eat too much but drink plenty of fluids."

As Pete and the medic led them into the mess hall, he spotted the Doctor with the mustache going through the line for food. Pete walked up to him and tapped him on the shoulder. The Doctor looked at Pete and saw the medic and the Delta Force coming in. The doctor threw his tray at Pete and ran for the far door. Pete shot him and the doctor fell to the floor. Pete walked over to the doctor and pulled him to his feet. "Someone handcuff this man and take him to the dispensary and have his shoulder fixed; I want this man alive." Two men came; one placed plastic ties on his hands which were now behind his back. The doctor was in pain and grimaced but did not say anything. Gen. Lawson and Col. Lindor had walked into the mess hall and seen the action. They walked over to Pete who still had his side arm in his hand. "Put it away, Pete." Pete placed his weapon in his holster and turned around and faced Gen. Lawson. "We have an urgent problem on our hands," said Pete. He motioned for two of his men who had just finished eating. "Get over to the dispensary and make sure our good doctor doesn't have any candy on him (cyanide); strip him and when they are through with him, have someone place an IV in his good arm."

Pete walked over to an empty table and sat down. Gen. Lawson and Col. Lindor joined him. Pete explained what Wallo had said and what had happened. "I thought these people were flown up to Loei Air Base yesterday?" He was looking at the General and Colonel. "I sent a C-123 up there. I didn't observe the loading. I'll give them a call. You know I haven't seen Bob Miller or Jack Martin since yesterday morning. Let me get on the horn." Pete looked at Gen. Lawson. "I don't know what the hell is going on but that doctor, whoever he is, will get my full attention. We almost lost 31 Delta Force people not to mention American POWs."

"Do we know where he came from or his name?"

"I have no idea; Wallo said his name was Zink and he would write a statement saying he was the one who had injected him and the other POWs. I have to go back and talk to Wallo, who by the way, says he is feeling better than he has in years. He stated that he had been in three different camps before he came to the holding area outside of Pakxe."

"You get with Wallo and I'll get with Col. Lindor and the other two doctors and find out what they know."

The medic who had helped Pete came over to their table as they were about to leave and asked if Pete needed him anymore. Pete looked at Gen. Lawson. "Yes, can you tell us anything about the vials of blood you drew from the POWs?"

"Sir, I helped package them, but the vials from the POWs were thrown away. The vials that went aboard the plane were from me and three other medics. Dr. Zink took the blood samples himself. He told us he wanted to make sure that we had not been infected." Col. Lindor came in and over to where they were standing. "We have a problem; I just got a message from Kadena; the blood they received was normal. The report from Loei is not any better; the only passengers aboard the C-123 were Miller and Martin and they had both been sedated. They are fine now. The pilot said a doctor brought them aboard the plane and told him to get those two up to Loei where they would be treated and that there would be no other passengers. I talked to our other two doctors and they didn't know where this Dr. Zink came from. He had told them he was part of our group that came in last week."

"I'm going over to see Wallo and then over to the dispensary to talk to Dr. Zink."

"Pete, use your head; don't go overboard in your interrogation – you have a round in your chamber, clear your weapon." Pete pulled his weapon out, cleared it and inserted the round into his clip. "I hope you never get mad at me; believe me, Nancy will hurt you," said Gen. Lawson slapping Pete on his shoulder as he left.

Pete went over to Wallo's bed. "Your observation of that doctor probably saved 31 of my men; they are okay now."

"What did you do to the doctor?"

"I shot him in the shoulder; he is being treated at the dispensary next door to you."

"You always were fast on the trigger. One of the camps I was in was on that plateau area in Laos; remember when we took off in the plane, it was like an aircraft carrier – the end of the runway had about a 500 ft. drop off. Our trucks had a hard time making it up there; I could see out the back it was the same place. The other two I don't know the location."

"How are you feeling?"

"I'm okay, like I told you, I haven't felt this good in years."

"I'll be back to see you later."

Pete headed for the dispensary. The doctor was strapped to the bed with an IV in his arm; two Delta Force men were standing on each side of his bed. "Has he said anything?" One of the men replied "no."

"That vial of blood we took from the one POW yesterday who died – get it and bring it in here; I want this good doctor to get the same stuff the POWs got." One of the men left and told Pete he would be right back. "How are you feeling?" Pete asked the doctor. "You bastard, you didn't have to shoot me."

"Dr. Zink, you have no idea what I'm going to do to you; when I get that vial of blood, it's going to be one on one." The Delta Force man came in with the vial of blood and he nodded to Pete. Pete told both men he wouldn't need them for a while but to stay outside the door and not let anyone in, no matter what their rank. They both pulled their side arms and left. Pete pulled the sheet off covering the doctor; he was naked underneath. Pete got a syringe and drew the blood out of the vial; he then inserted the point of the syringe into the aperture on the IV, but didn't inject it; he let the syringe just hang there.

"I want to explain something to you, Dr. Zink; no one knows about this place and you will be dropped into the jungle naked and bleeding, but alive. You know how the animals in the jungle get when they smell blood. You won't be able to walk because your knees will be broken, and minus your family jewels. Do you understand what I just told you?" Dr. Zink was pulling on his restraints and was hyperventilating. "Now the alternative to this will be your full cooperation and

I'm just saying this once cause I don't have much time – your answer please." The doctor was now staring at Pete. He let out a long sigh and tears were flowing down his cheeks. "Okay, I have a family," he managed to get out. "I don't care about your family, tell me where they live and I'll send someone to inject them with this contaminated blood from the POWs." Pete pulled out his small recorder. "I have less than half an hour, so start talking."

"The State Department has a section which goes into contested areas around the world and determines what the people need and tries to help them. The area my team and I were given was Cambodia. We went into Cambodia to a small town called Ba Kev, not far from the Vietnamese border and the town of Pleiku. There was a Vietnamese team there who controlled the town, even though it was in Cambodia. I was told by the Vietnamese that I would be working with them and to be ready to go in the morning." What about the rest of the American team in Ba Kev?"

"I don't know, I left the next morning and we traveled into Laos."

"How did you communicate with the Vietnamese?"

"Two of them spoke English."

"Go on."

"We went to about 10 camps, POW camps, and I injected the POWs with what the Vietnamese told us was an antibiotic to get them healthy because they were to be released. We stayed at one camp for about a month because of the rain; the roads became muddy and washed out. I noticed that some of the POWs were dying and asked the Vietnamese what we were injecting them with. I was told that the antibiotic came from Hanoi and that the POWs that died were weak and we had gotten to them too late."

"When we left the camp, all the POWs were dead and were

buried in two large graves."

"How many POWs are we talking about?"

"About 150 men."

"When you injected them, what kind of shape were they in?"

"The majority seemed okay but a little weak; they all had wounds which had healed but the Vietnamese said they had medics who took care of them. You have to believe me – I wanted to help them."

"Did the POWs know that you were an American?"

"No, I was not allowed to talk to them."

"All this time you were in the camp, you never had the opportunity to talk to the POWs? What kind of food were they given? Did you hear them talk amongst themselves?"

"The food was rice and something else, maybe some fish; like I told you, most were okay. There were others who were weak. I never heard them talk."

"In the month you were there, you never heard them talk; were they in cells or open camp?"

"It was an open camp."

"You are lying, doctor, and I think it's time for you to lose your family jewels."

Pete took out his knife and sat on the bed. The doctor started crying and tried to get free from his restraints. Pete made a slight cut in the doctor's groin area and the doctor screamed. "I merely tested the sharpness of my knife; the next cut will hurt. Tell me again about the POWs; did they talk amongst themselves?"

"Yes, one of the Vietnamese told them I was an American doctor from Washington, D.C. and had come to help them." The doctor was blurting out his answers and was trying to look at this groin area. "When were you told that the POWs would die from the injections you were giving them?"

"I was never told – you have to believe me. I asked the Vietnamese what we were injecting them with, but they told me not to ask that again, and if I didn't cooperate, I would get injected."

"You are lying again, doctor; my time is running out and I'm afraid you are of no use to me anymore."

"Please, I'll tell you. When I first starting injecting them I asked the Vietnamese why they didn't help; I was told they couldn't and if it got out that the POWs died and there was an International inquiry, they would leave a few POWs alive and they could say that an American doctor injected them."

"So you knew when you first started injecting them with this so-called antibiotic that it really wasn't an antibiotic but a poison of some sort?"

"Well, yes, I mean no; I didn't know until they started dying; you have to believe me."

The doctor started to pull on his restraints again and his left leg was almost free. Pete took out his weapon, grabbed it by the barrel, and hit the doctor's left knee with the butt of the pistol. The doctor screamed in pain. Pete got up from the bed and retied the restraints. "You bastard, I'll have your ass for torturing me; you have no idea who I work for in the State Department; if they don't hear from me, they will send people in here and take care of you." Pete went over to where the syringe was hanging from the IV. "How long after the POWs are injected do they get sick or die?" The doctor was looking at Pete and the IV. "About 2 weeks, maybe a little less."

"How many camps were you in, and how many camps are there?"

"I can't remember, it all happened so fast; I mean, maybe 8 or 10 camps, you have to believe me, I don't remember." Pete injected some of the blood into the IV. The doctor screamed this time loud and was thrashing around and pulling on his restraints while at the same time looking at the blood that was dripping into the IV. "Please, someone help me; oh God, please." He was now crying and coughing while watching the top of the IV tube turning red. He lost control of his bladder and peed over his thighs and bed. "Is there an antidote for this chemical you injected the POWs with?" The doctor wasn't listening to Pete. Pete grabbed the doctor's lower jaw and held his head still. "Is there an antidote for the so-called antibiotics you gave the POWs? I only have a few minutes left."

"I don't know, you have to believe me." The doctor was watching Pete as he injected the rest of the blood into the IV. "Yes, in my locker there is a container with a label which says "Ba Muoi Ba" on it."

"Ba Muoi Ba? That means "Beer 33" – I'm done here and so are you, Dr. Zink."

"You have to believe me." Pete placed his knife in the scabbard and walked over to the door and opened it.

General Lawson, Col. Lindor, and the Chief of Station were standing there with two guns pointed at them. "It's okay," Pete told his men who put their weapons in their holsters. "There is an antidote in Dr. Zink's locker." Col. Lindor and one of the Captains departed. Gen. Lawson took Pete by the arm and walked him over to the far end of the room. "What have you done here?"

"Nothing, I just had a talk with him; it's all here on the recorder."

"He poisoned me," yelled Dr. Zinc. Pete handed the recorder to Gen. Lawson. "What about the poison he says you gave him?"

"He thinks it's blood taken from one of the POWs; it's harmless, it's actually a vitamin which will make the doctor feel better; it just happened to be red in color. He works for the State Department, "Good Will" section; it's all on the recorder."

"You can't torture people, you are not above the law, Pete."

"That bastard has killed American POWs all over Laos, even tried to do away with 31 of my men. No one held a gun to his head; he knew exactly what he was doing. I should have killed the bastard; no one would have known about it."

"You would have, Pete!"

"Let's go over to the mess hall and talk to the Delta Force people who got injected. How could the doctor and medic inject 31 people?" said Gen. Lawson indicating for Pete to come with him. They found a few of the Delta Force men sitting at a table talking. The General and Pete grabbed some chairs and joined them. "How did the doctor inject you and what reason did he give?" Pete asked. "Well, we were getting ready to go up to Loei and this medic came and said one of the doctors wanted to see us. We went into this room next to the hospital where a bunch of cots had been set up. The doctor informed us that a medical problem had developed up at Loei and that Gen. Lawson told him to give us this injection so we wouldn't catch whatever they have gotten up there. He told us we would experience a little vertigo but to lay down on the cots and it would pass in about 10-15 minutes, and for us to help our buddies to lie down on the cots. We got injected and started getting drowsy and lay down. After we were all injected, we noticed all these IV bags already attached being brought in. Those of us who were not out yet started shouting and complaining, but soon we were out also. It wasn't until Col. Compton came in and started pulling the IVs out that we realized we had been had. Thanks, by the way."

"How are you feeling now?" asked Gen. Lawson. "Fine, sir, and ready to go; there is one thing we have talked about. Could this incident be held close? Our teammates will laugh for a week if they find out; we are good to go so we would appreciate if nothing was said. General Lawson smiled and told them to inform the rest of their friends that it was close hold, not a word would get out. He thanked them and told them to get ready to go. Col. Lindor, a Delta person, plus a doctor came into the mess hall. The Delta person was carrying a container which had a Ba Muoi Ba label on it. The doctor explained that he would run some tests on it, but from what he could tell, it was beer. Gen. Lawson looked at Pete. "Go back to our good doctor and find out what else he knows." Turning to the doctor, he asked if it was possible that the contents could be an antidote. "Sir, until we find out what the POWs were injected with, I don't know."

"We should have a lab here in a few hours so let's hope they can figure it out."

Pete went back to Dr. Zink's room where the two Delta men were guarding him. When Dr. Zink saw Pete he started shouting profanity. Pete sat down on the edge of the bed and just looked at him. "Can I borrow your wet stone?" he asked one of the guards. The man handed Pete a wet stone. "What's the matter, won't your knife hold an edge?"

"No, I just want to make sure my knife is really sharp; I have a little operation to perform." Dr. Zink started crying and shouting. Pete took his knife out and started sharpening it with the wet stone. "Dr. Zink, if you get thirsty let me know; we have some beer over in the mess hall; it's called Ba Muoi Ba, Beer 33; but then you couldn't possibly know that cause you were not in the war in Vietnam." Pete handed the wet stone back to the guard. Dr. Zink was now pulling against the leg restraints. Pete leaned over the left leg and grabbed some of Dr. Zink's groin hair and with the other hand, cut a fairly big swat of hair off. "I have to see where I need to make the incision." He looked at the doctor who had stopped struggling and was crying not moving. "Is there an antidote?" asked Pete in a calm voice. "I don't know," answered the doctor in a calm resigned voice. "Do you remember the location of the camps that you were in, and some of the others you were going to?"

"The only one I know of was NE of Vientiane, I think. They never told me where we were going next, but I overheard a conversation and the one camp by Vientiane was mentioned. We had to get a resupply of the antibiotics. My shoulder really hurts."

Pete got up and spoke quietly to the guards. "I'll send a doctor over to check his shoulder and give him a pain shot." Pete went into the mess hall but Gen. Lawson was not there. He saw one of the other doctors who was finished eating and asked him to look at Dr. Zink's shoulder and give him something for pain; and to check his IV also. Pete found Gen. Lawson in Col. Lindor's office along with the Chief of Station. "Well?" asked Gen. Lawson. "He doesn't know of an antidote. He still thinks I injected him with blood from the POWs."

"We have the planes from Okinawa landing in about 45 minutes. They have a lab with them, so we'll let them go to work. The other hospital we will send up to Loei. Our sources in Vientiane say there is a good chance to get the dead POWs out, but it has to be done quietly – no leaks or press."

"What about the graves/forensic people – they will talk when they get back to the States," said Pete looking at Gen. Lawson. "No, the ones who are coming are military and have signed the same secrecy act as us. Some have been working in North Vietnam for years; nothing has come out so far. We will head up to Loei in the morning with the other hospital and the people from Korea."

"When was the last time you ate?" Gen. Lawson was looking at Pete. "Last night, I think." Well, let's go over to the mess hall; we all deserve a good supper." Gen. Lawson led them out of Col. Lindor's office and was walking with Pete. "What do you want to do with Dr. Zink?"

"I had a doctor go over and look at his shoulder; he was complaining about it when I left him."

"Did you do anything to him before you left?"

"No, as a matter of fact, he was calm and told me the only other camp he had heard about was the one NE of Vientiane. None of the other camps he was in had any live POWs when he left. He thinks he was in 8-10 camps."

"Will it make any difference to our cause if we kill him; maybe make us feel good for a few hours and then we have lowered ourselves to his standards."

"He won't be punished by the State Department that we know, not with the culture there. They don't want any live POWs coming back to the States; remember "Peace with Honor" and the "Nobel Peace Prize.""

"When you think about the culture there, what as a nation have we become? I'm not going to get any great satisfaction in doing away with him; but when I saw the people we brought back from the ridge outside of Pakxe, don't we owe them something? What if we let him lose up in N. Laos at Muong Sai; the mountain people there are friendly towards Americans. There is a grave yard of POWs there; we can take him in and leave him. I think some of the people still remember me."

"But you will tell them to do away with him after we leave."

"Probably," said Pete opening the door to the mess hall.

Pete was starving; as they were eating they heard the unmistakable sound of the C-130s coming in. Col. Lindor got up and told them he wanted to brief the new arrivals and make sure they got setup in the correct hangers. Gen. Lawson told Pete and the Chief of Station that the Delta Force was assembled at Loei and would go in at early light, in the morning. They had been rehearsing and would hit the Ban Don POW camp NE of Vientiane. Jack Martin would go in with them along with an Air Force FAC (forward air controller) who would control the C-130 gun ship. "When they have completed their mission, I want you, Pete, to go into the plateau area at Muong Sai and bring the POW bodies out since you have been up there before."

"Do we have a green light from the Laotian to go in there?"

"Yes, they have pulled their people out of Ban Don and other camps of which there are 10 according to them, and have given us their locations. The Laotians want nothing to do with the Vietnamese anymore who have suggested that Vietnam and Laos become one country. The graves and forensic people will be here in the morning."

Chapter 19

Gen. Lawson and Pete flew up to Loei Air Field the next morning; the personnel from Korea and the mobile hospital had not arrived yet. The operation to free the POWs was under way. Bob Miller brought them up-to-date, as they monitored the radio transmission of the Delta Force. They received a message from the Delta leader that all POWs had been injected 2 days ago. They had 185 live and 14 dead. The two C-123s they had brought in were on the way back to Loei with POWs; they would return with three additional C-123s. Bob Miller coordinated with the Air Force and the additional planes were on the way. "Well, it sounds good," said Gen. Lawson. "All we need now is an antidote."

They received a message from Col. Lindor saying a mobile hospital plus medical personnel from Korea were on the way to Loei. The Walter Reed lab had arrived and was already at work. Col. Lindor's second in command had one doctor, three male nurses, and 10 medics standing by for the POWs arrival. A hanger had been designated for the mobile hospital plus

217

two air conditioned buildings had been set up with 200 cots and IVs all ready. They would use the same procedure for the POWs as used at Col. Lindor's location. The C-123s started arriving with POWs along with the mobile hospital and medical personnel from Korea, who arrived in two C-130s. After a short consultation with the Loei medical personnel, the team from Korea was integrated in handling the POWs. As soon as the C-123s were unloaded, they took off for Ban Don and more POWs.

In the evening, the C-123s arrived with the Delta Force who was escorted into a hanger set up as a conference room. The leader and Jack Martin chaired the meeting and briefed Gen. Lawson on the operation; no Delta Force personnel were lost. They had been able to take out the towers using sniper fire and were able to isolate the Vietnamese command center and their soldiers. No Vietnamese prisoners were taken. Five POWs were wounded by friendly fire; nothing serious. All the living POWs had been injected 2 days ago. The C-130 gun ship had returned to its base in Thailand. Jack Martin's only statement was he hoped that he never pissed off any Delta Force people because they were truly pros at their job. "Thank you for letting me go along with you to observe your capabilities." Gen. Lawson stood up and congratulated the Force. "What kind of shape were the POWs in?"

"You probably saw some of them when they were unloaded here; we sent out the weakest first, but even the best of them were in bad shape. No one should be treated like they had been; that's why it was easy to eliminate the Vietnamese of which there were many."

"Good job again; we will talk later – go and get some chow – the mess hall is ready and waiting."

Gen. Lawson indicated for the Delta Force leader and Jack Martin to stay. When they were alone, the General looked at them and asked about the Vietnamese cadre. "Were all of them male or were there female cadre present?"

"There were approximately 75 males and 23 female soldiers. There were two large excavations outside the perimeter fence, probably made for the POWs. We threw the Vietnamese bodies in the holes and poured gasoline on them and lit. The last thing we did before leaving was cover them with dirt. It took all of us about an hour to complete that and then rake the dirt. We brought back what we think was the injection they used. We inspected all the buildings and burned them to the ground; the same with the towers. Pictures were taken of the camp, but not any of the bodies before we destroyed the facilities."

"How do you know what you brought back was what they used to inject them?" Gen. Lawson was looking at the Delta Force leader. "That, I would rather not tell you at this time, Sir, with all due respect."

"Fair enough, give the stuff to Col. Compton. Pete – you and Bob Miller get on the C-130 that's heading down to Col. Lindor's place and give it to the Walter Reed team; they are there now."

"Will do, Sir; anything else?"

"Brief Col. Lindor and the Chief of Station on the operation; there will be nothing written down on what took place up here." They all left the hanger and Pete got with Bob Miller and told him they were returning to Col. Lindor's place. Pete gave the quart size container to a Dr. Thomas, the head of the Walter Reed team.

Bob Miller and Pete were sitting in Gen. Lawson's makeshift office going over the maps of Muong Sai. "There are approximately 150 bodies buried up there in two mass graves. I want to bring the graves people with us; it's going to be a bad job and we need to bring some form of clothing that can be burned. I'll get with the graves people and see what things they have with them. The Montagnards will not help with this – disturbing the dead is a big taboo. We will need some Delta people to go in with our team; utilize some of them here who have not had an adventure over here yet. Call up to Loei and bring about half of them down here in case something comes up."

"What are you going to do with Dr. Zink?"

"Between you and me, he is going to disappear. The General is after me to be a little humane. However, each time I see the POWs and the ones that didn't make it, I know what I'm going to do."

"Have you thought of the consequences if it leaks out? People saw you shoot him in the mess hall; it could get back to the State Department; you know the culture there – they will want some answers. It could have a severe detriment on your career."

"I don't care; I have enough years so I can retire. To be honest, I'm getting fed up with the status quo and the culture that's creeping into the military also. I'm not saying we haven't got great support for this operation, but that's thanks to Gen. Lawson and his contact at the Pentagon."

"I shouldn't tell you this cause it could influence your take on a lot of things, but according to my boss at Langley who swore me to secrecy, you will get your first star in about 5 months." Pete sat and looked at Bob and didn't say anything for a few minutes. "I'm not speaking from emotions when I say this; but a star or me having to leave the Army because of what I'm going to do will not alter my decision. That doctor is part of the culture I'm speaking of; the State Department caused the death of American soldiers under my command in Italy. That doctor will pay the ultimate price for what he has done here. I can always find a job; I'm too young to sit in a rocking chair and pester Betty for the rest of my life; although I don't think she would mind for a while. I have somehow gained a lot of friends since I have been in the Army, and I mean good friends, so I'm not worried about my future."

"Well, I have been told to keep an eye on you and if you do leave the Army, I know who will offer you a job."

"Getting back to Muong Sai, it would save us a lot of time if we could get a C-130 into that plateau. We could load all the POW bodies on that plane and the rest of us could fly out on C-123s. I haven't been in there in years, so I don't know what that air strip looks like or its condition."

"Didn't you say Dr. Zink had been in there and also your friend Wallo?"

"Hey, you're right! Let's go over and see both of them." Pete and Bob Miller visited Dr. Zink first. "How are you feeling?" asked Pete as he walked up to the doctor's bed. Dr. Zink looked at them with tears in his eyes. "Has he been behaving himself?" asked Pete directing his question at the two Delta guards. They both nodded in the affirmative. "Dr. Zink, I need your help; do you remember the air strip up on the plateau where you spent a month?" Dr. Zink looked at both Pete and Bob Miller with wild eyes; he didn't answer. "This is not a trick question, doctor; I need to know if I can get in there with a multi-engine plane and get those bodies out; believe me, it would help your situation if you cooperate." There was a long sigh from the doctor, but he was calm. "While I was there, we received more medicine delivered by a plane. The air strip is grass and the Vietnamese had some Yards cut the grass strip with sickles. We had received a lot of rain so everything was soft. The road leading up to the camp was washed out. A twin engine plane landed; I think it was a C-123 with Vietnamese markings, probably left over from the war. It stayed overnight and left the next morning. There is a sharp drop-off at the end of the runway. That's all I can remember."

All the while Dr. Zink had been talking he was calm and seemed resigned to his situation. "If I remember right, the rainy season is over up there so things should be drying out; anyway, it hadn't rained for almost a week when we left. The Vietnamese had the Yards fix the road so we could get out."

"Were the Yards friendly towards the Vietnamese and you?"

"To me, yes, but to the Vietnamese no - they didn't associate with them. There were six Vietnamese in our team and about 50 Vietnamese soldiers, some of them left on the plane. I told you about the rest, about twenty were there when we left. They were always armed; the Yards would not help the Vietnamese dig the graves."

"But you said they cut the grass on the air strip before the plane arrived?"

"Yes, but at the point of guns aimed at them."

"They treated you well, the Yards?"

"Yes, a few of the elder men could speak a little English."

"Did they offer you their women to sleep with for a night?" Dr. Zink's face turned beet red. "Well, no; I mean yes, they said it was their custom and to show friendship to Americans. It wasn't like I was cheating on my wife; it was part of their culture. To refuse would have been an insult."

"That's true, we are not judging your morals; thank you, Dr. Zink."

"Will you take off my restraints? I have helped you."

"No," said Pete, looking at the guards. "Have you two eaten? I will send someone to replace you in a few minutes," he said looking at the guards.

Pete and Bob went over to the hospital ward, donned masks and gloves, and headed over to Wallo's bed. "Good to see you, Lieutenant," said Wallo. "I used the bathroom – can you believe it. I needed a little help from the medic, but I feel good. The medic's parents came from Finland; he doesn't speak

Finish but I have a friend here besides you, Pete."

"Larry, I want you to meet Bob Miller, a good friend. He works for the Agency."

"I can tell, he has shifty eyes; I'm just kidding, nice to meet you, Bob. You have to excuse me, I feel so damn good and I can't believe I'm in friendly hands."

"Well, you're good compared to when we loaded you aboard the helicopter. Pete will probably have you in uniform in a few days."

"I don't think that's going to happen. I want to ask you how the operation NE of Vientiane went?"

"We got everyone out – 185 live, 14 dead; didn't lose a man."

"What about the Vietnamese in the camp?"

"That I don't know yet."

"It's okay, I know how it works; how is that doctor you shot doing?"

"He is next door to you - behaving himself. Can you enlighten us on the place up on the plateau? Did you see the air strip? Do you think we can get a C-130 in there?"

"I saw the strip, but it was overgrown with grass. If you remember, we landed in a twin engine Caribou and it had a hard time landing without running into the Yards' long houses. A C-123 can make it but not a C-130."

"Okay, thanks, I'll be back later."

When Pete and Bob Miller left, a medic came in and went over to Wallo's bed. "I can get you what you asked for tonight; are you sure you want it?"

"Yes, you have to help me next door; I will never tell."

"I know, but I heard one of the doctors from Walter Reed say that the container they brought down from Loei is highly toxic and that the Vietnamese had to dilute it with something otherwise the POWs would have died within hours."

"That's what I want, just a syringe of it."

"Are you sure you don't want me to administer it?"

"No, you won't know anything about it. I'll do it myself."

"Okay, I'll see you when it gets dark." Wallo laid there; he knew damn well what Pete was planning for the doctor; he owed Pete that much.

At night only, one guard stayed outside of Dr. Zink's door on a rotational basis. They gave Dr. Zink a sedative at night and he slept through the night. There was another door to his room which was locked from the outside and adjoined the hospital where the POWs were. It was 10:00pm and all the POWs were asleep having been given a sedative, except for Wallo. His fellow Finish medic came to his bed, helped him to the floor, disconnected the IV, and led him to the door. The medic opened the door and he and Wallo went over to Dr. Zink's bed. Wallo took the syringe from the medic and injected the entire contents into the aperture in the tube leading to the doctor's arm. In about 15 second, Dr. Zink felt the medication and opened his eyes; he tried to scream when he saw Wallo, but no sound came out. Wallo smiled at the doctor and said, "See you in hell." The medic took the syringe from Wallo and led him out and back to his bed. "Thanks," said Wallo as the medic hooked him back up to the IV. "I don't need any sleep medication tonight." The medic departed with the empty syringe.

The next morning there was a flurry of excitement. Gen. Lawson, Pete, Col. Lindor, the Chief of Station, Jack Martin, and Bob Miller were all seated around the table in Gen. Lawson's office. "We have a serious problem on our hands." The General looked grim as he spoke. "Dr. Zink was found dead in his bed this morning. When the two Delta guards went to check on him he was not responsive, so they called a doctor to examine him. He had died during the night. So how could this have happened with a guard outside his door and no one entering his room during the night? The guards, four of them on rotational basis, told me there was no entry the entire night and they did not hear anything; they showed me their schedule. Pete, that syringe you injected into the IV – I talked to the doctor who made it up for the Delta guard and he verified that it was a vitamin supplement; not toxic in any way. The forensic people are doing an autopsy on Dr. Zink as we speak. Now, who saw Dr. Zink yesterday afternoon?"

Pete related to the others about his and Bob Miller's visit to the doctor and what transpired. "What time was this?" Gen. Lawson was looking at Pete. "Let's see, Bob and I got back here from Loei about 1830 hours. We gave Dr. Thomas from Walter Reed the chemical we brought down from Loei and came over to this office and looked at some maps of Muong Sai. We then went over to Dr. Zink about 20 minutes later; talked to him for about 15 minutes and then went over to see Wallo; stayed there about 10 minutes. If I'm wrong about the times, Bob, correct me?"

"No, that's about right. Wallo said a C-130 could not land on the plateau up at Muong Sai; it had to be a C-123; the strip was too short. We thanked him and, oh, he said some demeaning things about me when he found out I worked for the Agency; told me he was just kidding and was feeling so good he had made it to the bathroom with the help of a medic. He couldn't believe he was back in friendly hands."

"He told us he hadn't felt this good in years; wanted to know what they were feeding him in the IV." Gen. Lawson was looking at both Pete and Bob. "Did he ask about Dr. Zink?"

"No, but 3 or 4 days ago he asked about him and wanted to know what I had done to him; someone must have told him he was in the dispensary. I told Wallo I had shot Dr. Zink in the shoulder. No, wait – I told him the doctor was in the dispensary getting fixed up."

"The reason I asked about visiting Wallo was that there is a door leading from the hospital where Wallo's bed is into the dispensary where Zink was being held; the door locks and opens from the hospital side. "What are you saying?" Pete was getting hot. "Take it easy, Pete, I'm not saying anything yet, but that door was not under guard and if there was foul play, they had to come through that door." The phone on Gen. Lawson's desk rang; he answered it but didn't say anything. "Thanks for the fast work; are you sure?" That was Forensics; Dr. Zink died of a highly toxic injection – the same stuff we brought down from Loei yesterday. Does anyone have anything else?"

"Do we know what was in the container I gave Dr. Thomas?"

"The only thing I know is that when we arrived it was highly toxic and they were trying to break it down. The lab people from Kadena have not had much luck with the new blood samples they took from the POWs. They are working with the Walter Reed team; we will just have to wait."

"You know, back in '69 we ran into a North Vietnamese unit; we were on the wrong side of the border and we surprised them, to say the least. They had a Russian doctor with them who was carrying about a pint or maybe a little more of some liquid chemical in a padded bag; very carefully concealed in a shoulder bag. We searched all the bodies, took their paperwork/wallets and turned the stuff over to MACV-G-2. Since this was not an authorized operation by MACV but by another agency, yours truly was kept down at Pentagon East and received several severe ass chewings. The day before they shipped me to the real Pentagon, a doctor introduced himself to me and asked if I was the one who brought in the chemical. I told him, yes; he asked if I knew what it was; I relayed that I took it off a Russian doctor – why? He thought it was made in East Germany and was the most toxic substance he had ever seen; sent it to Fort Detrick, MD, for analysis."

"What date was this - in 1969, Pete?"

Pete sat there thinking about the exact date. "I'm sorry but I have to think; Betty's father chewed me out; I can't think of the exact date."

"Wait a minute, are you saying you can't remember your first date with Betty? Wait till I tell her – you will definitely get another ass chewing," said Gen. Lawson laughing. "Pete here got lassoed and tattooed by the daughter of the Army Chief of Staff at that time."

"It was May 21, 1969 that I talked to the doctor at MACV, so they must have gotten it at Fort Detrick about May 24-25, 1969."

"Let me go and call a friend; Pete, come with me. Can I use you phone, Col. Lindor?"

"Be my guest; we'll go over to the mess hall and have some chow."

Gen. Lawson picked up the phone and "Bob" answered. "Can you give me the Pentagon, Chairman of the JCS office – a General Hammond? "Thanks." Gen. Lawson explained the situation and the problem they had; gave the approximate date that Ft. Detrick received the pint of chemicals. He told Gen. Hammond it was urgent and he would wait for his call. "Well, you don't have to worry about Dr. Zink anymore; do you have any thought, Pete?"

"Yes, I do but I need to do some checking first."

"Go easy on him, he has been through a lot and then to have an American doctor kill his fellow POWs, probably to include himself."

"I'll tell you he is the kind of guy you don't want to get mad at you; with him it's only one way. Shit, I hate to confront him; he saved my life once." The phone rang; Gen. Lawson answered and listened. "Thanks, Hammond, it was worth a try. They still have it at Ft. Detrick; know what it does but no antidote for it. They are in contact with Dr. Thomas' team from Walter Reed. According to Hammond, slim chance they think it originated in East Germany or Russia."

"I'll go see my friend," said Pete and left.

As Pete walked into the hospital and was about to grab a mask and glove, a doctor told him he didn't need it anymore; just don't have contact with the patient. "How are things going with the POWs?"

"We lost 8 in the last day and-a-half which makes a total of 17 dead; the 13 critical could go today or anytime; 12 are still hanging in there; I hope we get an antidote soon."

"Thanks, Doctor," Pete said as he went over to Wallo's bed. Wallo looked at Pete and shook his head. "It's getting sparse in here; empty beds are not good for morale. They have partitioned off part of the room, but we know what's going on. Heard a lot of noise from next door this morning; the doc must not be behaving himself; what's going on?"

"Dr. Zink is dead; died during the night in his sleep, I think."

"What did you use – a hollow point round when you shot him?"

"No, according to the forensic team, he died of a highly toxic injection, the same stuff we brought out from the POW camp at Ban Don, NE of Vientiane."

"I'll make it easy for you, Pete; I injected him last night with a syringe of the stuff. The shit head should have been tortured but I didn't have the strength to do to him what I wanted to do. He woke as the injection took affect and looked at me in the eyes and I told him I would see him in Hell, and he was no more; end of story. He was the one who injected me and the rest of the POWs. I'll sign a statement to that, but you better hurry cause my days are numbered. I feel good, Pete, especially after last night; I'm going to ask you a favor; actually two favors. I did this alone – no one else is involved so leave it at that. The other favor is I want my ashes buried in my home town in Finland in my family grave site. I had a medic write it down with the family name and the village NW of Helsinki. I have a brother and two sisters. Will you do that for me? You take it over there, and then we are even; your life in Vietnam that time and the favor I did for you regarding Dr. Zink. I know you and what you would do to him, but you have a future and a family waiting for you, so I took care of him for you and for all the POWs."

Pete looked at Wallo with tears in his eyes; he shook his head and left. Gen. Lawson was waiting outside the hospital as Pete walked out. Pete had tears running down his cheeks. "Let's go over to my office," said Gen. Lawson. Pete didn't say anything as they walked into the office and sat down. "I didn't have to ask him anything; he told me he injected Dr. Zink." Pete relayed everything Wallo had told him including what he asked him to do. "I have a little bottle here, do you want a drink?"

"No, thanks, but I have a favor to ask you."

"I know what it is Pete; Wallo acted alone, end of story; it will go no further."

"Thanks," said Pete, wiping his eyes. "I'll personally take care of Wallo's back pay and anything else he has coming, including promotions. If it comes to it, you and Betty fly over to Finland on Uncle Sam's dime; Nancy and I will take care of the girls. Let's get something to eat."

There was a meeting in the conference room that afternoon with Gen. Lawson chairing. "We are getting 30 Delta people here this afternoon. Pete, I want you and Bob Miller and your team of 8 plus any Delta soldiers we have down here who need to be utilized, to fly up to Muong Sai in the morning and check out that sir strip and make contact with your old friend. I'll have the graves' team and whatever else you need standing by; call me using the Burst radios. Any questions?"

"Yes, there are about 150 bodies up there; let's use body bags this time. We may need a few days to fix up the air strip; I'll send the C-123 back. It's the dry season up there so that should be in our favor. Is there a large motorized lawn mower or a tractor with grass cutting capability that we can take up there?"

"I have a small John Deer tractor with a grass cutter up at Loei; I'll have them send it down this afternoon and will go and make the call." Col. Lindor left the conference room.

"Christ, is there anything Col. Lindor doesn't have?" Pete asked. "You would be surprised," said the Chief of Station with a smile. "The reason I asked about the mower is I know the culture up there, and to cut the grass with a sickle is beneath them; I want to start off on the right foot. That reminds me, we need to wear green berets up there; they don't like baseball caps or floppy hats."

"Don't worry, Col. Lindor has all kinds of green berets," said Jack Martin. "Why am I not surprised," replied Pete. He got his team together and briefed them on the people at Muong Sai and their culture. There was laughter when Pete mentioned the first night sleeping arrangements and that the women were not Polynesian Nymphs. He had gotten out of it by claiming he had a sickness which they accepted. "Play it by ear," said Pete. They all knew about the graves. "Have your gear together and bring it in here at 1830 hours; any questions?" One hand was raised. "What about bringing in a GP tent up there and placing bodies in it since the people up there are against disturbing the dead? At least the bodies will be out of sight."

"Good idea; I'll see about a tent," answered Pete. One other hand was raised; it was a Captain that was part of Pete's team of 8. "We know there was a Vietnamese cargo plane in there awhile back; we also know the Yards are not fond of Vietnamese. I think maybe three of us should parachute in and check the air strip to make sure the Yards haven't altered it. It could be a mess if a C-123 crashes up there."

"Good idea; if they have dug holes or ditches, it could delay our mission. The C-123 should have plenty of fuel and it could circle the area while some of us check the strip. Let's take four chutes – I'll take one and the rest of you can draw straws for the other three. We'll go in at 400 feet; no reserves. See you all here at 1830 hrs."

Chapter 20

Pete and Bob Miller went over to the hospital to check on Wallo. They walked in and over to his bed. "You know, you are starting to look good enough to put on a uniform. We are paying you good money LTC, so start earning it. Oh shit, I wasn't supposed to say anything until the General got the official orders so don't say anything – act surprised."

"Are you serious?"

"Darn right I am."

"Is that business we talked about taken care of?"

"What business? I don't know what you are talking about." Pete nodded his head. "Thanks, Lt," said Wallo with a smile on his face. "You still feeling good?" asked Bob Miller who had not been privy to what had transpired. "Better than I have felt in years; they are starting some of us on solid food tomorrow. I only lost one tooth or molar; the dentist was in a while ago and checked us out, so things are looking good. Here come the doctor and his group to check me out; see you guys later." Wallo waved his hand at them.

Pete and Bob Miller went to the mess hall and sat down with Gen. Lawson, Col. Lindor, the Chief of Station, and Jack Martin. Pete mentioned their plan for the next morning's mission. Col. Lindor said their tractor had arrived; it not only could cut grass but also had a scoop on the front that could help them dig up the bodies. The tractor was tied down inside a C-123 that would take the first group up there. Pete asked if one of the follow-up planes could bring a GP tent up there to keep the bodies out of sight from the Yards. "The graves registration people have body bags so we can put the tent aboard with them. It would be the 2nd plane to land."

"Pete, I would fly the bodies out as soon as you can; put them in the bags and I would do that at the grave site; remember KISS (Keep It Simple Stupid). Oh, I talked to Hammond and made a special request to promote Wallo to LTC. They have a list of others who will also be promoted, mostly posthumously. We are no closer to an antidote than we were yesterday. I mentioned the death of Dr. Zink and the forensic report. Hammond will notify the State Department; the doctor must have gotten a little careless with the injections used on the POWs. I'll come by and see you a little later, Pete."

The inspection for the mission was held. Pete and three others would parachute in. The Air Force rep told them there would be no problem with fuel; they would circle until they saw green smoke. Take off would be 0600 hrs. Everyone was ready and Pete dismissed them. Gen. Lawson came in as Pete was about to leave. "We need to have a talk. Hammond said not to say anything about Dr. Zink's participation in the POW's injections and dying. The State Department is going to make a hero out of him so his family can receive a pension."

"That's so much crap – here we go again - hiding behind our jobs, the Pentagon and the State Department culture again. This has got to stop; are they not aware that Hanoi, working through Sweden, had sent large cash payments to Dr. Zink's family? Doesn't anyone care anymore?"

"Hold on, where are you getting this information from?"

"A friend who has a friend told me yesterday."

"Pete, this better not be a rumor; how sure are you?"

"I would not have told you if it was not true. I also heard it from Wallo who said the pilot who brought in the resupply at Muong Sai had told them to treat the American doctor good cause the leaders in Hanoi were going to use him if this ever got out, and they were financially securing his and his family's future."

"Shit, I've got to call Hammond again; come with me."

General Lawson used Col. Lindor's phone; it was just him and Pete in the office. He explained what Pete had just told him. Hammond told Lawson he would call him back the next morning (their time). Gen. Hammond explained to the Chairman of the JCS what Lawson had relayed. "Get our friends at the FBI over here ASAP; we need to do a little checking quietly; they should not have a problem with this."

"I saw Robert De Voe going into the Secretary of Defense's office; I'll get him."

Chapter 21

At 0600 hrs. the C-123 with Pete's team and a small tractor took off for Muong Sai. The red light came on about 1
hour and 10 minutes later. The four jumpers checked their
equipment. The green light came on and the four men exited
the plane. Pete landed on the strip and the three others about
50 ft. away. After collapsing their chutes and placing them in
their bags, they all put on a green beret. They observed the strip
which was overgrown with grass and small plants and headed
towards the village. Pete walked ahead of the men and they
met a small group of men who greeted them in a friendly but
reserved manner. Two of the men from the back of the group
came forward; one was the leader of the village. He looked at
Pete and said, "Dai Quy Peter" (Captain Peter). Pete held up
his right hand and greeted the leader. The leader spoke a little
English and looked up at the circling C-123. Pete asked if
the plane could land at the strip. "Yes, no problem," said the
leader. Pete told two of the men to smoke the air strip; a few
minutes later the plane landed.

The back door opened and men came out; a few of them helped the load master untie the tractor and one of the Delta men drove it out on the grassy strip. The plane turned around and took off for Col. Lindor's headquarters. Pete asked permission to cut the grass on the air strip. "No problem," said the leader explaining to the other men what the Americans were going to do. More people were gathering to see the American Green Berets and some came up to greet Pete and his men. They had never seen a tractor before and watched with awe as the American steering it cut the grass down to about 6 inches, making quick work of the air strip; it was obvious that the Delta man had done this before. Pete radioed back and gave the code word for friendly reception and for the next planes to bring more gas and oil for the tractor. The people who remembered Pete wanted to know what had happened and told him about the unfriendly Vietnamese who had been here and the American bac si (doctor). They pointed to the east of the village where the POW camp had been. The village people had burned the camp down after the American POWs were buried and the Vietnamese left. Pete explained what they were here to do. There was a murmur amongst the villagers; they did not like to disturb the dead. Pete explained that the dead POWs needed to go home to their villages in America and receive a respectful burial; not thrown in a mass grave. The ones that understood what Pete had said told the rest of the villagers who nodded in agreement.

The mowing was half done and it was starting to look like an air strip again. It was now 0845 and most of the villagers had returned to their homes to eat or work their fields of corn. About 20 women came out with homemade rakes and started gathering the cut grass into piles; other women came with large reed baskets, which they carried on their backs, and filled them with the grass then carried them back to the village.

This continued all morning until the air strip was all cut and the grass removed. The first plane arrived to green smoke on a neat looking air strip; the plane never shut down, but turned around and took off. A large GP (General Purpose) tent approximately 12' x 35' was taken by the scoop or bucket on the tractor and placed near where the POW camp had been. This was after Pete had received permission on where to erect the tent by the leader of the village.

The graves' team came in on the next plane. The tractor operator had scooped the top layer of the graves and people in protective clothing started to carefully dig for bodies. When they reached the POWs, they cleaned the dirt off them with a brush-like instrument and placed them in body bags which were then placed in the C-123 by the Delta group. Due to the short length of the air strip and the altitude, heat, and humidity, only 35 bodies could be taken out and flown back to Col. Lindor's HQ. The procedure was repeated with a total of 70 of the deceased taken out the first day. The C-123 came in the late afternoon and shut down; it would remain overnight. It had brought in thermos containers of hot food which were placed in the tent along with trays and utensils. The work continued as long as there was enough light to see; 45 body bags were placed aboard the plane. The crew had explained that they could take the extra load since it would be cool in the morning and the plane could easily handle it. Pete gathered the Delta Force, the graves personnel, and air crew and thanked them for an outstanding job; they would need one plane tomorrow for the POW bodies.

Pete explained the culture of the tribe where they were located. He explained the old tradition of the first night sleeping arrangements; however some of the village men had watched the work being done; no invitation had been rendered so he thought maybe they were off the hook. "Let's get some food and we can utilize the tent for sleeping; guards tonight per SOP (Standard Operating Procedure). Our tractor operator has dug a trench up by the POW camp near the trees that we can use as a latrine; which some of you have used already." They had just finished eating when a delegation of village men came and talked to Pete. They wanted to know if Pete and his men needed anything. Pete told them they were fine and that they would be out of there the next day. He told them he appreciated the help in clearing the grass off the strip and was there anything they could do for them? The village men looked around and saw there were about 45 men. The leader explained to Pete that one of the Vietnamese soldiers had forced one of their young women to lie with him the night before they left and had given the woman a sickness; did they have a bac si (doctor) with them? Pete told the leader that they did and nodded to the Delta man to get his medical bag. The leader asked that Pete also accompany them to the sick woman.

Pete and the medic followed the delegation and arrived at a long house. The leader went into the house and ushered everyone out except for a young woman lying on a straw mat. Pete told the leader that he wanted a woman to go into the house with the bac si. The leader said something and a young woman came forward and followed the medic into the long house. Pete asked that everyone leave the front of the house to give the bac si light and the woman privacy. The leader said something and all the people departed except for him and Pete. The leader told Pete the Vietnamese had been very bad and had killed the American POWs and treated the villagers like prisoners. The medic came out and said the woman had been a virgin when taken by the Vietnamese and had some tears which had become infected. "It's not bad, so I gave her a shot of antibiotic, cleaned her, and will leave antibiotic pills for her to take over 11 days, one tablet each day." The leader said he understood. He called the young woman who had gone in with the medic and explained that she had to give the patient one pill each day starting tomorrow with water: she took the bottle.

Pete told the leader they would be back in 11 days to check on the woman but that she would be healthy by then. The leader invited Pete and the medic into his long house. He told them that the normal custom in his village was for them to sleep with a woman on the first night there. However, due to what had happened to the young woman, the men in the village were reluctant to let any stranger sleep with their women. The leader said that Dai Que Peter was aware of the custom, but he hoped that he understood why the offer was not being extended. Pete said he understood and that he appreciated all the help he and his men had been given in returning the POWs to their home villages in America so they could be given proper burials. Pete also told him they would fill in the two burial holes the Vietnamese had dug and return the area to the way it was when they arrived; they would talk before they left the next day. The leader held up his right hand and Pete and the medic returned the gesture and departed.

The next morning the last 35 bodies were placed aboard a waiting plane. Pete radioed Gen. Lawson and requested three planes be sent to his location to take the men and equipment back. He gave the code word for mission accomplished. Pete had brought an M-1 carbine with a folding stock, 5 magazines, a metal box with 500 rounds of ammunition, a green beret with the cloth emblem that he had worn when he was there as a Captain, and a silver eagle pined to it designating it as a Col. Beret. He gave these items to the leader. The men of the village came forward and gave each of the men with Pete a bracelet designating them members of the tribe. The planes came in and took their equipment, tractor, tent, and plastic bags with garbage. The area was clean and neat when they left.

Chapter 22

Gen. Lawson, Col. Lindor, the Chief of Station, and Jack Miller ushered Pete and Bob Miller and the rest of the men into the conference room upon their return. Gen. Lawson thanked them for a sad, but job well done. He told the graves' team he knew their job was just beginning but thanked them for their effort at Muong Sai. The men were told that an antidote had not yet been produced and more POWs had died. Gen. Lawson told them to get cleaned up and get some chow. He told Pete and Bob Miller to stay. He told them what Gen. Hammond had told him about an hour ago. There would be a ceremony at the State Department and a funeral when Dr. Zink's body was returned. His family would receive a pension and be told that Dr. Zink had been part of a humanitarian mission in Cambodia and had contracted a disease and unfortunately passed away before the State Department reps were able to help him. This was a joint solution to the problem by the Pentagon and State Department. Pete walked out and slammed the door; he headed over to the hospital and to Wallo's bed.

"What's the matter, Lt., you look pissed?" Pete tried to smile. Wallo was now clad in blue Army hospital pajamas, but there was something about his eyes that was different. Pete was about to say something when Gen. Lawson, Col. Lindor, the Chief of Station, Jack Martin, and Bob Miller walked over to Wallo's bed. Bob Miller said "Attention to Orders" and read the promotion order for Larry Wallo, promoting him to Lieutenant Colonel. Gen. Lawson pinned the silver leaf on Wallo's blue pajama collar. Bob Miller read three more citations, one for the Silver Star, the Purple Heart, and the Legion of Merit, which Gen. Lawson pinned on the left pocket of Wallo's pajamas. Tears were running down Wallo's face. "Well, aren't you going to say something; you usually have some smart remark when high ranking officers are around," said Pete reaching into his pocket and pulling out a bullet. "Here is an award from the Russians; they apologized and said they wanted to give you a bullet for years, so they asked me to give it to you." That brought laughter from everyone including Wallo. "I want to thank you all for this, as Pete knows, I'm not good with words."

"Good with words, hell – you can barely speak English, you old DP (Displaced Person – a term used primarily for refugees coming into the U.S. after WWII). You have said enough; Uncle Sam is not paying you good money to lay around in his hotel/spa all day – it's time you did something to earn your keep."

"I think Pete has said it all." Wallo reached out and shook everyone's hands; when he shook Pete's, which was the last one, Pete had tears in his eyes as he looked at Wallo. "It's been a hell of an adventure, LTC. Larry Wallo; I'll never forget you and you have my promise, if it comes to that."

As others left, Pete sat down on the edge of Wallo's bed. "If I bring you a small recorder, can you talk about what happened to you from the events in the Tri Border area to the present;

just what you remember, including Dr. Zink's injections of the POWs?"

"You better get the recorder now; I might not be here tomorrow."

"You'll be here; I'll go and get it now." After delivering the recorder and showing Wallo how it worked, Pete headed to the mess hall; it was crowded but the food was excellent. Pete sat down at Gen. Lawson's table with the others. "That was a good ceremony, thanks," said Pete and started eating. It was a quiet meal.

Dr. Thomas, the Walter Reed leader came over to the table and sat down. "We are running the analysis on the chemical you brought us around the clock; we are getting a new piece of equipment from John Hopkins Research Lab which should be here tomorrow. So far we have nothing; we know what it's made up of; it's really strange we received a sample from Ft. Detrick, MD, back in '69; it's the same stuff – we couldn't figure that one out either. When you look at the different components which make up this chemical, it's not rocket science; it's actually very simple. We isolated the components and came up with what we thought was an antidote, but no go. I wish I had more positive news, but I'm afraid we are going to lose more POWs before we are successful. I have talked to a POW by the name of Wallo; he is very clear in his statements, but according to him the last group of which he is one, will die three days from now. The thing that bothers me is he is so upbeat just to be back in friendly hands, as he calls it. He doesn't mind if he dies knowing he is among friends. I don't know where we got these soldiers from but they are a cut above the rest. I just left him, he is recording his adventure, his word not mine, so maybe in the future captured American soldiers can learn what to expect. Well, that's my two cents worth; I have to get back to the lab. If we get a break, I'll let you know."

Pete explained about the woman they treated at Muong Sai. He needed to take a medic and a doctor with him and stay for a few days; he had observed a lot of open TB sores on the people up there. "It would be 11 days from now. I know we have a lot of work to do here, but this is the dominant tribe in northern Laos and are very pro-American. I think we should take care of them."

"I'm not sure what our doctors will have to do in 11 days if we don't get an antidote, all we will have is body bags and they are being transported to Hawaii; so plan on it," said Gen. Lawson getting up from the table.

Chapter 23

The task of digging up the 35 graves in Pakxe was given to Jack Martin, who requested Andy as his advisor. Andy had spent most of his time so far fixing up Col. Lindor's vehicles. Jack Martin would take 30 Delta Force personnel and the graves' people. It was decided to use two CH-53s (Jolly Green Giants) to ferry the force in and the bodies out. The graves were located north of Pakxe away from the town and room for the helicopters to land. The team took off at 0700 hrs. the next day. There was no interference from local people. One of Jack Martin's sources came and informed him there were two other places which they had just been alerted to about 5 kilometers east of Pakxe which held live POWs. Jack radioed back to HQ and informed them about this news. There was a place near the two camps where C-123s could land. Vietnamese soldiers were at both of the camps which were adjacent to each other. The layout of the camps was sketchy. Gen. Lawson called a meeting of Col. Lindor, the Chief of Station, Pete, and Bob Miller. He informed them about Jack's transmission.

"Get half of the Delta Force down from Loei today; that's about 30 men and we have another 20 here. Do we have any pictures of the area 5 km east of Pakxe."

"The pictures we have are in your office when we blew that ridge about 2 weeks ago; those pictures covered at least 15 km east of Pakxe."

"Go get them, Pete, they are in my middle drawer. Bob, get on the horn and get those Delta people own here today."

Pete brought back the photos and spread them on the table. "Here is the ridge where we were; 5 km is about here; there is something there; the two camps are almost next to each other. How the hell could we have missed these; there are no towers shown, but there are shadows there and they are people."

"Have Andy come back on the next helicopter; he might know this area; we need to do something for that man when this is over," said the General. "I already have him on my pay-roll," said Col. Lindor. "I might add he is well taken care of."

"That's good to hear; he is definitely in our camp. Those people up in Muong Sai – we need to take care of them also. Make sure you are up there in 11 days, Pete; you never know when we might need them, especially Col. Lindor here with his program. When Andy gets here, let's formulate a plan; I'll get Jack Martin on the horn and see if he can use his resources to look at the area and make sure we can land a C-123 there." General Lawson left the group.

"I'm going over to see Wallo," said Pete. Walking into the hospital, Pete looked over to Wallo's bed where he was speaking into the recorder and looked animated, like he had something important to tell. "What is so important?" asked Pete as he walked up to the bed. "I have been talking into this machine for hours now and things are shaking loose in my head. I have recorded what I'm about to say to you, but handle it carefully cause it's sensitive. In early '73 we got some new people in the camp I was in. There was a guy I got friendly with who looked familiar. He was on his 3rd tour and had been assigned to that MACV Intel program we had up at Pleiku. He was telling me about the crap he witnessed in the Saigon HQ back in '69 when he was assigned to the MACV-G-2 section.

They had gotten a small quantity of some chemicals taken off a Russian doctor and some documents written in Russian. The documents were translated and one in particular was the formula and the antidote for the chemicals which had been sent to Fort Detrick, MD. This guy's boss was a LTC Hammond. When he brought the translation to Hammond, the LTC asked my friend if anyone else had seen the translation. My friend told him that only the translator and the two of them had seen the report. My friend, a Captain at the time, was told by Hammond not to mention this translation to anyone and that he himself would take care of it. Hammond stamped the translation and original documents "Top Secret" which he was *not* authorized to do, then placed the documents and translation in his safe. A month or so later there was an inquiry by the MACV G-2, a two star General, as to where the translation was along with the original documents. LTC Hammond, when asked, told the General that he had not received the document and had been told by his boss (a Colonel now deceased per a vehicle accident in Saigon 3 weeks earlier) that he would handle the documents and for Hammond not to get involved. Hammond told the G-2 General that he thought it strange because he usually was the one who verified translations with the translator before it went further. The G-2 General told Hammond he knew the translator, a WO (Warrant Officer) named Timko, had been killed in a helicopter crash 2 weeks earlier, but to go through his desk and see if he could find anything and to report to him only.

Hammond gave the task to my friend who worked directly

for Hammond and was on friendly terms with him. My friend had been present during the meeting with the G-2 and went through WO Timko's desk but found nothing. He reported back to Hammond who told my friend that he had sent the documents/translation to his friend at the State Department in D.C. and to say nothing about it; that he, Hammond, would handle it.

"Are you sure about this?"

"Hell, yes I'm sure, since my friend and I talked about it several times and the other crap that went on at the Pentagon East in Saigon."

"What is your friend's name, and do you know where he is?"

"His name was LTC Fred Hayes and you carried his body out when you rescued us. He was one of the first to get injected; didn't make it."

"Continue recording things, but give the recorder back to me and only me."

"You got it, I should be done today."

Pete headed back to Gen. Lawson's office and sat down. It was just the two of them. Gen. Lawson was about to say something but he looked at Pete and remained silent. "Sir, do you know anything about Gen. Hammond's tour in Vietnam?"

"What's going on; you know when you get that look on your face, I know there's trouble."

"I was just wondering about Gen. Hammond's Vietnam duties."

"Well, he and I were advisors to Vietnamese units in 1966-67. I was with an Airborne Battalion; Hammond was with the Vietnamese 23rd Division outside Ban Me Thuot. In '68-69, Hammond was at MACV G-2 section in Saigon. I had a Battalion in the 101st Airborne up in I Corps (U.S. Army), why?"

"We have a big problem on our hands and I don't know how to explain it."

"Try me; we have solved some problems before – what is so different about this one?"

"To your knowledge, did Gen. Hammond have a friend in the State Department back in 1969?"

"I don't know; wait – we had a classmate who went to the State Department after he had served his West Point obligation in the Army, why?"

"Was Hammond close to this officer?"

"They were roommates at the Point. Where is this going, Pete?"

"In '69 Hammond sent the Russian documents and translation including the formula of the chemicals plus the antidote to his friend in the State Department."

"Where the hell are you getting this crap?"

"You will have the tape and the story this afternoon."

"If it was anyone but you telling me this shit, I would cold cock them. You and I and only us will talk about this; not another person, no matter his rank. Is that understood?"

"Yes, Sir, I hate to bring this to you, but I'm afraid it's true."

"Who told you this?"

"Wallo's prisoner friend told him about all the crap he witnessed at MACV-G-2 section in 1969. This friend was a Captain at that time and worked directly for LTC Hammond. The timeframe and the chemicals all fit. Wallo does not know that the chemicals that were sent to Ft. Detrick, MD were the same stuff they were injected with; he is just relating what he and his fellow prisoner talked about. I told him when I gave him the recorder to tell everything no matter how insignificant. His friend was one of the first in Wallo's group to receive the injection and was one of the bodies we brought back from the ridge."

"Jesus Christ, how do we handle this, Pete? Hammond and I go back to the Point. He, as you know, has run interference for us on numerous problems and has been a true friend. What I am about to say now is between us. Hammond's friend and mine, Roger Carpenter, is still at the State Department. How did the SD find out about the Delta Force and its ultimate mission? Hammond was playing both sides, but why? "Could it be for financial gains?" asked Pete. "It's a stretch, but you might be on to something. Hammond came from a really poor background, financially that is. His roommate's parents were richer than God. I don't know, but you might have to go and see your friend Senator Clifton and tell him this sordid affair; but he'll have to keep it close hold. I'll borrow Col. Lindor's phone and you and I will call him and only him, tell him it's urgent and that American lives depend on it. I guess he will have to get the FBI involved. I don't know if Hammond has friends there; he probably does and they will tip him off. Jesus, I hate this, but let's go. Clifton is majority leader now so he must have friends."

They walked into Col. Lindor's office; it was empty. Gen. Lawson picked up the phone and recognized Bob's voice. "Bob, this is Gen. Lawson. Can you please get me Senator Clifton, the Senate Majority Leader?"

"Give me a few minutes, I may have to go to his home."

"Thanks, I'll wait." Gen. Lawson heard a female voice announcing that it was Senator Clifton's office. "This is Gen. Lawson calling long distance; I have an urgent call for the Senator."

"Senator Clifton is in a meeting, can I have him call you back? I see you are on a secure line."

"I'm sorry, but I have a friend of his here and this involves National Security."

"Just a minute."

"This is Senator Clifton, who am I talking to?"

"Sir, this is Gen. Lawson; I have a friend of yours here, a

Colonel Peter Compton and he needs to talk to you."

"Pete is with you? Hold a second and let me clear this line; okay, we are alone. Pete, how are you?"

Pete told Senator Clifton he needed to see him alone in the next few days and it would take him about 2 days to get to D.C. "Where are you, Pete? I know you are not in Italy; last I heard you were at Ft. Bragg, N.C. and in Paris."

"I'm in Thailand and it involves the lives of 100s of POWs."

"Pete, copy this address – it's my home; I don't want to meet you on the Hill; also, you will stay at my house; looking forward to seeing you." There was a click. Pete finished writing down the phone number. "Okay, I got a meeting with him at his home; now all I have to do is get there."

"I'll take care of that," said Gen. Lawson and he left the office.

The General walked into the Chief of Station office and sat down on a chair. "I need a fast plane, destination Andrews Air Base; one passenger; need to have him there in 2 days." The Chief of Station lifted his phone and pressed a button. "Roger, I need a fast bird, destination Andrews, one passenger." The Chief listened to whoever was on the other end of the line. "Gen. Lawson, can your passenger leave this afternoon?"

"Hell yes, anytime."

"Okay, the bird will be here in about 2 hours; was scheduled to leave for Andrew's; will stop by and pick up your passenger."

"Thanks, I'll get him ready." Gen. Lawson briefed Pete; told him to travel in his fatigues, and take civilian clothes with him. "I don't want you to contact Betty until this is over. I'll take care of the POWs east of Pakxe in the morning. Go and see Wallo and tell him you will be gone a few days, but not where."

"Okay, I'll pack my bags and then go over."

Pete walked into the hospital; Wallo was lying with his head propped up. He glanced at Pete as he walked over to his bed, then handed him the recorder. "I'm done with this, Lieutenant. There might be some jumble and timeframe overlaps, but I think it's complete."

"Thanks, I'll be gone a few days; don't do anything crazy while I'm gone."

"Lieutenant, have you known me to do anything that was not above board?"

"Oh, God, I haven't got the time to remind you. You take care and I'll see you in a few days."

"Just remember your promise, Lt. I'll see you when I see you; have a good trip."

Chapter 24

Pete landed at Andrews Air Base; he and one other passenger deplaned inside a large hanger. He was wearing his Delta Force camouflage fatigues and his green beret. Looking around, he saw a young woman standing just inside the hanger doors waving at him. Carrying his hanging bag and utility grip, he walked over to her. "Pete? I was told by my father to just call you Pete. I'm your driver, Pat."

"Nice to see you again, Pat; I remember when you were just a teenage girl; nature has been kind to you."

"My Dad said to be careful of you."

"Oh! I think your Dad has me mixed up with someone else," said Pete as they walked up to a large black sedan. "There is a hook inside the back door where you can hang your bag; just place the other bag on the back seat."

"How did you get through the security gate?"

"My Dad knows a lot of people."

"You have to excuse me, Pat; it has been a long trip and my brain is not awake yet."

The drive was pleasant and the heavy sedan was comfortable and could easily lull you to sleep. "I have been told not to ask you any questions about where you came from or what you are doing; so you have to carry on the conversation because it's easy to lose your concentration driving this big tank."

"Yes, I see what you mean; tell me about yourself; I know you don't want to me to remind you about the last time I saw you and the bad news I brought."

"Oh, God, a lot has happened since then - college, growing up, marriage, working to help put my husband through Law School, buying a house, and two children – a boy and girl."

"Didn't you marry a soldier?"

"Yes, Army, Delta Force; was going to make the Army his career but was badly wounded in that rescue fiasco in Iran and lost his right foot at the ankle."

"What is your married name?"

"Kennedy."

"Know your husband well; went through the 2nd Delta Force class at Ft. Bragg; damn good man. I didn't go to Iran; I stayed at Ft. Bragg and kept the Delta Force training going. Charlie Beckwith took the Force over there."

"Please don't mention Beckwith's name if you meet my husband; there is a lot of hidden anger there."

"You don't have to explain; your husband and I are on the same page there."

They were now driving on a tree-lined road over in Virginia. The homes had land around them and were definitely in the high rent district across from D.C. Pat pulled into a long graveled driveway and up to an old mansion. "Are you sure this is the correct address?"

"Yes, this had been in the family for generations; gets upgraded about every 10-15 years. My Dad wouldn't live anywhere else." Pete grabbed his bags and followed Pat into the house. To say it was well decorated would be an understatement. Pat's Mom came and greeted Pete. "Nice to see you again; you certainly have moved up in the ranks since I last saw you. You look good but tired, Peter." Mrs. Clifton gave Pete a hug and told him a room had been prepared for him and to get some rest; it would be 3-4 hrs. before her husband came home and to make himself comfortable. Pete thanked her and followed Pat upstairs to a large room. "We try to make our guests comfortable." She opened the door to a large bathroom. "If you need anything, just dial 0 on the phone and a maid will come up and help you." Pete looked at her. "You know, Pat, you are still the Pat I remember from 1969; it's a good thing your husband went through our Delta course, otherwise I don't think he could handle you."

"Keep your comments to yourself, mister, or I'll tell my Dad you tried to grab me," said Pat with a smile on her face as she was leaving the room. "Thanks for picking me up, Pat, and say hello to your husband."

"See you later snake eater," she said as she closed the door.

Pete put his things way and took a long hot shower, shaved, and brushed his teeth. Putting on his jogging outfit and sweat socks, he laid down on the bed and fell asleep. He felt someone shaking his shoulder; slowly opening his eyes he was looking at Senator Clifton. Pete sat up rubbing his eyes. "I'm sorry, but I fell asleep."

"Don't be sorry, that's a hell of a long flight, Pete, go wash up and I'll meet you downstairs. Your outfit is fine." The Senator left. Pete did his toiletry and put on a pair of jogging shoes; good thing they were new. He went downstairs and the Senator, dressed in a jogging suit, greeted him. "Thank you for seeing me and putting me up in your home," said Pete shaking the Senator's hand. "Let's go out on the back porch, I'm having a beer, how about you?" Pete told him that sounded great. They sat down in overstuffed chairs in a large screened-in porch. "We are completely alone and I have given instructions that we are not to be disturbed, so start from the beginning."

Pete related the entire story leaving nothing out. The Senator would interrupt him once in a while asking Pete to repeat something. "This is totally incredible that we are treating American POWs in this way. I'm glad you came to me; we have to tread carefully on how we handle this, which I don't have to tell you."

"I think General Hammond has friends in the FBI and Mr. Carpenter has moved up in the State Department hierarchy so there is that to take into consideration," said Pete putting his beer can on a small table. "Do you remember Senator Rose?"

"Yes, I do," said Pete with a smile. "Well, he is one of the few Senators I trust. He is Chairman of the Intelligence Committee and has deep resources. The problem is how much we tell anyone; the other concern is that we need to act fast; we have a lot of lives that depend on it. Let me give Senator Rose a call to see if he can come over tonight." Senator Clifton left to make the call. Pete thought about Senator Rose when he had met him some years back. Senator Clifton came back. "Rose will be here tonight; let's go in and have some supper; I'm starving."

The Senator led the way into the dining room; it was just the two of them and Mrs. Clifton. The talk around the able was light and touched upon Pete's visit in n'69, when he had brought the news of their nephew's death in Vietnam. Pete mentioned Pat and what a great looking young lady their daughter had become. "She definitely takes after her mother," said Pete. "They have two young children; you would think that they are something special and are smarter and better behaved and better looking than any other children in the U.S. the way she hovers over them," said the Senator with a smile on his face. "I have a wife and two daughters back at Ft. Bragg and I can tell you I know exactly what you mean," said Pete smiling at both of them. "Will you get a chance to go down there or call them while you are here?"

"No, that I can't do." Mrs. Clifton looked at her husband who shook his head. The topic was dropped.

"Sam Rose is coming over in a few minutes; no calls or interruptions no matter who it is." The Senator placed his napkin on the table and rose. "If you need to use the facilities, Pete, it would be a good idea to do so. You remember Senator Rose."

"Yes, Sir, how could I forget? Thank you for a delicious meal, Mrs. Clifton."

"Pete, please call me Liz, Mrs. Clifton sounds so formal and to be quite frank with you, so old."

"That is not going to be easy for me, so if I slip, well, it's just that you being a Senator's wife and me being in the military. I think I've said it, but thank you for making me feel so welcome in your home and stealing your husband's attention when you two should be having quality time."

"Have you ever thought about becoming a politician, Pete, you certainly have the personality for getting votes."

"I mentioned the very same thing to him some years ago when he came to see me on the Hill," said the Senator. "If you ever meet my wife, she will tell you I would fail miserably as a politician considering the work I do."

Pete went up to his room and freshened up. He had mixed feelings about meeting Senator Rose again. The Senator had been very vocal the last time Pete had met him. If Senator Clifton felt that he could be of some help that was what mattered. Pete went downstairs and was met by Senator Rose who had just arrived. "Is this to be a continuing saga of Peter Compton?" asked Senator Rose holding out his hand to Pete smiling. "It's a pleasure to meet you again, Senator Rose, and

I'm afraid that again like last time I'm emotionally attached to a sordid affair."

"This young soldier doesn't forget much, does he, throwing my own words back at me from the last time we met." Senator Rose was directing his comments to Senator Clifton. "No, he doesn't, but let's head out to the porch and get a plan worked out."

"Can I get you gentlemen something to drink? asked Senator Clifton's wife. "Water would be welcome, Liz," replied Senator Rose. She brought them each a glass of ice water.

"Okay, Pete, let's have it" said Senator Rose. Pete related everything he had told Senator Clifton. The Senator interrupted Pete several time asking him to repeat something. When Pete had finished, Senator Rose looked at him. "We are talking about a tragedy of monumental proportion here, Pete. This is a crime that has to be taken care of immediately. We need two people here tonight, the Chairman of the Joint Chief of Staff and Holbrook from State. I don't want any staff members here. I need to use your phone. I have their home phone numbers."

"Use the gray phone in my study, Sam." Senator Rose came back. "They were both on their way out to a function; the chairman will have his driver with him; Holbrook is alone and should be here in about 45 minutes. "Pete, you do make waves; are you sure we have a go from the Laotians to hit the other camps?"

"As long as we keep it low key and no news media or political ramifications; they want nothing to do with the Vietnamese anymore."

"Do we need to send more troops over there or medical people?"

"No, we are fine; more people will only muddy the water; we just need an antidote for these poor POWs, and Carpenter has what we need. I know he won't or hasn't destroyed the documents because he can use them in the future when the time is right for promotion or job assignment. General Hammond, I don't know, he has been more than helpful, but he has an agenda, whatever it is."

Mrs. Clifton escorted two men into the porch. The two Senators and Pete stood up as introductions were made. "I know Col. Compton; good to you again," said the Chairman. Mrs. Clifton brought in two more ice water glasses and then excused herself. "We asked you over here to listen to Pete; when he is through, we have to formulate a plan that cannot leak out to anyone - friends or staff members. The President will not be briefed."

Pete again narrated the story and events leaving nothing out. When he was finished, the two new arrivals just sat and looked at Pete. "You know Hammond and Lawson are the best of friends," said the Chairman. "Yes, Sir, Gen. Lawson was devastated when I told him. Gen. Hammond has helped us on numerous occasions over the past years and it was a shock to the both of us, but if we look at the timeline of events, it coincides with everything that has happened. The question that Gen. Lawson and I talked about was did someone higher at MACV HQ instruct Gen. Hammond to send the translation and documents to the State Department or the ambassador to Vietnam at that time? That could make sense. This is not a witch hunt by Gen. Lawson or myself, but to see the POWs dying in front of us, you do become emotionally attached to this sordid affair. The doctors are working literally around the clock; they have the latest equipment and each time we have asked for help, Gen. Hammond has been there for us. He might not be aware that the documents he sent to the State Department have a bearing on this; we didn't think that we should be the ones that told him."

"Carpenter has influence through his family; his is ambitious but we are talking about hundreds of POWs, maybe thousands. Okay, what to do?" said Holbrook. Senator Rose looked around. "Who knows you are here, Pete?"

"Only this household."

"Good, you go and relax and we'll take it from here. Thanks for doing what you are doing professionally and for bringing this to our attention." Pete left and went up to his room and fell asleep.

"Before we start, I want to say something about Gen. Lawson and Col. Compton. I want them promoted when they return from Thailand." Senator Clifton was addressing the Chairman of the JCS. "I second that," said Senator Rose. "This is the 2nd time that young Colonel has prevented a news media extravaganza."

"Gen. Lawson is slated to get his 3rd star when he returns and will take over the 18th Airborne Corps at Ft. Bragg. Col. Compton will get his first star in about 4 months, but we can promote him and the General when they return. Col. Compton will take over the JFK Center for Special Warfare. He will probably have my job someday."

Early the next morning, Pete was awakened by Senator Clifton. "Get your traveling clothes on; you are heading back to Thailand. There is a plane waiting for you at Andrews. Breakfast is waiting downstairs and so is your driver." Pete got up and dressed in the same fatigues he arrived in, packed his bags, and carried them downstairs. Pat greeted him and led him into the kitchen. "How do you want your eggs, Pete?" Mrs. Clifton asked. "Sunny side up – firm if it's not too much trouble," he said taking a cup of coffee from Pat. "Pat, have you made your father mad at you by not only picking me up but also driving me back to the airport?"

"It's only a short distance this morning; a helicopter is flying you to Andrews; too much traffic in the morning." Breakfast was ham, eggs, toast, and strong coffee, Pete's favorite. "Mrs. Clifton, I mean Liz, is there any chance of you adopting me? I have never eaten so good in my life."

"I wanted to adopt a young Captain some years back that seemed lost trying to explain the death of our nephew, with tears in his eyes. I know Pat here had a crush on you."

"Mom, please let some things be; I was in high school then. I will admit that after you left, Pete, I became very interested in the Green Berets." Pete finished his breakfast and stood up, gave Mrs. Clifton a hug and told Pat to lead the way.

The Senator came out of his study and gave Pete a large envelope. "Everything was taken care of last night, Pete; this is the original document with the translation; take good care of it. We contacted Col. Lindor's HQ and the doctors have the antidote now." Pete shook his hand and thanked him and Mrs. Clifton for making him feel so welcome in their home. Pete walked out to the car with Pat and deposited his bags in the back seat. The ride was short. "I didn't tell my husband you were here; Dad said it was close hold."

"Tom understands; treat him good, Pat, he was one of the best that has gone through that course, and believe me it's tough!" They were at an old air strip where Pat pulled onto the runway and up to a hangar where a helicopter had its rotors turning. Pete collected his bags and walked over to where Pat was standing and gave her a kiss on her cheek as he thanked her. "See you snake eater, have a good trip back." Pat got back in the car and dabbed her eyes as she watched Pete climb into the helicopter. How could she still have feelings for that man? "Grow up, Pat," she said out loud to herself as she drove on. Back at the house, Mrs. Clifton was having a cup of coffee with her husband. "You know, Liz, if it was up to Pat she would have kept Pete here."

"I know, she never got over that man; she and Tom have

a good life, but I know her."

"Liz, that train is long gone."

Chapter 25

Pete was the only passenger on the plane, it was a luxury model and he made himself comfortable. He was introduced to two other pilots who sat in the back. When they stopped for refueling, the crew switched giving the initial pilots a break. The last refueling stop was Bangkok and then on to Col. Lindor's Headquarters. Pete got out and was greeted by Gen. Lawson and Col. Lindor. The plane never shut down but turned around and took off. "Let's go over to the mess hall. I know you're hungry," said the General. They joined the Chief of Station, Jack Martin, and Bob Miller at their table. "Well," said Gen. Lawson. Pete related everything that had happened. He started eating and noticed Bob Miller's bandaged arm. "What happened to our arm?"

"Bob went in with the Delta Force east of Pakxe and got wounded along with five of the Delta Force," said Gen. Lawson.

"When the Vietnamese at the two camps saw the C-123s land, they shot all the POWs – 42 of them. There were 35 Vietnamese soldiers there including a Colonel; none of them made it; both camps were burned - only ashes remain."

Pete pushed his half eaten meal away. "How are the Delta Force people?" Pete asked not looking at anyone. "Four were lightly wounded and still in the hospital. The 5^(th) one is serious and might lose his right hand," said Jack Martin. "No, he won't," said Pete opening his bag and taking out a large thick envelope which he handed to Gen. Lawson. "From Senator Clifton."

"I'm going to my quarters and get rid of my baggage then over to the hospital to check on the men."

"We are having a meeting in Col. Lindor's office in half an hour," said Gen. Lawson. Pete left not saying a word. He went to the hospital and asked a doctor how the men were doing, specifically about the most serious one.

The doctor went over to his desk and placed some x-rays on a light board. "We have taken care of the major problems and he is resting; I would like to say he is stable, but I can't. His right hand is a big if – it might have to come off. Here's the x-ray." Pete looked at it and smiled. "Have you talked to the Walter Reed doctors about the hand?"

"No, should I?"

"Keep that hand elevated and I'll be right back." Pete went over to where Dr. Thomas and his Walter Reed team were working and asked if they had the antidote. Dr. Thomas looked up from his microscope at Pete and shook his head. Pete was dumbfounded. "What do you mean; you got it two days ago your time."

"We have been at it around the clock but nothing yet; sorry Pete."

"Have any of you done any orthopedic work?" Dr. Thomas said he had spent 5 years in that field before he went into research. Pete asked if he could come with him for a few minutes. They headed over to the area where Pete had just left the doctor.

"Will you show Dr. Thomas the x-ray of the hand you just showed me?" The doctor again placed it on the light board. "That can be fixed; I don't see any foreign matter in there; keep giving him antibiotics and keep his hand elevated." Pete showed both doctors his own right hand. Dr. Thomas stared at Pete. "I saw pictures of that hand in my text book some years back. So you were the one at Walter Reed back in 1965-66?" Pete told them about it and excused himself. He went over to Wallo's section and asked a doctor how he was doing. The doctor looked at Pete and shook his head. Pete thanked the doctor and went over towards Col. Lindor's office. "Son of a bitch," he said out loud. Wallo was gone.

Pete took a seat; everyone was there. Gen. Lawson handed Pete the envelope he had brought back. Pete took out the papers and read the note Senator Clifton had written stating that these were the original documents that Carpenter had in his safe. Pete studied the papers and the translation. He looked around at the faces looking at him. "These are bogus, the original documents were written in Cyrillic Russian letters; these are in our letters but in the Russian language; believe me, I saw them numerous times while getting my ass chewed by Pentagon East warriors in Saigon. I just talked to Dr. Thomas and his team; they are not happy campers. We have been had and by people I know and trusted except by Holbrook from State; I had never met him before. The documents I handed in to MACV G-2 had two bullet holes in them; these are forged and furthermore I will bet you the two people involved have been given new jobs. This stinks, not to mention the con job I was given. I will tell you all this - I will someday somewhere confront those two individuals responsible for this. Our POWs never had a chance and neither will these two individuals, that's a promise."

"Pete, I think you owe it to Senator Clifton to tell him

about the documents; I don't think he knew about them. Col. Lindor handed Pete the phone; the call went through. Pete asked whoever answered the phone to speak to Senator Clifton, giving his name. Pete listened as a frown formed on his face. "Thank you," was all he said. Pete was staring at Gen. Lawson. "The Senator's car was hit by a garbage truck; the driver of the car was killed instantly; Senator Clifton is in the hospital not expected to make it. The driver of the garbage truck escaped – no one saw him or could identify him. This is how Hammond's boss in the G-2 section was killed in Saigon. You were right, Gen. Lawson; I don't think Senator Clifton knew. The Senate is holding an emergency meeting to designate an interim majority leader and according to Senator's Clifton's secretary, it will be Senator Rose. How interesting the same guy who didn't want me at the meeting; I was the only one who could identify the documents."

General Lawson picked up the phone and asked for the Chairman of the JCS office. A man answered but it wasn't Hammond. The General asked for Hammond but was told that Gen. Hammond was on leave and was then heading for his new job at NATO HQ in Brussels."

"Are you his replacement, this is Gen. Lawson, a good friend of his?"

"Yes, Sir, I'm Colonel Graham, can I help you, Gen. Lawson? As a matter of fact, I have a note from the Chairman to give you a call. The old man wants to know how many camps you have left that the Laotians have told you about."

"We are going into the last two as we speak."

"He will send you orders to terminate your operation when the two camps are taken care of. The Air Force will send planes, C141s, to Bangkok when your operation is complete; send all remains to Hawaii even if they have not been processed."

"Will do, good to talk to you Col. Graham and congratulations on your new job; looking forward to meeting you."

"Yes, Sir, the same here, General."

General Lawson looked around at the others. "Well, Hammond has a new job; I'm sure Carpenter has a new assignment also. We are to terminate our operation as soon as the last two camps are taken care of; orders are on their way." Col. Lindor's phone rang; he answered and listened. "Thanks," was all he said. "That was my assistant at Loei; got a message from both Delta Force leaders. Only dead POWs in both camps; one of them had POWs not buried, while the other had shallow graves; 64 POWs total between the two camps. They are placing the unburied POWs in body bags and will terminate the mission today; the other camp, it will be tomorrow before they will be back in Loei. In both camps it looked like the Vietnamese left recently and in a hurry. They sent out two small recon units to see if they can locate the Vietnamese," said Col. Lindor leaning back in his chair.

"Are we missing something?" General Lawson was looking at Pete. "We have checked 10 camps but only 6 had POWs. There were 150 POWs' bodies at Muong Sai; at Ban Don there were 199; at the other camps the totals were a lot lower. Pete, take your team up to Muong Sai tomorrow morning and take a doctor with you. I know it haven't been 11 days yet, but spend some time up there; check on the sick woman and the ones with TB sores. Talk to the leader and see if he has communication with their other villages. I know it's a long shot, but like you said, it's the largest tribe in northern Laos and who knows, we might learn something. If nothing else it will show good will and that they can rely on our word or promise; also Col. Lindor can benefit for future help."

"Okay, I'll get the men. Bob, check which of the doctors are getting bored here and would like to have an adventure and meet some nice people. Let's meet in the conference room with gear in an hour. Col. Lindor, can we borrow that GP tent again?"

"You got it; I'll have it placed aboard your plane and I'll alert the Air Force to have reps at your meeting." Everyone going into the meeting was briefed and a pallet of rations was added since they would be in there a week.

Chapter 26

At 0830 they landed at Muong Sai. A small delegation of villagers came out to the air strip to greet Pete and his team. He explained to the leader of the village that they had come back to check on the woman who had been sick and also help anyone else who had any ailments. The leader told the rest of the men what Pete had said and they all nodded and smiled. Pete was told he could place the tent where it had been before. The plane took off for Col. Lindor's HQ. The doctor and medic checked the woman who had been sick. She was fine, but was told to take the pills the medic had given her each day. The sick call was started and the doctor and medic had their hands full.

Pete, Bob, and two of the Captains who spoke Laotian (spoken by the leader and some of the elders) talked to them about the Vietnamese and if the other villages in the tribe had seen POWs and Vietnamese. The leader and his men talked among themselves. They have not heard anything but would send men to the villages and question them. They should be back within 2 days. Pete had brought a map and the two Captains showed them where Muong Sai was located and wanted to know where the other villages were. They had not seen a map before and were having a difficult time pointing out the other villages, but pointed in the direction where they were located. The team was at Muong Sai for 4 days before the men came back from the distant villages. None of the villages had seen Vietnamese or American POWs. Pete radioed back to Gen. Lawson and told him. The General said it was worth a try and the Chief of Station had used his resources, but no new camps.

Gen. Lawson had received orders to close down the operation. He had talked to Col. Graham and Wallo's urn with ashes was waiting in Hawaii and Col. Peter Compton could claim it on his way home. Gen. Hammond had taken care of Wallo's back pay and for Pete to let them know how and when he wanted to pick it up. The Army would pay for Pete and his wife to go to Finland and settle with Wallo's family there. Gen. Hammond had arranged it all. The POWs' bodies were now all in Hawaii and Loei had been closed down as far as medical personnel. The Delta Force was on its way back to Ft. Bragg. The mobile hospitals were back in Okinawa. Gen. Lawson had told Pete he wouldn't recognize Col. Lindor's HQ when he got back. Pete told Gen. Lawson to send a plane in 2 days to pick them up. The villagers were grateful for the medical treatment; the doctor said they should be done tomorrow with sick call and that he was overcome by the generosity of the villagers. They had brought him and the medic bracelets and colorful woven blankets. "I think we have scored some points with the village, and they don't forget. Gen. Lawson sent the plane and the villagers lined the air strip as they took off.

The return to Col. Lindor's HQ brought some interesting news. The Chief of Station told Pete and Bob Miller that Roger Carpenter was now at the U.S. Embassy in Helsinki, Finland; not as the Ambassador but as 1st Secretary, a definite promotion. Pete looked at Gen. Lawson but nothing was said. Later that afternoon, Pete was sitting in Gen. Lawson's office – just the two of them. "Pete, I know what is going through that head of yours, but don't act on it. You and Betty will fly over to Finland; don't do anything that will upset her. We and your team will leave here in 3 days, stop for 2 days in Hawaii, pick up Wallo's urn, and then travel to Travis AFB and back to Ft. Bragg. Three days later you and I will report to the Chairman of the JCS office - for what I don't know, but I'm not looking forward to it. According to Col. Graham, we can bring our wives, which seems kind of strange."

"I would like to bring Betty and visit Senator Clifton's family and pay my respects; that's going to be a tough one – his family was very close."

"I think we should give them one of those small statues of a paratrooper inscribed to him and his family for the help he has been to us; I know the silver ones cost, but I'll chip in and you can give it to them."

"That would be nice; I saw his study and I know he doesn't have one – he was a true friend."

The departure from Col. Lindor's HQ was solemn. Col. Lindor informed them he had been extended and his program would continue with help from Langley. Goodbyes were said and the team climbed aboard the C-123 for the trip to Bangkok and onto Hawaii aboard a C-141. At Hickam AB, a representative from the Graves Registration met the plane and Pete signed for Wallo's urn. At Pope AB, next to Ft. Bragg, they were greeted by Nancy and Betty who escorted them over to two brand new cars. "So your money is safe, is it? I told you when these two ladies get together, it's going to cost us."

"They are devious and bear watching," said Pete giving Betty another kiss. "I'll stop by the JFK Center and get that statue and have it inscribed; it will be ready in a day or so;

I'll see you in 3 days," said Gen. Lawson getting into Nancy's new sports car.

"Well, what do you think? It's not a sports car but it's what we need," said Betty getting into the new station wagon and heading for home. "The girls are at their tennis lessons so you'll have to put up with their mother for a few hours."

"I guess I can handle that," said Pete with a smile. The reunion was great; the girls were full of news and it was good to be home. "Nancy and I got a message; we are to accompany you and the General to Washington in 3 days. My parents are coming down to stay with the girls; what's that all about?"

"I don't know, our trip to Thailand was a disaster; I'll tell you what I can. You and I are going to Finland in a week or so."

"What are we going to do in Finland?" Pete told her about Wallo and what he had promised, but not the circumstances. A military sedan picked them up and drove them to Pope AB where Gen. Lawson and Nancy were waiting aboard a small Air Force plane. They brought their luggage aboard and got comfortable.

"I picked up the paratrooper statue we talked about; they did a nice job with the inscription. I'll give it to you when we get to our hotel in Washington."

"Who are you giving a statue to?" asked Nancy as they were taking off. "It's for a Senator's family who are friends of Pete. He did us some favors." Their hotel accommodations were luxurious; at dinner that night the conversation was light; the main topic was whether the General and Pete were getting kicked out of the Army and why; not a word was said about Thailand.

The next morning at 11:00 a.m. they were picked up in an Army sedan. The General and Pete were in their Class A greens; the ladies looked stunning. They were escorted up to the Army's Chief of Staff office where introductions were made. The Chief of Staff walked them down to the Chairman of the JCS Office where a small crowd of senior officers were waiting. The Chairman walked in and a Colonel read the first order, "Attention to orders." Col. Compton was promoted to a one-star General and General Lawson received his 3rd star. Congratulations were offered by the Chairman who knew Betty's father. The other officers chimed in their congratulations. The Chairman asked the Army Chief of Staff, Gen. Lawson, Gen. Compton, and their wives to come into his office. They all took seats and the Army Chief of Staff told the two newly promoted Generals their new assignments. The wives thanked them for leaving them at Ft. Bragg. The Chairman asked if the wives had been briefed on the operation in Thailand. The answer, of course, was "no."

"I'm just going to tell you two ladies that your husbands performed a delicate and tragic mission over there; a mission they will never forget nor can they adequately be thanked for. The details of this mission is classified beyond Top Secret and as a nation, we are extremely grateful to you. General Compton and your wife will leave for Finland from Andrews AB a week from today. Transportation from Ft. Bragg has been laid onto Andrews. If you have any problems, please contact my aide, Col. Graham. Again, congratulations for well-deserved promotions to both of you and your wives."

They returned to the Army Chief of Staff's office. He briefed them on the change of command ceremonies which would take place in 3 weeks for Gen. Lawson and in a month for Gen. Compton. "Call me if you need anything. You have 2 days here in Washington; I know you, Gen. Compton, want to visit Senator Clifton's family; tell your driver when you want to go over there and he will take you. The two newly promoted Generals along with their wives thanked the Army Chief of Staff for everything and departed. No one said anything until they arrived at their hotel. Pete told the driver to pick him up tomorrow at 11:30 for the trip over to Virginia.

"Well, this calls for a nice lunch and I will make the arrangements," said Betty. "Your uniforms, Generals, are the correct dress." Betty went over to the hotel concierge and talked to him. She returned and said, "We have reservations at a very famous restaurant in 1 hour; where Pete took me on our first date."

"Pete, do you remember the date back in '69 when you asked Betty out?"

"First of all, I didn't ask her out; she asked me out and even picked the restaurant. Right now my mind is in overload; I don't even remember my birthday right now."

"Let's powder our noses, Betty, and let these senior officers chat," said Nancy guiding Betty to the powder room. "Well, General, how does it feel and did you know about the promotion?"

"Yes, I knew but not officially. I thought it would be some months from now."

"So did I," said General Lawson. "Who told you?"

"I got it from the Agency; but the word was 5 months from now"

"You have too many friends," said Gen. Lawson as the ladies joined them. The lunch was great and Betty related the story about her and Pete's short courtship. "Betty, you don't have to tell everything, Nancy and the General will think we had to get married."

"Well we almost did, Pete, let's be honest." Back at their room in the hotel, Betty gave Pete a nice soft kiss. "You, know, Pete, I have never been to bed with a General, let's go."

The next morning, an Army sedan picked up Pete and Betty for the drive over to the Virginia address of the Clifton's. Pete had the nice statue wrapped in a box to present to Mrs.

Clifton. He had called last night to make sure they were home. They pulled up to the house and Pat and her husband, Tom, came out and greeted them. Introductions were made. Mrs. Clifton was waiting in the house for them. She came forward and hugged Pete and held him. She looked up at him and said, "My husband thought of you, Pete, as the son we never had." Tears were flowing down her cheeks. Pete gave her a kiss on the cheek and then introduced Betty. "Let's sit down," said Mrs. Clifton. Pete got up and presented her with the box containing the statue. Upon unwrapping it, she lifted it up so everyone could see it. Gen. Lawson had gotten the exclusive statue reserved for high ranking dignitaries. Mrs. Clifton read the inscription out loud as more tears flowed down her face. "My husband would have considered this a high honor and he would have kept it in a place of honor in his study; he was very fond of you, Pete. You are a very lucky woman, Betty, to have such a fine husband."

"Would you please say that a little louder, Mrs. Clifton?" Everyone laughed; the tension was broken. "Pete, you can't fool an old woman, you know you are very lucky to have a wife who supports a soldier husband; let's go into the dining room and have some lunch."

The conversation around the table was flowing and light. Pete related about Tom going through the Delta Force and being the outstanding graduate; something his wife Pat had not heard before. Pete was congratulated on his promotion and on his new assignment. Pat asked Betty about when and how she had met Pete. Betty told "almost" everything and had the others laughing; she told them Pete had no chance – she knew she was going to marry him. Mrs. Clifton took a quick glance at her daughter Pat, whose eyes were on Pete. When they walked out of the house, Tom walked them to the car and was making small talk with Pete. Mrs. Clifton and Pat were having another cup of coffee. "Let it go, Pat," said her mother. "Like your father told you, "that train is long gone.""

"He is quite a man," said Pat and sipped her coffee.

On the way back to the hotel, Pete stopped by the Pentagon and went up to the Chairman's office and talked to Col. Graham who had Wallo's back pay in the form of a government check, as well as, Pete and Betty's travel orders to Finland. Pete thanked Col. Graham for his help and departed. Back at the hotel, Gen. Lawson and Pete talked about the Finland trip; the ladies were out shopping. Pete informed the General that he had Wallo's medals and decorations being framed back at Ft. Bragg and that he would present them to his brother and sisters. "Pete, Wallo's brother, who by the way is almost 20 yrs. younger than Larry, is in what Finland calls their Secret Service and is the number two man in that service. I will never admit that I told you this, and if it comes up you will deny that I told you, understand? What I'm saying is don't get too friendly with Larry's brother. Travel in civilian clothes and keep a low profile; you know who is in our Embassy over there and you know the protocol. You have to visit the Embassy within 3 days because of your rank; they already have a copy of your travel orders."

"I know, Betty and I will make arrangements to meet the two sisters and his brother, relay Larry's request, hand over the urn, check, and decorations, then head back to the States on the first available plane. I want to be at Ft. Bragg for the change of command ceremony where you become the C.G. of the 18th Airborne Corps. Did you ever in your wildest dream think that you would get such an assignment?"

"I'll tell you, and it's between us, there was a time when I had serious doubts about making Captain; in fact, when I was a Captain I knew for sure I would not make the rank of Major. I had a hard time convincing Nancy to marry me and

I was a Major then. She had heard too many stories about me as a Lieutenant and as a Captain. There are no secrets in the Army and at Ft. Bragg where I spent most of my junior years; it's a very small community. It was after I got married and had responsibilities, at least I thought I had, that I started getting serious about my career. When Nancy had her miscarriage and we found out she couldn't have any more children, we really became close and I was determined to see that she had a good life and a secure one. I have never told this to anyone else, Pete. I don't know if Nancy has told Betty; it she did, it was on the QT, and girls talk."

"I didn't know, and knowing Betty, if Nancy had told her not to tell anyone – I would never hear of it. There has never been any pillow talk in our house. Can I ask you one question?"

"Go ahead."

"Did you have something to do with my star?"

"The short and long of it is no. I knew when I came back from the Pentagon prior to our Thailand mission that you would get your star in about 6 months. I was told by the Army Chief of Staff not to say anything to you. I told Nancy, how should I phrase it, "under extreme duress.""

"These ladies have their ways. Speaking of which, here they come with bags of new clothes and accessories. They are hard on the wallet."

"What was that?" asked Nancy. "Pete here was just saying you two deserve everything and anything."

"Well, it's good to hear you have learned as General's wives we need to dress the part."

"Let's go up to our rooms and we'll show you what we have bought with your promotion pay."

Chapter 27

Betty's mom and dad stayed and took care of the girls while Pete and Betty headed for Finland. It was an upscale Air Force fleet passenger plane with about 20 passengers, mostly Embassy or State Department people. As Betty and Pete walked into the terminal in Helsinki, a man in civilian clothes walked up to them and told them to come with him; they had not gone through customs which would only be a formality; they followed him and arrived at the small luggage area. Pete was carrying the wrapped decoration and awards display. The man asked in good English which suitcases belonged to them. Pete pointed them out and the man signaled to two men who came over and took their luggage. They were escorted out of the terminal to the waiting cars. He then introduced himself as Jonas Wallo, Larry's brother. Pete gave the display to Betty and hugged Jonas and shook his hand; he introduced Betty to Jonas. "Let's get in the first car; your luggage is safe with my two men and they will follow us. I didn't want you to go through customs which would only have been a formality, but you would then appear in our computer system. Here in Finland, the Government knows when you go to the toilet; it's the same in Sweden and Norway. It's our way of keeping track of people. I know all about you; had a letter from a medic who took care of Larry after you rescued him. It was a sad business but here you are keeping your promise to my brother, and for that we are grateful. You will stay in my country house and rest for a day or so; traveling east is rough on your system. In 2 days my two sisters will join us and we will celebrate Larry's life. You have no idea how much the family appreciates you two taking the time to do this – not only for Larry but for his family also. I have done all the talking; please ask any questions you have."

"Betty and I are grateful for our reception here in Finland, but let me make one thing clear, Larry was one of my best friends – he saved my life in Vietnam in 1965 - so there is that."

"I know - the last letter I had from my brother written in April of '65, which I still have, described a young Lieutenant who reminded him of himself, totally reckless and quick on the trigger; could that be you?"

"You have just described my husband," said Betty with a smile. "Although I didn't know him until 1969, he hasn't changed to this day." They all laughed. "I also have to report to my Embassy within 3 days or they will red flag me."

"I know, after you rest a car will take you to your Embassy and bring you back to my house. We are here, even though it's wooded, Finland distances are not like in America where you travel for days and days. We are only 25 minutes from your Embassy."

It was a beautiful timbered house with furnishings of wood and leather; they were escorted in by Larry's brother. "This is a typically Finish country house; it is larger than I wanted it to be, but then I'm married and I don't know about America, but here in Finland the wife is the boss and she got it the way she wanted it."

"It's the same in America, the wives are the boss," said Pete. "We use it on weekends and in the summer. There is a nice lake adjoining the property and we have a sauna there which we will use. A maid and handyman are also here; the maid speaks a little English." They were taken up to their rooms and the two men brought their luggage up. "Make yourselves at home; I will see you tonight for dinner. If you get hungry, the maid will fix you a meal. See you tonight – get some rest."

Betty looked at Pete and around the room, went into the bathroom and came back. "This is the kind of house we should have for weekend getaways; my God, did you know about this, Pete, these people are seriously rich; wait until you see the bathroom – it's got everything."

"No, I had no idea; I know that Larry's brother had a good job, but not this good." They unpacked their luggage in an empty closet. "I'm going to take a shower and put something comfortable on; I'm tired," said Betty and went into the bathroom. Pete got undressed and laid down on the bed and fell asleep; Betty returned and fell asleep also.

There was knocking on the door and Pete got up; it was Larry's brother. Pete looked at his watch and saw it was 1830 hrs. "I'm sorry," said Pete. "I guess you were right; we were tired."

"Don't be sorry; we'll eat in 1½ hours if that's alright; casual dress – I'm going to put on my jogging suit. See you later." Pete told Betty who was still not quite awake and then took a shower. They were both wearing jogging suits and sneakers as they came downstairs. The maid met them and escorted them into a casual room where Larry's brother and wife were sitting sipping a drink. Introductions were made. His wife, Laura, was tall and blond, a striking middle aged woman in excellent shape. The maid asked what they would like to drink. Pete looked at his host and asked, "What do you recommend, Jonas?"

"I think something mild, you haven't eaten since you arrived and I want you to enjoy your dinner. Betty, what do you usually drink?"

"A little wine if you have it would be fine and a beer for my husband." Jonas nodded to the maid who brought them their drinks.

Betty and Laura started talking and the word "shopping" was heard. "Pete, let's take a walk around the grounds while the ladies talk shopping." They walked out where it was light and took a trail which led them to a bench with a view over the lake. "This property has been in the family for generations; we had a cabin here but it was old so I tore it down and built the house. My sisters are married and are more comfortable in the city, but come out here on birthdays and at Christmas. What I wanted to ask you is how Larry died; the letter I received from the medic indicated that you would tell me."

"What I'm about to tell you has the highest U.S. classification and I would like it to remain between you and me."

"That's not a problem, you have my word."

Pete told him the entire story. "Are you saying one of the people is at your Embassy here now?"

"Yes he is; his name is Roger Carpenter." Pete told Jonas how he felt about Carpenter, not only because of Larry, but also about the hundreds or perhaps thousands of other American POWs. Jonas remained silent for a while. "You know who I work for, don't you?" Pete nodded his head. "If something were to happen to Mr. Carpenter, does he have a family?"

"No, he is not married."

"We are not allowed to harm people in our organization, but there have been instances. What I'm saying is, if Mr. Carpenter had an accident, it could not happen for at least a year so that you would not be implicated, having been in Finland and met with me."

"I understand and would be forever grateful."

"You know Larry was right about you, you are a lot like him; take that as a compliment."

"Thank you, I will."

"When you leave Finland, you and I will never have any contact; no Christmas cards, no thank you notes, etc. Is that understood?"

"Perfectly," said Pete. "Okay, we will not talk about this again, but know this – I'm in complete agreement with you. Let's finish our walk; the small house you see down here is the sauna; we will use it while you are here; after we get hot and steamy, we jump in the lake to cool off; believe me, we will cool off – the lake is cold. Is your wife a good sport?"

"Oh, yes, she likes adventures."

They rejoined the ladies who were laughing as they walked in. "Pete, we have a problem. I hope you brought your American Express card and your Visa, for when my wife laughs like that, it means it's going to cost me money."

"I'm married to her sister, Jonas, I'm used to it." They all laughed and Laura said the meal was ready. The meal was delicious consisting of medallions of reindeer (fillet mignon), lingonberry, potatoes, and white asparagus. "Everything you are eating comes from Finland including the wine. We call it "humans kost" – "everyday fare." Pete raised his glass to Laura. "If this is "humans kost," you have just got yourselves two new relatives that are staying permanently. I was born and grew up in Norway, so I know what "humans kost is" – "skal."

"You have to excuse my husband," said Betty. "There is only one thing my husband likes more than food; he will do anything for a good meal." Laura looked at Betty and said,

"Are you telling me that Pete and Jonas are related; men have a one-track mind, but you and I wouldn't have it any other way." They all laughed.

"So that you two won't be overwhelmed tomorrow evening when the others get here, I had a fire built in the sauna and you can get initiated to an old Finish custom." They were having desert ice cream with whipped cream and cloudberries on top when Laura explained the sauna to them. "It sounds interesting, and as they say "when in Rome" we would love to participate," said Betty. "The clothes you are wearing are fine; if you need to use the facilities, I would recommend that you use them now." Betty and Laura excused themselves. "When my sisters get here and after our little get-together, they will head to the sauna; they are getting older but they are true Fins." They headed down to the sauna; walking in was almost a shock. The walls and floors were made of birch; one could eat off the floor. It was almost sterile. There were wooden hooks to hang your clothes on and benches on two walls. "This is beautiful," said Betty looking around. "You have to keep the dressing room clean and the sauna itself," said Laura taking her clothes off. Betty looked at Pete who smiled at her and started to undress. When they were naked, Laura said to take a towel from the bench to sit on. Jonas opened the door; there was the smell of steam; benches lined two of the walls and were tiered so you could sit on the upper level where they headed, except for Jonas who took a ladle from a wooden bucket of water and poured out water over an iron grid which contained the hot rocks underneath. Soon the room was steamed; a temperature gauge was on the wall showing the temperature. Soon sweat was pouring out of the occupants. Pete noticed the good shape Laura and Jonas were in. Betty was toned from playing tennis and golf. "Where did you get your scars from, Peter?" asked Laura looking hard at Pete. "Do you want the truth?"

"Of course."

"Being married to Betty is not always easy; she can be rough on you." They all laughed.

"Peter was in Vietnam with Larry and spent some time there," said Jonas. "Oh, I didn't mean to pry, but they are very noticeable; I think, Peter, you are a lucky men to even be here and obviously didn't fight the war sitting behind a desk. You are a fortunate woman, Betty, in more ways than one."

"Oh, I just string along," said Betty giving Pete a kiss on the cheek. After another 5 minutes, Jonas announced they were ready for step #2, and opened the door; they followed Jonas out to the dock and jumped into the lake. There were cries of shock as they hit the cold water; they only stayed in a short while before getting out and back to the dressing room to towel themselves off. "The cold water has a detrimental effect on the men," said Laura looking at Pete and her husband; but fortunately it's not permanent," she said laughing.

"Laura is going into Helsinki around noon, do you want to ride in with her and check in with your Embassy?"

"That would be great, if we are not imposing?"

"No, I'm just going in to pick up something; does Betty have to check-in also?"

"No, I just need her passport."

"Good, Betty and I will do a little window shopping." They were walking up to the house. "Does anyone care for a night cap?" asked Jonas. "Can we beg off?" asked Betty. "After seeing two handsome and virile males, I'm not afraid to say it – I'm ready for bed."

"I am too," said Laura. "Come on, Jonas, its homework time." They slept late; Betty and Pete were ready at noon after a light breakfast and Laura drove to the U.S. Embassy. "I'll pick you up in an hour," said Laura as her and Betty took off.

Pete went into the Embassy after showing the guards his

military identification. He walked up to a desk where a Marine Captain sat and introduced himself. "I would like to see your Military attaché."

"One moment, General Compton." The Captain spoke to someone; a door down the hall opened and a LTC came out and introduced himself to Pete. "Please come with me, Gen. Compton." They entered a large office with a secretary sitting across the room. Pete took a seat and took out his and Betty's passports. The LTC studied them and gave them back to Pete. "We expected you yesterday," he said. "Yes, we were picked up by friends," said Pete. The LTC asked Pete if he knew the person who picked him up at the airport. "No, I had not met Jonas before but he is the brother of a dear departed friend of mine."

"Yes, I know; do you have any idea what your friend's brother's occupation is?"

"No, I don't; in Europe it is impolite to ask a newly acquainted person what he does for a living; didn't they teach you that in Alexandria when you went through the attaché course? I'm here to deliver the urn of his brother's ashes to him and his sisters tonight. I would like to depart Finland on the next available military plane. This is not a social visit."

"I understand; there is a scheduled military plane leaving in 3 days at 0700 hrs. local time. Do you need hotel accommodations until then?"

"No, my friend's brother has placed his country home at our disposal, thank you."

"Do you plan on traveling around the country while you are here?"

"No, I don't and if you have any more questions, call the Chairman of the JCS at the Pentagon; he is the one who sent me here; talk to a Col. Graham – he will patch you through to the old man. If there is nothing else, I have preparations to make for the family's services tonight." Pete stood up and walked to the door. The LTC got up and opened it for him; Pete went out and stood outside the Embassy; he had a feeling someone was looking at him through the upper windows. He walked out through the gates and stood waiting for Laura and Betty to pick him up. He was not happy with the LTC attaché interview. As he was standing there, he brushed the left pocket of his jacket; there was something in it – he let his hand gently brush against the small lump in the pocket; it was hard, probably metal; he didn't want to take it out and look at it here; he had the strange feeling he was being observed.

Laura pulled up and he got in the back seat; placing his finger over his lips, he indicated to Betty he needed some paper to write on. She handed him an envelope she found in the glove compartment. Pete wrote on the envelope, "don't go directly home – drive in the opposite direction then get into traffic." Betty whispered it to Laura who understood. While driving in heavy traffic, Pete took the circular metallic device out of his pocket; he opened the rear window and tossed the device into the open rear window of a passing car with camping gear on its roof; it was heading in the same direction but turned onto a highway going out of town. "Sorry about that but I think our Embassy is playing games with me."

"What are you talking about?" asked Betty with a concerned look on her face. "If I'm not mistaken, they placed a tracking device in my jacket pocket." Betty was about to say something but changed her mind. They were now on the road to Laura's house. When Jonas came home, Pete looked at him and motioned with is head to go outside. He explained about his meeting at the Embassy and the device the LTC has slipped into his pocket. "Was it gray and black in color?"

"Yes," answered Pete. "Well, they can track it on their new computer. The car you placed it in – was it going in your direction?"

"Yes, but it turned and headed out of town on an angle to us."

"That's good; did you see the car's license plate?"

"Yes, it was Swedish, why?"

"Well, if they track it, they will be busy for the next few hours. Let's join the ladies and have a cocktail; my sisters and their husbands will be here shortly.

As they were sitting having a cocktail, Pete explained what he had brought for them. The check was a U.S. Treasury check which Larry wanted them to divide equally amongst the three. He wanted to be buried in the family burial plot. Pete had brought down the large board with a green felt cover with Larry's medals and decorations; also a small picture of Larry from the waist up of Larry in his green beret. The picture was placed in the upper portion of the display case which was covered entirely by glass. It was impressive, to say the least, for Larry was a well decorated officer. "Peter, place the display against the wall with the back to us so when my sisters come they can't see what it is."

There was a knock on the door and the maid let in two elderly women followed by two men. Introductions were made and Pete and Betty met Larry's sisters - Suvi who appeared to be older, and Mariana along with their husbands. They all spoke English to a varying degree of efficiency. The maid got them all a drink as they sat down. Jonas explained what was about to happen and introduced Pete; "the floor is yours, Peter." Pete thanked the sisters for coming and explained his relationship to Larry and their long friendship. He told them he had helped rescue their brother Larry from a Vietnamese prison camp in Laos and brought him and his fellow prisoners to Thailand 2 months ago. The prisoners were weak and had suffered starvation and other diseases. Larry had gotten to the point where he said he felt better than he had in years; it was then that he had told Peter what he wanted done with his years of back pay and where he wanted to be buried.

Larry was a LTC in the U.S. Army Special Forces. Jonas interrupted, "Oberst Lieutenant in Commando Jager." The people in the room were impressed; tears were flowing from his sisters and Laura. Pete got the display case and turned it around leaning it against a small table so they all could see. Pete explained the various medals for bravery which included 3 Purple Hearts. Pete also explained how Larry had saved his life in Vietnam in 1965. Betty handed Pete the urn which he placed on the table and handed the check to Jonas. Pete explained that although Larry had suffered in the prison camps, he had died without pain and like Larry said, "among friends." There was not a dry eye in the room. Pete's last words were, "it was a distinct honor for him to bring Larry back home to the people and country he loved and had fought for."

Everyone got up and hugged and kissed Pete and Betty and thanked them for coming all this way. They took their seats and Jonas took the check, looked at it, and converted the dollar amount to the Finish currency; he told his sisters what their share would be. There was a gasp of disbelief from everyone; the sisters came forward and thanked Pete again and hugged him. He explained that this was not from him but from their brother Larry. "But you brought it to us," said Suvi. Laura came up to Pete and hugged and kissed him again as she thanked him. Laura then announced that the meal was ready. Everyone was seated around the dining room table; the talk around the table was both Finish and English and sometimes mixed. The meal was delicious and one of the sisters sitting next to Pete pointed at a dish and said to "eat those round items," it will make your wife very happy for the next week. The others laughed and Pete ate about four of them.

Jonas announced that he had made arrangements with the

church for tomorrow; the pastor would say a few words at the grave site and Larry's urn would be buried in the family plot. He had ordered a stone with the appropriate inscriptions, but it would take a week for the stone to be ready. Mariana, the youngest sister, asked Betty and Pete if they had ever experienced a Finish sauna. Betty looked at Jonas and Laura and said, "What is a sauna?"

"Oh, we have a surprise for both of you; remember, you have to do exactly what we do," said Mariana laughing. "You Americans are so prudish when it comes to certain things." After the meal, they all headed for the sauna; Betty and Pete took off their clothes and hung them on the wooden pegs. The sisters looked at them and said, "Are you sure you are Americans?"

The ceremony at the church graveyard was short and Larry's urn was buried. Laura took Betty and Pete around Helsinki; it was a modern city. Betty bought necklaces for their daughters. The evening before their departure, Jonas and Laura presented Betty and Pete with a crystal vase made by a prominent Finish artist. On one side was written, "Thank you for being our friends." Betty had tears in her eyes as she thanked them. Jonas drove them to the airport and Betty and Pete boarded their Air Force fleet jet.

Chapter 28

The homecoming was great. Betty's parents told them they were getting too old to keep up with the girls and were happy to see their daughter and son-in-law back. They all attended Gen. Lawson's change of command ceremony. Pete's own change of command was coming up. Gen. Lawson received housing on post - where Generals were required to live. Gen. Lawson and Pete had a chance to talk and Pete briefed him on his Finland travels and also his visit to the U.S. Embassy. Gen. Lawson was dumbfounded when told about the tracking device. "Were you satisfied with the trip and was everything taken care of?"

"Yes, Sir," answered Pete.

A few weeks after Pete's change of command, he was sitting in his office when his aide came in and said there were two gentlemen to see him. Two men in civilian suits were ushered in and introduced themselves. Pete told them he was about to have a cup of coffee and would they like a cup; both said that would be great. Pete took a chair by a small table and his visitors also sat down opposite him. "What can I do for you?"

asked Pete. They both showed their IDs with the FBI. They asked about his trip to Finland and the U.S. Embassy. Pete related the entire trip leaving out the sauna. He thought the LTC at the Embassy was a little aggressive and did not reflect well as an American representative. He had not seen much of the country as this was not a pleasure trip but a promise kept for a soldier friend. "Did you stay at the brother's house?"

"Yes, we did; very nice people."

"Did the brother and his wife stay there also?"

"One of the four nights they stayed; otherwise we were alone with the caretakers, a man and a woman. One afternoon the brother and his two sisters along with their husbands were at the house and we had a little ceremony celebrating my friend's life. It was an emotional time to say the least; the next day we had a ceremony at the grave site by their church, where the urn was buried."

"Were you aware who or what position your host held?"

"Yes, my friend told me before he died that his brother had a good job with Nokia Electronics in Helsinki, why?"

The two FBI agents looked at each other. "When you left the Embassy, did you find anything?"

"No, my host's wife and my wife picked me up and when we were stopped at a traffic light, the car next to us with camping gear on its roof and two children in the back seat were singing and one was hanging out the window of their car; my wife had told me to give them something because they were so cute. I didn't have anything; I checked my pockets and found I had a medallion, grayish in color, so I gave them that and they thought it was nice. My wife said they were from Sweden according to the license plate and emblem. I think that was the only unusual thing, why?"

"The emblem you gave them – had you seen that or anything like it before?"

"You know, now that you mention it, I can't remember picking it up; I think there was some black on it; I'm not sure – I usually don't pick up things and place it in my pocket. What's going on; there must be a reason why you're here? I don't believe my wife and I violated any protocol or broke any laws while we were over there."

"Before you went over to Finland, you visited Senator Clifton's family in Virginia, why?"

"That, gentlemen, is none of your business! Let me just say this – Senator Clifton and his family are very close friends. If you have any more questions, go and see the Chairman of the JCS and the Chief of Staff of the Army; they may or may not fill you in. If there is nothing else, your little fishing expedition is over. Pete got up and pressed a button. His aide came in and escorted the FBI agents out. Pete pushed the red button on his phone and General Lawson answered. "Can we meet for lunch at the Officer's Club today or anywhere else?"

"The Officer's Club in 1 hour."

Pete related to Gen. Lawson his visit by the FBI and what was said. "I can understand the tracking device, but Senator Clifton's family - that sounded like a fishing expedition or else someone is getting nervous."

"I don't know if I told you, but while I was waiting to get picked up at the Embassy, I had the feeling someone was looking at me from the upper windows of the Embassy. I don't know, but you know how you get that sense that someone is at your back or watching you?"

"Let's just drop it and play it low key."

"One other thing - is Gen. Hammond married?"

"No, he is not."

"I remember in Italy when you talked to him, you said - give your regards to his better half."

"That was something which started at West Point when we

were pleabs; you couldn't be married so we thought we would use that phrase when the upper class men were around; for some reason, it irritated them. So we have used it through the years, why?"

"Well, Carpenter is not married either."

"Believe me, I have mulled that one around many times; I don't know, it could be; you think you know people and then, well, you don't. How are things going at the JFK Center?"

"I'm going to move some people; there is definitely nepotism/favoritism. It's time some of the entrenched get their hands dirty and their feet wet; their boots are too shiny and their bodies too out of shape. After all, we have an image to maintain."

"Yeah, I know; I have a LTC and a Major that have been there for 12 years; they think they own the place and have all the answers. Continuity is one thing, but homesteading is another. They don't know it, but they are both getting orders next week. Just remember I never told you what Larry's brother did. I think you and Betty are coming over for drinks and dinner tonight, or maybe its tomorrow; check with Betty. I'll see you when I see you."

They both headed back to their offices. Pete called over to Bob Miller's office. "Come over and see me soonest," said Pete and hung up. A few minutes later Bob Miller was escorted into his office. "General, you wanted to see your favorite servant."

"Have you been into the fire water already or are you bored in the new office I gave you?"

"Neither, I had two gentlemen visiting me a few hours ago."

"Have you been a bad boy again?"

"Shit, Bob, I have a short story to tell you." Pete explained his trip to Finland leaving nothing out. Bob just looked at Pete and said, "Do you have any idea what those tracking devices cost?"

"In all seriousness, they were on a fishing expedition; let me ask you, was the problem where you were taken care of?" Pete looked at Bob and nodded his head. "What about the other party?" Pete shook his head in the negative. "My old partner from the Cambodia fiasco is assigned to the same place. I was just about to write him a note congratulating him."

"This office is sterile; you and I need to talk but not here. By the way, do you need a pay jump? I have a helicopter laid on for tomorrow – Holland DZ (Drop Zone) – nice soft sand to land in; if you want an easy jump, be here at 1100 hours."

"Sounds good, I'll see you in the morning, we can talk on the DZ."

Their jump was referred to as a Hollywood jump due to the lack of wind from the propeller engines of a C-130 or a C-141. It was like falling out of bed. Pete and Bob Miller were sitting on the bags containing their used parachute and the reserve. The helicopter was taking other soldiers up for their jump. "I want that person taken care of, Bob, but it has to look like an accident. "Okay, consider it done." I haven't told anyone else this but after a year in my job, I'm retiring. I would like to work for your Agency. I'm slated to get another star in little over a year or it could be sooner according to my father-in-law who is a friend of the Chairman of the JCS. The fact that the two people from the FBI were down here yesterday is a good indicator that the rot and culture hasn't changed either at the State Department or the Pentagon. Someone sent those two agents down here."

"They are not local, are they?"

"No, they wanted to know about you and the operation in Thailand, they were from D.C."

"So why didn't they go to the Pentagon and who is interested in the Thailand operation; I'll tell you it's the State Department. Did you say anything about Thailand?"

"Not a word; I told them they should check with the Pentagon."

"Alert your boss; if the job offer is still there, I'm interested. Betty will understand but General Lawson will be pissed. I sit in my office and referee squabbles among my department heads; some are like kids and I'm going to get rid of some of them."

Pete walked in the door of his new house (old houses that Generals were required to live in on post). Betty greeted him in a sweat-soaked tennis outfit. He grabbed her and held her close. "I love the smell of sweat on you," said Pete removing her top. "Where are the girls?"

"Tennis lessons" was all she could get out as Pete steered her into the bedroom. They just lay there afterwards; her head on his arm. "You know, Pete, that strange food you ate that night at Laura's house really doesn't work; they were the testicles of reindeer; Laura said it's just a cultural thing that they make bridegrooms eat on their wedding night."

"Are you saying they don't work; Mariana said you would be happy."

"Pete, I am, I am, but you need to rest; it's been every day since we got back; don't get me wrong, I'm not complaining, but I should have had my period over a week ago and we weren't planning for any more children." Pete took her in his arms and kissed her softly on the lips. "You taste good, Betty."

"Pete, we are invited to the Lawson's in 3 hrs."

"Plenty of time."

"Pete!"

The girls came home and greeted their father who was in the kitchen fixing them cheeseburgers and French fries. "Dad, don't overcook them like you usually do." It was the youngest 9 year-old girl. "Are you telling a General how to cook cheeseburgers?"

"Rank has not improved your cooking, Dad; even Mom said that."

"Okay, we are going to have a family meeting and I'm cutting your rations in half."

"You always say that; your cooking is fine; don't criticize his cooking." It was the oldest who was almost 12 years-old. Their mother came into the kitchen and said, "We're going over to the Lawson's; you girls do your homework when you have eaten; keep the doors locked and take a shower – you both smell of sweat; place your dishes in the dishwasher and behave."

"Will you ask Gen. Lawson to take a look at my bike when he has a chance?"

"I'll check your bike," said Pete. "No, please Dad, you remember last time, it took Gen. Lawson almost 2 hrs. to put it together again."

"Let's go, Betty, I know when I'm not wanted."

"We love you, Dad, but you know skiing is your thing."

"As they were walking over to the Lawson's, Betty announced that while taking a shower, she got her period. "I was wondering what was taking you so long."

They were the only ones at the Lawson's. Nancy looked at Betty and asked if she would give her a hand in the kitchen. "You look pale, Betty, are you okay"

"That husband of mine is out of control; every night since we have been back from Finland and twice before we came over. I finally got my period when I showered, a week and a half late. He also has some news which he will share with you." They returned to where the men were sitting. "I guess I might as well tell you; I'm going to retire from the Army."

"Say that again – slower. I'm on my 2nd drink and sometimes I don't hear so good." Pete repeated what he had said. Gen. Lawson just sat there; no one said a word. "Are you aware that you are getting another star in the near future – when you have been in your present job a year?"

"I'm bored to death; I have been offered a job at the Agency. I haven't been to the War College yet and I'm not sitting in a classroom for a year listening to a bunch of has-beens. I'll be working in Operations, western/northern Europe. Betty's parents have given us their house ½ hr. from Langley; beautiful place; they are heading to Arizona."

"Betty, are you aboard with this?" Gen. Lawson was looking hard at her. "I'm aboard with anything Pete wants to do. My father tried to talk him out of retiring; this has been coming since he got back from Thailand. We have talked about it."

"Jesus, Pete, why didn't you talk to me about it? I know you are playing nursemaid to a bunch of Dept. heads, but retiring? You have a bright future."

"I'm not deceiving myself about the Agency, but the culture in the State Department and the Pentagon is so overt, it's not for me anymore."

"Nancy, we better eat or I'll have another drink which I don't need." The dinner was great and the talk was light, but there was an underlying current. Pete and Gen. Lawson were sitting alone in the living room while the ladies were cleaning up. "I'm not going to try to change your mind, Pete; have you notified the Pentagon?"

"No, not yet, but I will in a week or two."

Pete was enjoying a night cap at home later that night. He looked satisfied as he thought to himself, "the job with the Agency would require some traveling to his areas of operation in western and northern Europe; however, it was where he needed to be to make sure his two targets were neutralized."

"He owed that much to the 100s of dead United States Prisoners of War."

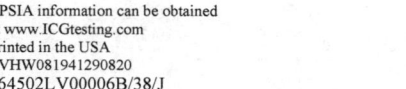

9 781733 314954